THE PARIS THIEF

THE PARIS THIEF

LISA ROCHON

REVIEW

First published in Canada by Harper Avenue, an imprint of HarperCollins Publishers Ltd

First published in Great Britain in 2026 by Headline Review
An imprint of Headline Publishing Group Limited

1

Cataloguing in Publication Data is available from the British Library

Trade paperback ISBN 978 1 0354 4291 1

Offset in 12.72/18.02pt Garamond Premier Pro by Six Red Marbles UK, Thetford, Norfolk

Printed and bound in Great Britain by Clays Ltd, Elcograf S.p.A.

FSC www.fsc.org MIX Paper | Supporting responsible forestry FSC® C104740

Headline's policy is to use papers that are natural, renewable and recyclable products and made from wood grown in well-managed forests and other controlled sources. The logging and manufacturing processes are expected to conform to the environmental regulations of the country of origin.

Headline Publishing Group Limited
An Hachette UK Company
Carmelite House
50 Victoria Embankment
London EC4Y 0DZ

The authorised representative in the EEA is Hachette Ireland,
8 Castlecourt Centre, Dublin 15, D15 XTP3, Ireland (email: info@hbgi.ie)

www.headline.co.uk
www.hachette.co.uk

For John, and our children,
Geneviève, Alexander, Hannah, and Dylan
And for Olivier

Love is the emblem of eternity; it confounds all notion of time, erases all memory of a beginning, all fear of an end.

—Madame de Staël, *Corinne*

CHAPTER ONE

Château de Chambord, 1939

Mathilde stands at the edge of the forest, blue shirt, canvas pants, a thin gold chain around her neck. The late morning sun beats down on the top of her head. Glistening above her lips, a slick of sweat. There is no breeze. She wants to be in control like a ship's captain or a French patron, the way that men look puffed up with their own magnificence. She crosses her arms in front of her chest but thinks it too casual. She sets her shoulders and clasps her hands behind her back. This seems unnatural to her, one wrist slapped on top of the other, as if arresting herself. Finally, she shoves her hands into the pockets of her pants to hide the trembling of her fingers. Church bells clang in the distance; there is the unrelenting buzz of a cicada. She feels more animal than human; she senses everything, all the uninvited changes in her world.

Behind her rises the forest, vast and unknown, bigger than all of Paris. She has been warned that wild boar and deer rut and stampede here. But not in the summer. Not now. This is not their season. Now the land is sleepy. The people are sleepy. Ahead, an epic grassy courtyard parched by the sun. Beyond the courtyard, there is a château, a folly of ostentation that looms impossibly large on the horizon. She had imagined a robust hunting lodge low to the floor of the Loire Valley but instead, rising before her, a spectacle of vanity and wealth, hundreds of chimneys and towers spiralling into the sky. Her fingers tighten inside her pant pockets. She imagines trying to draw the monument and running out of paper.

More than four hundred rooms inside. Likely many of them never occupied. Designed for a king to impress other kings. She doubts the ancient castle can resist fire and rain, or those who want what she has.

"Madame, it is time."

She exhales loudly and nods at the soldier, distracted. She tastes lavender on her tongue, smells engine oil, fresh straw pressed into wooden crates.

She fixes her gaze on the château, this place she must occupy to stay safe, and hesitates because of its grasping, wheezing self-importance. Heaps and heaps of stone quarried and stacked by unlucky men, spires, chimneys and towers enough for ten villages, all collaged together to bring an old French king closer to God.

The soldier positions himself in front of her, his rifle at the ready. Another has arrived behind her, carrying Mathilde's leather bag in one hand, manoeuvring a luggage cart with the other. He pushes the load onto the gravel path and it lurches forward. The sharp edge rams into Mathilde's ankles. She turns, dazzled by the pain, but is subdued by the sight of the large wooden case sitting pristinely on the metal cart. With a jerk of her head, she signals for the soldier to step away to make room for her. Moving into position, she wraps her fingers around the handles of the cart. They are crusted with dirt but she cares not at all. During the long drive from Paris, she rehearsed the unloading. Her grip is sure. Small discomforts will not interfere.

"Madame, you're a long way from the city. This path is for pigs." The soldier in the front scoffs and kicks a boot at the pebbled track.

She squints at the sun and does not look at the soldiers. Her dark bangs hang bluntly above her eyebrows. "I will manage."

"But, madame," says the other, his face slick with the heat, "the cart will be a brute to push."

"Thank you for stepping away." There is a long silence and she knows the soldiers are exchanging glances. She smells their onion sweat, their ignorance about the treasure they are shepherding along an inglorious path. "She is my responsibility."

The sun pounds down its terrible heat. She steps her feet back to gain purchase and channels the energy of a stubborn mule. The wheels spit and pop. The cart advances.

"Well, look at that, this one's stronger than I thought," mutters the older soldier to the other.

She thinks, *Va te faire foutre*. Instead, she leans her body hard against the metal bars and advances, fixing her gaze on the château far, far ahead.

Suddenly the cart lunges sideways and the wooden case wobbles before hitting the grass. "No damage," she says, whispering through her teeth. "No damage." The soldier from behind pulls a length of rope from his satchel. He shows the cord to Mathilde and raises his eyebrows, asking for approval. She nods, giving him permission to rope the box to the cart. He works carefully and efficiently. She straightens the wheels to centre them on the path. The cart inches ahead. In her estimation, there are two hundred more steps to accomplish. She does not concentrate on the soldiers but on the figure who has appeared at the front entrance of Chambord, who has travelled down the elegant stone stairs, where a small stone bridge crosses over the moat. He is wearing a suit and is walking briskly toward her. The sun is punishing her entire body. She wants to rest her head on the handles of the cart but wills herself to move forward. This is her job, she has been commissioned to do this; she will find the power and there will be no goddamn damage. She can see the man's face, angled cheekbones, eyes shaded below his straw hat. Wearing a bow tie. How absurd, she thinks, in this heat and with their nation on the brink of collapse. His leather shoes crunching lightly, all efficiency, on the gravel. "Welcome. Welcome to your humble new home," he says, extending his hand, laughing. "Pierre Schommer, special envoy."

She nods and shakes his hand. "Mathilde." She does not use her last name, she rarely does. She notices the slight lift of his eyebrows, his surprise at the sight of her. A woman with large circles of sweat blooming over her shirt, a tiny ivory button that has been lost, her dusty shoes.

Pierre's brown eyes are alert and watchful. He offers her a cigarette and lights hers with his. "It's a strange world," he says. "Great artworks are created. And war decides where they end up."

She watches him cast his eyes over the wooden case, taking in the leather handles, the custom fittings, the three red circles painted in a row. He nods as if in agreement with something she has thought, not said. They stand under the sun and take the heat. She inhales the last of the cigarette and drops the butt to the gravel. "Monsieur, I would be grateful if you could . . ."

She stops herself, aware that she is being unfriendly. A pushy bureaucrat from Paris. If only he knew that she comes from humble stock. She needs to reset her watch and get on rural time. Forcing a smile, she looks down at her shoes and back at her host. "If you would show me where the work will be kept safe."

Pierre pulls a large clutch of keys from his satchel. They are orange with rust. "Four hundred keys, none of them marked." He waves a hand at the enormous château. "Welcome to Chambord. Pick a room. Pick some stairs. There are seventy-seven of them. It's all yours."

She has studied the interior from her desk in Paris, knows about the rooms and the stairs, the dozens of vast courtyards big enough to launch hot-air balloons or grow bushels of tomatoes. To the west is a soaring chapel, and above that architectural elegance, timbered bedrooms set high above the moat, that incision cut into the earth holding lightless water. "This box will stay with me in my room. I'll need a guard with a gun."

The man lifts his hat, fans his face, and settles it back on his head. "Madame, with the greatest respect"—she follows his gaze to the single duck floating in the moat and catches a whiff of the still, fetid water—"our staff is not as extensive as you might expect."

"Monsieur Schommer, I need a man with a gun," she repeats, looking steadily at his eyes below the brim of his hat. "Can you provide that?"

She can hear the soldiers shifting on their feet, growing impatient.

"The cook's husband," he says at last. "Bad leg from the last great war, but a good shot."

These crates are not filled with oats for the horses, she wants to say. But this man is from Paris, he is her boss, responsible for the Chambord depot, with more experience than she can imagine. Instead, lowering her voice, she says, "You and I understand these are masterpieces."

The roar of the trucks pulling up at the edge of the forest distracts them, the squeal of the brakes being applied hard.

"These are world treasures," she says, bending toward him, shouting to be heard above the noise.

He smiles and shrugs, indicating that, of course, he already knows this.

She feels stupid, stating the obvious, and yet she needed to say it out loud, to steady her mind, her commitment to the project. She looks again at the trucks. There are at least fifty of them. Drivers are yelling, horns are blowing loudly. "We'll protect them as best we can, madame," he says. "I only arrived a few days ago. There is much work to be done."

They walk together, taking turns pushing the cart.

"Are there locks on the rooms? We'll need iron security bars . . ." She can't help herself.

"Madame, where there are shutters, there are no windows. No locks that function," he says, frowning. "The château is old, Renaissance era, the biggest in France. Built by King Francois I as a hunting lodge, used occasionally, infrequently, by Henry II and Louis XIV. Hundreds of rooms, as you know. One working toilet. I'm afraid it's a relic from the past."

"Electricity? Lights?"

He shakes his head. "Oil lamps and torches are the best we can do but we rarely use them."

She stiffens. She needs to recalibrate. After tending to every detail of her fastidious plan in Paris, she had forgotten to consider all of this. This was not part of her mind's rehearsal. Her system is broken. The château is not safe.

"Fire risk?"

"Of course."

"The men will have to unload the trucks as fast as they can before nightfall."

He stops abruptly and looks over at her. "Madame, may I call you by your first name?"

She hesitates and finally offers something like a smile.

"Mathilde, perhaps you will grant me a personal inquiry."

With the back of her hand, she wipes the sweat from her mouth. The heat has given her away. She is nothing if not coarse.

"Why are you here? Surely you have a family?" He reaches into a pants pocket and pulls out a linen handkerchief. "It's clean," he says, handing it to her, sniffing with a touch of Parisian arrogance.

"I do. I have a son."

She already misses Philippe, brilliant at law school, talented in art, handsome and shy. She said goodbye to him that morning at their apartment on the Left Bank, forcing a smile and calling out, "See you soon! I'll be back for your birthday. Twenty-one candles!" He did not roll his eyes and say something witty or sarcastic in return as he normally would have. Instead, he looked at her with intensity, his eyes locked with hers, willing her to stay, asking her to, until she offered a final wave. She went alone down the spiral staircase, and when she was sure to be out of sight, she collapsed against the carved wooden banister, sick with grief as the weight of the new reality, the imminent occupation of her beloved country, suddenly came crashing down. One year ago, Germany had annexed Austria and hung their flags of Nazi swastikas throughout Vienna and Strasbourg. Fascist Italy had invaded and annexed Albania in the springtime. All of the papers in the Paris newsstands were reporting that the next country to be seized by the Nazis would be Poland, which would provoke a world war to erupt in a matter of weeks. France, everybody assumed, would be quickly mowed down.

Her fear changed the smell of her sweat. She washed her cotton shirts daily and still the stench of the unknown seeped from her pores into her clothes. The Nazi military was equipped with modern firepower, a formidable Luftwaffe air force, and one million highly disciplined soldiers. By comparison, France was preparing to fight with obsolescent planes and tanks.

"Mathilde, there is still time. Go back to him and save yourselves," Monsieur Schommer says.

She looks to the sky to stop the tears. She will not cry in front of this man.

"You're a pretty woman. War is never pretty. It is ugly."

"This is my job." She touches one hand to her gold necklace and rubs her stiff neck. She wants to tell him that she is frightened and cannot do this. The secret of what lies packed inside the wooden case must be hers alone to bear. She feels the knowledge as a weight, something of a new, uninvited circumstance, like Persephone eating pomegranate seeds. Did the goddess happily munch the seeds to satisfy her need for deceit or was she forced to choke them back in some dark, forbidden corner? Mathilde considers this, looking to the magnificent, monstrous castle. She only wants to do her job and go back home to her son in Paris, reclaim the banality of the familiar. Her sweet morning pleasures, the feel of her linen sheets against her skin, the trace of daylight pressing through the metal shutters of her apartment, the smell of coffee lifting from her glass French press. Even the sound of Philippe in the mornings, his feet slapping along the wooden floors, how he looked half asleep, lost to the world, while eating jam on a baguette. All the daily routines and familiar comforts are gone. The odds are against her now. She feels herself spinning, rudderless, unmoored. One minute frying an egg in an iron skillet, wondering whether to flip or go for sunny side up, and the next forced to grapple with the wretched shape and depth of human evil. Foreigners—uninvited, illegally, aggressively—will march in heavy boots over her city. At least that is the nightmarish vision invading the minds of the French. The Nazis will be armed with machine guns, mortars, and howitzers. They will follow orders, no matter how brutal. She wonders how much she will have to endure, as a mother, as a French citizen.

Pierre nods in agreement and leans toward her. "I'm not trying to push you away. You come highly recommended from your superiors at the Louvre. It's an honour to have you here."

She does not acknowledge his kindness but pauses to look back again at the mounting chaos behind them. Crammed onto the driveway and the lawn is a crush of vehicles, Citroën light lorries and a handful of cube trucks typically used to move stage sets from the Comédie-Française. She sees the small florist's delivery truck she and her guards travelled in from Paris, avoiding all the major roads heading south. Unpacked on the lawn, there are rolls of carpets and tapestries wrapped in brown paper. Next to them, stone sculptures of Roman gladiators and disc throwers. She sees the wings of a white marble goddess glinting in the sunshine. Advancing fast along the path, dozens of soldiers and volunteers pushing buggies, carts, and dollies heaped with crates. "Now it begins," she says, signalling to the soldiers to lift the heavy wooden case from its cart, leading them over the narrow stone bridge spanning the moat. The lone duck beats its wings in panic, desperate to fly, sending ripples across the black water. "Show me to my room," she says. A trail of sweat trickles down her chest. Pierre heaves open the thick wooden doors and waves her inside the château. She feels cool air on her face, sees the heads of antlered deer mounted inside on the walls.

"Madame, may I help carry something?" he asks, extending his arms.

"No, thank you." She hoists her leather bag over her shoulder and jerks her head to the soldiers. "I only need—" She thinks of everything that is wrong with the day, the absurdity of the evacuation, the civic panic that's careening through Paris like a mudslide. She knows that the château is in the safe zone. She knows this is why the masterworks from the Louvre museum have been evacuated here so that no harm can come to them. But who can say that a mudslide obeys borders drawn on paper? Her voice is rough with emotion: "I'm here to save some of the beauty. Please, call the man with the gun."

CHAPTER TWO

Paris, 1910

Picasso has told Mathilde that Montmartre is a dump for all the rejects of the world. He tells her this with a shrug of his shoulders. "Naturally, it's the same here or in Spain, everywhere you go, the artists, the insane people, the workers who break their backs and fail to get ahead." She can see what he means. The housing is squalid. It's easy to tell who belongs to the doomed of the city by their appendages. Red, bloated hands on the women who wash clothes in scalding water all day; purple, frozen feet of children without shoes. But sometimes Montmartre feels like enlightenment. There's a conviction that, perched high above Paris, the artists working on the hilltop are creating a new world. She has seen the soft northern light washing over Picasso's studio like a gentle baptism. All the rules chucked aside so that a new kind of jagged art can be born.

Mathilde walks up the steep hill, past construction workers dragging shovels and picks behind them, heading back from work sites in the city to their shanty homes, pack horses trudging beside them. The air in Montmartre seems heavier than in the rest of Paris below, as if the dust from the old gypsum mine on its slope is still gathering in its particles. The rain has stopped, the roads are slick. She passes a couple kissing in a doorway, knocking over pots of geraniums to get at each other's bodies. She walks toward Place Ravignan, where iron street lights flicker next to a few ragged trees. It's hard to know how to navigate through the crowd. Barely 9 p.m., and everywhere are artists in berets, women in dresses hiked seductively above their ankles. A mime with a white powdered face and red lipstick smeared over his mouth pulls Mathilde into a swirling dance. They make several rounds on the square, bumping hard into other people, and the man laughs with his ghoulish head thrown back before tossing her aside.

Released, she steps lightly to the low-lying building at the far side of the square. The double wooden doors are painted green and adorned with a single sign: *Ateliers du Bateau-Lavoir.* She travels up some rotting wooden stairs, glad to be off the streets and inside the old piano factory where artists have staked a claim. It's dirty. It's cheap. The plaster on the walls is faded and chipped. There's a single faucet and one toilet with a broken door for all twelve tenants to share. Ignoring the scattering mice, she walks down a hallway, cloudy with plaster dust, toward the sound of laughter and shouting. Her heart is pounding. Eighteen years old. She feels exhilarated and terribly alone.

It takes her eyes several minutes to adjust. The smoke is heavy in the studio, and the crowd of artists seems heaved against her. She does not recognize individuals, only shapes and lines. Arms hoisting drinks to lips as diagonals, heads as ovals, bodies as cylinders. Her clothes feel suddenly all wrong. Her long hair, caught in a loose ponytail with some of it coiled on top of her head, is too provincial. She has been living several months in Paris and modelled for Picasso for some of that. But here in the studio, among these artists, she can't shake the feeling that she's an imposter who has come empty-handed.

"The beautiful blonde from Alsace. You must be Mathilde." A

woman approaches and kisses her cheeks three times, Paris-style. "I'm Suzanne Valadon." She steps back and waits to be recognized.

Mathilde stares at the woman, at her glittering blue eyes, her shock of red hair. "*Enchantée*," she says at last, using an expression that Parisians use and overuse. It seems to cover a lot of territory: acceptance, engagement, civilization.

The woman pouts, her lips dipping wide and full. "You do not recognize me? I will give you a hint. I grew up rough in Montmartre, did circus acts, often on a horse, mostly naked. My mother was a laundress. Renoir has painted my portrait many times."

Mathilde is desperate to touch this woman, discover her source of power. "And so you are famous," she says, resisting the urge, spreading her arms wide instead.

"Let Henri Matisse be famous with money from his Russian patrons," says the woman. "Being famous does not interest me. Degas is my friend. Do you know him?"

"No, not yet, but . . ."

"Montmartre is like an opera that never stops. All day. All night. Get on stage with it. I am showing my latest oil painting about Adam and Eve for the Salon d'Automne this year. Make sure you attend."

Mathilde feels Suzanne's eyes taking in her oversized canvas pants and embroidered white blouse.

Her heart is pounding, trying to keep up. "Why Adam and Eve? I thought the Bible wrote enough about them."

"Oh, that old story. The God-controlled world." Suzanne swirls her wine and tips the glass to Mathilde's mouth for her to taste. "You will appreciate my interpretation. Mine depicts an older woman with her much younger lover."

"An older woman with a younger man?" says Mathilde. "No judgment?"

"No sin. No Catholic guilt. Freedom! And who said she's with a man?"

"That sounds"—*strange* is what she is thinking, but she searches for the right word—"like intoxication," she says, smiling.

"Exactly right," Suzanne says. "I like your honesty." She kisses Mathilde on the lips. "Come visit me at my studio down the hall."

"Have a real drink," says another man, handing her a glass of green liquid. The smell of anise pierces her nose. Absinthe. Not her favourite. "I'm Giorgio de Chirico. Welcome to my party."

She takes the drink and glances at the colourful canvases hanging on the walls. "These are yours?" she asks him.

"Tell me, what do you think?" he asks, lifting his chin, showing the extent of his bulbous nose and a brow that seems furrowed with invisible mathematical equations.

She looks closely at his paintings of human figures looming large and silent like statues. "They're menacing," she says, peering at the way they seem to be guarding ancient Italian piazzas and colonnades.

"Art needs to destroy the rules of the past."

She has heard this before from artists who take themselves very seriously. "Why destroy?"

"So that people can see the world, how tragic and empty; that's what I want to capture in my paintings, the truth of the human condition. Life is *molto povera*," he says, looking sadly out the window. "It makes me want to cry."

She laughs at the way Giorgio delivers the speech like an old Greek philosopher, or a statue of one.

"You're laughing at me?"

"Not at you. Just the way you speak like an actor in a theatre."

"That's from my mother. My father was Greek. Both of them from the Italian aristocracy."

"I'm glad for you." She suddenly feels resentful. Recovering herself, she says, "You sound very wise. But how old are you?"

"Twenty-one. But I have lived many lives, like a *gatto*," he says, meowing loudly.

She laughs and meows back at him.

"You're an artist?" asks Giorgio.

"I guess. But I don't know," says Mathilde. She feels nervous and restless, looking around at these people. All of them are artists with the guts to throw themselves fearlessly at the making of art. She knows that her art is technically proficient, but, compared to the visions produced by Giorgio or Suzanne, it lacks originality, as if she were a dull student copying lines on a blackboard.

"Why doubt yourself?" he says, shrugging his shoulders, gesturing to all his paintings on the wall. "Pick up your golden thread and let it guide you."

"I should. I'll try. I need to find . . ." But before she can finish, another man approaches the artist. They clink glasses and start speaking in Italian. Finally, Giorgio introduces Vincenzo Peruggia. Mathilde eyes his tweed suit and high-necked white shirt, the formal style of his clothes in this, the most unleashed neighbourhood of Paris. Maybe the absinthe is clouding her judgment but she feels drawn to this man, his dark moustache and sculpted face, even the square of his shoulders. The men switch to French and now Mathilde overhears that this man in the tweed has left his village in Italy to experience the City of Light. Mathilde learns he is an artist, but he pays his rent as a carpenter and glazier working on contract at the Louvre museum.

She reaches for his cigarette, touching her fingers to his mouth, and takes a drag. "Go on," she says, turning the conversation away from Giorgio. Vincenzo slides his eyes over to her, taking his cigarette back, smiling.

She has caught his attention, of that she can be sure. But the men do not ask about her work. Finding her golden thread, whatever that might be, she should do that. Or stay hidden and afraid, like the badger that lived in an oak tree near the family barn, only daring to come out of the hollow at night when nobody was looking. She squints her eyes at the smoky room, thinking it's a very long way from Montmartre, where strangers become family, back to her village of Haguenau, Alsace, where families become strangers.

"I'm at the Louvre much of the week," she says, speaking loudly and gazing at them, emboldened by the drink. Perhaps this is her trying to come out of her hollow. "Copying the masters. It's amazing how stupid they make me feel."

She intends this as a joke, but the men do not laugh. They shift on their feet, empty their glasses. "Copying the past no longer interests me," says Giorgio. "I want to look into the future, celebrate the machines, the speed of the automobiles."

"Aluminum and chromium," says Vincenzo. "The Eiffel Tower. One thousand glorious feet tall."

"Mass production for everything. Dishes, clothes, desks and chairs."

"Burn the old ways," says Vincenzo.

"Except for your paintbrushes and the Bateau-Lavoir," says Mathilde.

Vincenzo hesitates and then steps close to her. "You are a smart girl, and a beautiful one."

"You're very bold," she says.

"I think you are very bold too," he says, whispering in her ear.

Giorgio jerks his head to the far corner of the studio. "Picasso is over there with his Spanish friends. You know him, yes? He'll want to see you."

She nods her thanks and angles her body through the crowd, lifting her glass in the air, glad for her height.

"Fernande Olivier," says a tall woman in a long skirt and turtleneck when Mathilde approaches. Her auburn hair is heaped on top of her head and rolled over her forehead. "*Enchantée.*" She offers her cheeks to be kissed. "Fabulous ensemble," she adds, scrutinizing her. The women clink glasses. Fernande, whose large green eyes are set against pale skin, is not a beauty like Suzanne, thinks Mathilde, but there is something fierce about the way she occupies space, feet set wide below her skirts, something that declares, "Don't even think of messing with me."

"You must be the new muse," says Fernande. "Well, don't just stand there. Picasso will want you to say hello. But remember, don't get too friendly." She jabs a finger several times at Mathilde before turning away, back into the crowd.

Picasso kisses her once on each cheek in the Spanish tradition, says her name affectionately, "Mathi." She stands next to him motionless, sipping her drink, vibrating from the way he purrs her name. The green liquid tastes like bitter mushrooms. Picasso seems to guess the sensation in her mouth. "Eh, *por favor*, don't drink that," he says, taking the glass away from her. "Try this. *Vino tinto* from Spain." She smiles her thanks and looks across the crowded room to Fernande, who is watching her.

"Don't worry about Fernande," he says in his accented French. "She's the jealous type. But you and I, we have done nothing wrong."

Mathilde feels that Picasso is a spider at the centre of an intricate gossamer web. A very large spider with a balding head. She has come to know him these last months and is fully aware that he enjoys the company of only a few artists, preferring to spend his precious time with irreverent writers and critics, or serious collectors, like the Americans Leo and Gertrude Stein. He is twenty-eight years old and already at the top of his game. Tonight, he seems relaxed, smoking a pipe and wearing pleated pants and a navy-blue sailor's sweater. Other artists flit nearby, the brave approach him tentatively. They are looking for his blessing but they will be disappointed. He is the originator. The creative mind behind Cubist art, along with his friend Georges Braque. Still they come. Circling the man. Like moths. They might as well kneel at his altar—*bless us, Picasso*, Mathilde thinks—and offer him gifts of myrrh and frankincense.

Many times, he has kissed her in the studio, and she has allowed it, not because she desires him but because the passion in his mouth amazes her. At the party, his hands trace lines in the air and they are mesmerizing to watch, but his fingers are weak when they touch hers, and she does not like the feeling. During breaks modelling for him in the studio, she has managed, so far, to escape his hands. That is her backstory with Picasso. Pleasing him but also managing him.

She notices the Italian man, Vincenzo, is staring at her. She walks back to him, smiling a little. He has a sharp animal scent that draws her close, and, tipsy, she allows herself to rub against his chest. "You're my new friend." She smiles at him. "My first Italian friend."

He leads her to a wall of windows in a corner of the studio, and he touches one finger to her lips and moves his face next to hers. They stare at each other. She touches her lips to his and he allows it but only barely; this suggestion of a kiss, she thinks, must be an Italian invention, maybe by popes or priests in shadowy ancient churches.

He tells her that he grew up poor in Italy, that he likes to draw on wooden boards and sculpt in clay. She tells him that she draws portraits of people crossing city streets and travelling underground in the new Métro, all in shades of black and white, pencil, ink and conté, no colour. "Colour is overrated. It's not as important as lines and form and textures, the real essence. Colour is used by the church to make people believe in God."

"You see, you too are a Futurist," he says, speaking softly. He touches her hair, the side of her neck. "But where did you learn to paint?" His moustache caresses her cheek.

"By whitewashing our barn." She smiles, feeling as if she were floating off the floor. "Mostly, I was self-taught with a little encouragement from my grandmother. She was a landscape painter. High realism. A bunch of her paintings hang in my bedroom back home." He nods, waiting for her to continue. "And by luck, I was taught by an artist visiting Alsace from Germany. He was . . ."

"He was what?"

"He was quite . . ."

"He was quite what?" It's obvious that Vincenzo won't let the subject drop. Mathilde decides to indulge him with a little bit of her history.

"We were together. I trusted him. We were very . . . you know."

"No, I don't know. Tell me."

"Here," she says, linking her fingers together into a ball. Words failing her and a little drunk, she spontaneously decides to show him. "Try to pull my hands apart." Hesitating, he reaches over. She feels his rough, calloused hands as he attempts to break apart her fingers.

"You see?" she says, shaking her fists free. "We were like that. Unbreakable."

His hands move to her waist and he pulls her by her leather belt toward him. "And now you are here, in Paris, far away from your past. You can trust other people," he says, kissing her neck.

Vincenzo's soft lips make it difficult to gather her thoughts.

"Maybe. You could be right." Mathilde nods and shrugs her shoulders. She touches the gold chain around her neck, a gift from Franz. She wears it even when she sleeps.

Finally, she pushes him away, dumps the rest of her red wine in a potted plant. "I pay my rent by working as a cook at Lipp," she says, abruptly. "We can eat there for nothing as long as we stand outside at the back."

She does not mention to Vincenzo that it was at the Brasserie Lipp, while taking a smoke break, that Picasso had first noticed her. She was leaning against a stone wall, a tall, lanky eighteen-year-old with a long blonde ponytail, thinking about all the potatoes she would still have to peel before her shift ended. The garbage overflowed the metal cans next to her. She wondered, as she often did, if there were any hills in Paris where she might run and feel like she was back in the verdant countryside of Alsace.

She noticed his energy before she noticed his face. Powering forward, eyes flashing, rugged with animal intensity. He charged past her, and she thought she might like to draw the shape of his square back and shoulders bulging below a navy-blue sweater. One minute later he had returned, his hand on his quizzical brow. "*Alors?*" she said, more of a challenge than a greeting. The man was circling her, looking down on the ground as if tracking prey. Finally, he stopped, and because she was taller than him, he had to look up to her. "*Bonsoir*," he said. His mouth was a fine, generous shape, his eyes were iron black. "My name is Picasso. I am an artist. Will you please come to my studio to model?"

She laughed at his question.

"I see," he said, nodding appreciatively at her. "You are young. And so you laugh."

"I don't always laugh," said Mathilde.

"No, you should. Life is cruel. Laugh now, cry later."

That was several months ago. Now she is standing at a party with all the artists who matter in Paris. The Cubists. The Futurists. The writers. The poets. She needs to learn how to be fearless like them. But for the first time, she feels that she could belong in this city, that maybe, right now, she does.

"I'd like to see you again," says Vincenzo to Mathilde, whispering in her ear. His cheek grazes the side of her face.

She looks around the room for Picasso, but he is sharing a wicker chair with a woman whose neck is adorned with indigo-blue tattoos. They seem to be engaged in a soulful conversation, the kind in which he does all the talking. She agrees to meet Vincenzo, this dark romantic, in the morning. Café de la Rotonde in the Latin Quarter, down the hill, far away from Montmartre. Taking her leave, she walks into the deep night and bends to gulp water at the fountain at Place Ravignan. She never feels afraid walking through the streets, as there are people laughing and shouting, providing companionship all around, just like the stars dazzling overhead. Finally, she reaches the Pigalle Métro stop and sits, exhausted, on a park bench. She unlaces her leather shoes, kicks them aside, and pulls Picasso's pipe from her satchel. After filling its bowl with tobacco and striking a match, she takes a draw on the shank, wafting the earthy smell from her mouth through her nose. It's almost as if the Spanish artist is sitting beside her, keeping her company, speaking softly to her: "Mathi, *biens, biens*. . . . Look at you, once a farm girl, now a model with long legs and silky blonde hair."

"A potato peeler," she imagines saying back to him.

"You are an artist."

"Let me hope."

"I am so happy you came to my studio." He says this with a big, luscious smile even as his eyes stay serious. She hands him his pipe for a smoke and he hands it back to her. No accusations, no guilt, but a sweet harmony flowing between them. She lies down on the bench to contemplate the sky but she is thinking about the land she comes from. So much of her past seems foreign to her, as if she were a sojourner merely passing through Alsace. But she won't give in to a chafing self-pity. She feels at this exact moment to be adored, laced with delight. She puffs again and blows out. The smoke rises grey and sinewy against the night.

CHAPTER THREE

Paris, 1910

Artists gather at La Rotonde because it's grand, it's airy, and it's cheap. Anyone who can't afford a ten-centime café crème can draw something on a napkin and offer the art to Papa Libion, the restaurant owner. Mathilde sees that Picasso and Suzanne Valadon have their sketches taped to the wall. A naked woman on one napkin drawn in a single line with a pen. A naked man on another drawn with deep shadows and cross-hatching.

She smiles at the memory of Vincenzo's body pressing against hers in the corner of the studio last night, his hand touching her face, his lips on her neck. She feels desire between her legs and realizes it will be very nice to see him this morning. Outside, the city is quiet and dreamy below soft June skies. She sees herself reflected in the many grand mirrors of the café and does not look away but stares at her reflection, the way Parisiennes do without lifting their gaze. And then she sees her Italian romantic, a basket under his arm, toppling a chair in his rush to greet her. He grips her hands and then stands back to admire her, taking in the light blue dress that falls loosely below her knees, her blonde ponytail hanging down her back below a wide straw hat. "*Dio mio*," he says quietly. "How is this possible?"

"How is what possible?" she asks, looking up at him from the café table.

"That you are more beautiful than even I knew last night." She likes the way he speaks French imperfectly with an Italian accent.

She gestures at the basket stuffed with blankets and a bottle of wine.

"Did you cook pasta for me like a good Italian mama's boy?"

He looks hurt by her comment. She likes to be sarcastic and realizes sometimes too late that her words cut people in the wrong way.

"I do things. And I say things that are reckless. I don't know why. Maybe because I was raised rough on a farm. I'm sorry, come and sit, everything looks lovely."

"If you don't want me here, I can go," he says, his face darkening.

"No, not at all. Please," she says, patting the chair next to her. "Let's order something to eat."

He sits down and Mathilde kisses him on the cheek. She takes off her straw hat, loosens her hair from its ribbon, and pulls her chair closer. The waiter brings them their coffees and croissants. Hovering next to her, the waiter asks if he can also bring her some brioches and fresh strawberry jam. Surprised, she shrugs her shoulders, flicks her eyes flirtatiously at him, then turns back to Vincenzo. "I have a dream," she says. "Can I tell you?" He winds his fingers around hers. "If I can save enough money, I hope to attend École des Beaux-Arts. It just opened its doors to female students."

He considers this information and nods earnestly. "Why not? You should do it." He leans forward and takes both of her hands in his. "Tell me more of your *fantasia*, your *sogni*."

"My dreams?"

"Yes, your dreams."

She hesitates for a moment, examining his face with her pale blue eyes, wondering if she can trust him. "To be perfectly honest," she says at last, "someday I hope to exhibit my original paintings in a gallery."

"That's a big dream."

"You don't think I'm good enough?"

"I cannot say. I have never seen what you make."

She relaxes back in her chair, pulling up her dress, crossing her legs, showing her knees, a habit from the kitchen table in Alsace, telling stories, playing cards. "Want to know my other dream?"

"Tell me," says Vincenzo.

"I'd like to be paid by the Louvre to copy some of their masterworks. I mean, not now, down the road, if I'm good enough. Otherwise, I will nail my original art up here." She angles her head to the wall of artists' works. She leans forward to down her espresso and heap jam on her croissant. "But you, Vincenzo, tell me about you." She leans closer to him, enjoying the sight.

Vincenzo puts down his coffee. "One day a lonely Italian man met a beautiful woman at a party in Paris. Her name was Mathilde. They fell in love. Together they became one." He clenches his hands tightly into one ball. "That's it. Conclusion. End of my story!"

Astonished at his words, she is catapulted from her dreamy state to a sudden reckoning. Here is a man easily seduced, who she would very much like to have for a while. She twirls a finger around a length of her blonde hair and lifts her lips into a gentle, seductive smile. Reaching a hand to Vincenzo, she urges him to go on with his story. After devouring his croissant, he tells her he started one year ago as a general labourer at the Louvre, but his skills as a carpenter got him quickly promoted. Leaning toward her, checking to make sure no one's eavesdropping, he confides that there is little security at the Louvre, although recent small thieveries have prompted an effort to safeguard the important works. She feels a slight thrill at the mention of theft and draws her chair closer. The clatter of cups on saucers, the barking of orders between the waiters and baristas, all the noise fades away.

"Tell me," she instructs.

"These days, they've got me building shadow boxes with thick glass," he says.

"Why?"

"To protect the masterpieces. Hundreds of them."

"The masterpieces, of course." She nods, feeling a kindred spirit in Vincenzo, that they are akin to a couple of fireflies buzzing around, looking for meaning, in this city of dazzling light.

"Most of them are by Italian greats, the Renaissance artists, Michelangelo, Botticelli, Leonardo da Vinci," he says, his eyes darkening. "Stolen by Napoleon during ten years of pillage by his armies, all of them thugs." Mathilde sits up straight. "Every one of those paintings should go back to Italy." He bangs his fist on the table and then puts a finger below one of his eyes. "*Occhio.*" He glowers at her. She takes this to mean *beware*, all Italians are watching.

Mathilde had never considered this before, that war decides where the most desirable art will end up, but she feels it in her heart. Her homeland of Alsace was long ago seized by Germany, and ever since, the orchards, the vineyards, the highbush blueberries with their dazzling sweetness, all that once grew on the quiet land had been corrupted by an occupying enemy.

The light-filled room where they sit faces the busy boulevard of Montparnasse. Time feels wonderfully slow inside the café. Mathilde likes the company of Vincenzo; he makes her feel desired, maybe a little cherished. She talks about her favourite places to visit in Paris—the Île Saint-Louis and the Pont Neuf over the Seine at sunset—and he agrees with her, adding that he feels most comfortable going to the

Italian eateries in his neighbourhood in the city's 10th arrondissement, where he can fill his stomach eating good pasta and drinking Italian red wine that's perfect even if it's cheap. She likes his appetite. She likes the way he is awake to the wrongs of the world. She strokes the cracks in his fingers with her hands, caressing the rough patches, telling him that she admires the way they have held countless artworks with tenderness. She looks up at him. Soon they will make love, of that she is sure.

Vincenzo speaks French with a heavy Italian accent, and sometimes, unable to find the right word, he'll blurt out *bellissimo* or *allora* and kiss his fingers before sending them flying into the air. His eyes are warm and penetrating, searching for everything beautiful and unique in the world. In contrast, Picasso's eyes rarely sweep the horizon but focus intensely on particular objects. Mathilde has seen him drill into the essence of a face, into one lurid eye or part of a woman's broken nose, where grief or shame resides. Vincenzo is different. He speaks with sensitivity about cityscapes, about Milan for its monumental piazza—more impressive than any of the public squares in Paris, of that he is quite sure! Once, he tells her, he visited Florence with his father to stand in awe of the duomo and admire the magnificent *David* by Michelangelo. He dreams of someday visiting Rome to see the Colosseum, and Venice, where the water flows through the city the way blood travels through our veins. She can see the yearning in his eyes, his love for his country. When he speaks of Italy, his words become poetry even if he dropped out of school when he was ten years old.

Next to their table is a man who looks up from his napkin sketch and introduces himself as Modigliani. His thick black hair pushes wildly from beneath his broad felt hat. Knotted around his neck is a brilliant yellow scarf, but Mathilde notices that the man's eyes are darkened by shadows. Vincenzo stands quickly to shake the man's hand and blurts out, "One of the great new artists. Another from the Italy!" Vincenzo is blushing, such is his admiration for the man. Modigliani kisses Mathilde kindly on both cheeks. "I'm at the Bateau-Lavoir," he says, looking intently at her. "I've seen you around. Come visit me. My friends call me Modi." He sits back down and crumples up the sketch, throwing it to the floor. Seated next to him is a woman with an elegant, long face and pouting red lips. He reaches for another napkin and begins to sketch her with a pencil.

Mathilde does not know why, but the waiter brings them another basket of croissants with more jam. "On the house," he says, shrugging his shoulders. She feels as if she is floating through a moment in history in which kindness and creativity are privileged rather than repressed. Who knows what the future will bring? Someday, her luck might change and she will feel less like an interloper. But for now, there is this, all of this, she thinks, looking around at the café, people thriving because of other people. A city in exaltation.

A man smoking a pipe rumbles through the café, his large frame tilting metal tables at precarious angles. He throws himself into a chair and looks over at Mathilde and Vincenzo, greeting them with meaty pink hands. Perhaps he is an artist *and* a butcher, she thinks, but in the next moment, he introduces himself: "Apollinaire."

He looks directly at Mathilde, who absorbs his long, horsey face and worried eyes. "I saw you last night at de Chirico's party," she says, allowing him to hold her hands in his.

"And I saw you," he says, wagging a finger at Vincenzo. "You dare to rob Picasso of his blonde muse?"

"This is a free country, no? She's with me of her own will."

"But it's uncivilized to steal somebody's girlfriend," says Apollinaire. "At least in France. But I can tell from your accent that you are a foreigner accustomed to a more vulgar society. With time, you might learn about the ways of French civilization."

"I'm not Picasso's girlfriend," says Mathilde, and now it's her turn to blush.

Vincenzo sits back in his chair and laughs at Apollinaire. "Your arrogance amuses me." Then he leans forward. "The ways of French civilization? You mean your oppressive colonialism, or your Napoleonic looting? Without Italian genius, your art collections would be worthless!"

Mathilde finds this a wheezy performance by Vincenzo and wishes he hadn't bothered. It is morning. The birds are chirping outside. People are nursing hangovers and negotiating the day with little sleep. Apollinaire shrugs and sips from his coffee. "And yet here you are in the City of Light. We who are constantly fighting along the radical creative edges. This is why I live here. Maybe you should go back to your Italian countryside and lick your wounds."

Vincenzo stands and kicks back his chair. He is a small man but solidly built, and it looks like he wants to fight Apollinaire. Mathilde places a hand on the arm of her new friend, though she is somewhat impressed by his show of bravado, and tries to ease him away. "Let's not waste our time here."

Apollinaire, taller and bigger, rises to meet his aggressor. He seizes Vincenzo's hands. "I was born in Rome. My father was the pope." His entire body shakes with laughter. "Like you, like most of us, I'm an expatriate, so let's rebel altogether."

"Italian? *Allora*, I should have guessed." The men laugh and embrace each other.

"By the way," Apollinaire continues, "Picasso is a genius with a girlish handshake. He's afraid of hurting his hands." He throws back his head and roars. "Let's raise a glass of absinthe. *Garçon!*" He motions to the bartender. "Paris glitters from the brilliance of the Italians. Bring us some of your green fairy!"

Together with Mathilde, the men drink the bitter liquid, clinking the thick, fluted goblets, speaking excitedly in Italian and French.

"What do you mean, your father was the pope?" she says, her eyes twinkling.

"That's what Picasso believes. Who really knows? Men like to spread their seeds far and wide, especially the priests, the bishops, and the popes," says Apollinaire, taking a pipe from his mouth and booming with laughter. They drink the absinthe, the smell of anise wafting in the air, and promise to meet up at the Bateau-Lavoir at an upcoming party. As the men say their goodbyes, Mathilde slips a pair of the goblets into Vincenzo's basket, before tipping her hat to the poet.

Outside on the boulevard, two-wheeled carts pulled by horses trundle by in both directions.

Mathilde walks quietly beside Vincenzo. He tries to hold her hand but she brushes him away. They walk to a quiet corner of the Luxembourg Gardens to bask in the sun next to a long reflecting pool framed by thick garlands of ivy. Vincenzo uncorks the red wine from the basket and prepares to drink directly from the bottle. "Wait," says Mathilde, producing the pair of stolen glasses. "Surprise!" she says. "A gift for us, the little people, from La Rotonde."

Hesitating, a look of confusion on his face, Vincenzo pours two glasses of wine. "To the little people," he finally says, nodding, seeming to approve of the way she has lashed them together with most of the other people in the world, clinking his glass to hers. They talk about Apollinaire, Modigliani, and Suzanne Valadon, how dazzling their commitment to their art, as if they knew from birth what they needed to write or paint. Vincenzo places a wedge of Camembert on a piece of baguette, stuffing some into Mathilde's mouth and then his own. Chewing methodically, for the bread bought in the morning is no longer soft, Mathilde thinks some people, the great artists, are like carrier pigeons, bred to reach lofty ideas at high altitudes, eyes bulging, beak forward, nothing to distract them from their winged journey.

"That god looks very angry," says Vincenzo, gesturing with the baguette at the far end of the pool with a sculpture of an overbearing giant leering at a pair of lovers.

"Maybe he should mind his own business," says Mathilde, resigned to being distracted by the dazzling ancient beauty of Paris. "Let people love who they want to love." They finish eating, and she drinks another glass of wine, glad for the alcohol's misting of her brain. He suddenly reaches for her face and pulls her toward him. In the leafy undergrowth of an oak tree, they kiss deeply and she crawls into his lap, hungry for him, as oblivious as if they were in a garret floating above a sea of zinc-grey rooftops.

Later, they walk across the Seine, moving from the Left Bank to the Right, and arrive at the Louvre without ever making a plan to do so. Because Mathilde and Vincenzo are both familiar to the guard, they are quickly waved through at the arched entrance. She pulls her new Italian friend down a long hallway and through several galleries to show him a painting called *Pastoral Concert* by Titian, which she has been copying at a smaller dimension. She tells him that it reminds her of the woodlands of Alsace where she grew up before coming to Paris. They move past many artists they know, men and women, who have pitched their easels next to masterworks they're copying. Picasso is one of them. He is staring intensely at Eugene Delacroix's *The Women of Algiers* while holding a paintbrush mid-air. In the painting, three women wearing silk pants are relaxing on a colourful carpet, their hair adorned with flowers. Picasso looks over at the couple. “The bastard,” he says, referring to Delacroix and the large canvas. “He’s really good.” He pushes a dark lock of hair from his forehead and stares at Mathilde, his enormous eyes resting quietly on her as if reading her life story. She thinks, *I should go to him now.* But, abruptly, he turns back to copying Delacroix’s painting. His rejection stiffens her yearning and, suddenly, she despises everything about him, his animal energy, his indigo-black eyes fixated on the canvas in front of him. She reaches for Vincenzo and, together, they walk through the gallery holding hands as pretty couples typically do, the drumming of Picasso’s heart filling her head.

CHAPTER FOUR

Paris, 1910

"I want to show you something," says Vincenzo, and they walk through the museum crowded with visitors. Mathilde looks back one last time at Picasso. As much as she despises him in this moment, she longs for him to purr her name, *Mathi*, and beckon her again with his black eyes. But his gaze is fixed on his canvas. She hopes he will contact her soon for another modelling session. Picasso's new work fascinates her, all of its sharp angles and layered forms. Even if she isn't recognizable in his shadowy, geometric works, she wants to be part of this radical kind of painting he and his friends call Cubism. Picasso seems to trust Mathilde with his passion for art. In his studio last time, he showed her a painting with large letters set against a wild collage of cylindrical and circular shapes. He told her it was inspired by a bottle of rum he was drinking at the time.

"Here we are," says Vincenzo, his voice suddenly dark and sombre. He has led her into the heart of the vast museum to a large gallery filled with great paintings by Italian masters. Mathilde stops to take in the magnificent gallery, the Salon Carré. She looks up to gaze at the monumental skylight surrounded on the ceiling by gilded figures and the names of many famous artists. This is the showstopper gallery in the Louvre, renowned not only for its ornate baroque design but for its masterpieces. She has visited it many times. There are no guards and none of the paintings are bolted to the walls. The gallery has become the living room of copyists—seasoned and emerging artists—who perch on stools or stepladders to commit their likenesses.

"Do you know this one?" asks Vincenzo, turning to Mathilde. Of course, she does. It's *The Wedding Feast at Cana* by the great Italian painter Paolo Veronese. Her eyes float over more than one hundred people populating the canvas, most of them men, dining at a grand banquet in Venice. Another artist had explained it to her a year ago. Veronese and some other art geniuses are playing instruments. Jesus, at the centre, has transformed water to wine, and now it is flowing from a large stone urn. Only five women sit at the dining table, beautifully coiffed. She wonders who they are. The truth is she doesn't much care about all the pomp and circumstance displayed in this revered painting. She is a simple country girl, trained to run fast and spit as coarsely as her brothers. But she has the burning desire for something greater within her. And so, she has cut the ties to her past, to her suffocating kin and that small, closed-minded village. Becoming a Parisian, that's what matters now, to step into the anonymous crowd and make something of herself. She has put many miles between herself and Alsace. Damn the paralyzing guilt and shame of religion, damn the reverence for obedience and family hierarchy. She wants to step onto the stage of the opera, as Suzanne advised, to breathe with the city. For she is young, willing to spill blood to learn, to be carefree, to inhale the present and breathe out all the rigid ways.

Vincenzo speaks softly to her. "The canvas was torn off the wall of a major Venice monastery in the late 1700s," he says. "Look at it"—he points to the monumental artwork stretched across an entire wall—

"how it was ripped in half when they stole it from Italy and carried it with the rest of the war loot back to France."

Mathilde stares carefully at the painting. "Who did this?"

"Napoleon's army. The assholes," he whispers, clutching her hand.

Mathilde allows the moment of intimacy before stepping slowly along the painting's great expanse. She admires the shine of the gold and silver plates on the wedding table. Some of the cloaks the men are wearing are deep orange; others are grassy green decorated with circles of gold thread. She sees the rip in the painting across its length, just above the head of Jesus Christ; there's no mistaking it, and the stitching that came later. "The French stole the best works from the Italy and have treated them badly ever since," Vincenzo says, his voice half choked.

He guides her to the opposite wall. They stand in front of a small portrait of a woman who looks to be from the Renaissance. She is without jewels and is looking directly out at the world.

"By another Italian?" asks Mathilde.

"The French call it *La Joconde*," says Vincenzo. "In the Italy it's called the *Mona Lisa*. Leonardo da Vinci started painting the portrait in Florence during the early 1500s."

"Mona?"

"*Monna* is the little word for *Madonna*," he says.

Strange, thinks Mathilde, she had never noticed this portrait before, but it seems familiar. Not a classic beauty. But the look of defiance in the woman's eyes amazes her. Her enlightenment. As if she has just been effortlessly born or is about to die a noble death.

Lisa. The name of Mathilde's mother.

The portrait is surrounded on the wall by dozens of other paintings. Vincenzo explains passionately the story of how the Renaissance master portrayed Lisa Gherardini—a grieving mother and silk merchant's wife—against a shifting Italian landscape, brushing barely pigmented oils on a poplar board. "I still don't understand her but I want to know her," he says, standing within inches of the painting and breathing deeply. The wood that the portrait is painted on comes from the eastern region of Italy, where he grew up, he tells her. He says he can smell the lush valleys and dense forests of Lombardy. But soon that smell will disappear behind the shadow box and protective glass he is charged to build next week as a security measure.

They stand quietly in front of the *Mona Lisa*. For a long time, they do not speak. Mathilde slides her fingers to the gold chain at her neck, something she does when she is puzzling her way through a problem. She steps forward, her eyelashes almost touching the woman's. Who is she, Mathilde wonders, and what does she know? There seems to be some information, some painful truth, that the *Mona Lisa* is carrying inside. And despite her secrets, she is attempting to put up a brave face. Vincenzo interrupts, whispering to Mathilde, "This portrait by Leonardo should be back in Florence, where it was painted, not in a glass cage here in this foreign city."

He excuses himself to leave her in peace. She stares for a long while at the woman sitting on a balcony with a landscape in the background that curves across the ages. She sees rocky outcrops jutting from steep hills and rivers surging from different lands. There is a tiny detail of an old stone bridge with multiple arches, which makes her think of crossing from life to death. There is something about the expression on the woman's face that mesmerizes Mathilde, a combination of sorrow and life experience. Unadorned, looking bravely out into the world. Lisa. My lady Lisa. She is not pretty but she has a woman's story to tell. Mathilde decides to copy the portrait after finishing her Titian.

After they leave the room with the Italian masterworks, Mathilde wants to shake off the serious turn the afternoon has taken. If a fountain presented itself, she would strip off her clothes and jump in. Instead she asks Vincenzo to take her somewhere private in the museum. He hesitates, trying to understand her meaning, and when he sees one of her eyebrows lift ever so slightly, he grabs her hand and turns on his heel. In a poorly lit passageway, he finds a low, thick door and, with a shaking hand, pulls a clutch of skeleton keys, one of which turns the small bronze handle. Inside, lit by an upper clerestory window, she sees that this is a storage room for carpenters such as Vincenzo. The shelves hold a carefully ordered arrangement of tools and discarded gold frames. A tapestry thick with golden threads hangs on one wall. On another, opposite the window, is an oil painting in the Renaissance style: Venus is naked, her suitors draped in gorgeous robes, the entire scene bathed in the afternoon's apricot light. It might be an original. It might be a copy by a gifted female artist. She feels hot and craves release. Eyes wide, Mathilde takes in all the details of the room while kissing Vincenzo hungrily.

He loosens the ribbons at the back of her dress and it falls to the ground. She grabs at the buttons on his white shirt, running her hands over his shoulders and down his stomach to the snaps on his pants. He makes sounds, not Italian or French, but a dialect that seems to be invented for her, for both of them, in the little room. Quickly they are naked and down on the floor. She lies against him, the better to feel his skin, her hands and breasts caressing his thighs, his stomach, his face. But he lifts her up to her feet and presses her against the wall, winding her legs around his back. They make love while she stares past his shoulder at the painting of Venus, her nakedness arousing Mathilde, and the forbidden room where they are pounding loudly against the wall. Even the nails and screws rattling on the shelf seem to be alive with desire. A small golden frame flips over. Mathilde will think back on this as funny, but not now. Now, she inhales Vincenzo's animal cries into her mouth.

When they leave the Louvre at last, the evening sky lifts a dome of ethereal blue over the city. Crowds of people have gathered on the bridges to gaze at the Eiffel Tower. "A structure already twenty years old, but it still carries the shock of the new," says Mathilde to no one in particular. "We need to remember that." They stand on the Pont des Arts to gaze at the insanity of its height, a monument dreamed up by an engineer, a celebration of iron beams criss-crossing to show off modern strength. She has made a collage of the Eiffel Tower, pasting large black and white sketches on top of each other as if to represent stages of construction. She dared herself to make the artwork. It seemed radical at the time. But then in Picasso's studio, she saw that he had already painted the tower with him pointing at it, a cartoon character dwarfed by the monument. His work was far more interesting.

Vincenzo wants to kiss Mathilde on the bridge but she pushes him away. "Not now," she says, looking down the river, half-fleeced clouds along the horizon. Her eyes are pale and restless. He shrugs and smiles, touches a hand toward her, then lets it fall by his side. "*Va bene*, but I'd like to see you again."

She looks at him and smiles. "My sweet Italian friend. Yes, I'll see you again."

"I don't know why. I mean, how many hours have I known you?"

"Depends if you're measuring time on a farm or in a city."

He brings his face close to hers: "I know both of those clocks," he says. "I can go fast or I can go slow." She nods, liking the sound of that. So many women get obsessed over children and birds. She'd rather keep her sights on the future; upright and ironclad, like the Eiffel Tower.

CHAPTER FIVE

Château de Chambord, 1939

When, in her youth, Mathilde experienced love from her father or older brothers, it was spooned out as thin watery gruel, lacking regular nurturing and forgiveness, rudimentary principles necessary for a selfless and empathetic kind of love. For this reason, when she feels fear about the occupation, she wants to forget about everybody else, bar the doors, save herself. Her fingers twitch to bolt the double and triple locks. In that moment, she knows herself to be cruel and deranged. She was never taught love the way she was taught the alphabet and the basics of math by her conscientious schoolteachers. Forget the truck drivers, the castle staff, and the curators. Forget beauty. Somebody can paint something new when the nightmare is over. In her panic, Paris seems distant, her apartment, her clothes, all of it insignificant. Her greatest obsession is herself. But Philippe snaps her back. She sees him in the city, alone at the kitchen table, and she recoils at the error of her calculation. Leaving him there, knowing that the enemy could arrive in a matter of months or even weeks, waving goodbye that morning as if there were nothing to worry about, as if the sugar cubes would forever shine in the French cafés.

But no. This war. This nightmare. The horror is coming.

"I need a room with a door that locks, close to the exit," she says to Pierre Schommer.

She watches the endless crates being unloaded from the truck and rolling toward her. She feels sick about the impossibility of her task, to keep the artwork safe from the enemy. "This way, Mathilde," he says, all formality. "Watch your step."

She stops. "Is there another entrance without stairs?" He looks at her, hesitates, and she understands that he is wondering if she has a bad heart. "Not for me. For the men and the carts. It'll save so much time if they can roll their carts in without lifting."

"I'm afraid not." By now they have crossed a grand interior courtyard and entered a hall with richly coloured tapestries adorning the stone walls. In front of them rises a monumental staircase carved from white stone. "Unfortunately for us, Chambord is all about stairs," says Pierre. "All floors are accessed by this double helical staircase. Designed by Leonardo da Vinci."

"Clever, I'm sure," says Mathilde, "but a nightmare for men carrying heavy crates." She is eyeing the soldiers who are labouring under the weight of the double-walled wooden box.

"You and your prize," says Pierre, glancing down at the box, motioning with his chin, "are best to go here." They cross an enormous room with antlers mounted over a white fireplace to a short door tucked into the far corner.

"Here, this is about the only room with a working lock," says Pierre, handing her a pair of rusty iron keys. Inside the room, there is a canopy bed, a chair, and a washing basin on an ancient chest of drawers. She tells the soldiers to leave her luggage and go. Alone, she slides the wooden case below the bed, along with her large leather bag. It's stuffed with clothes and her old rifle from Alsace wrapped in a chenille blanket. She wipes her face on the towel by the basin and thirsts badly for a glass of water. A pitcher of boiled water—she will arrange that with the kitchen staff.

Out of the room, she turns the bolt twice, pockets the keys, and walks past Pierre at the entrance to the château. Two dozen men have already gathered, each standing beside large wooden crates, much bigger and heavier than her slim case. The sun is relentless. There is no wind. She walks quickly to the cases and checks their labels. In Paris, she was responsible for overseeing the packing of the entire collection of the Louvre museum: the historic archives; the Renaissance paintings from the Denon wing; the ancient Etruscan, Greek, and Roman sculptures and artifacts. The crown jewels, whose worth was incalculable, were sent to Château de Valençay farther south, as were the Louvre's most monumental of the sculptures, the *Venus de Milo* and the *Winged Victory of Samothrace*.

She steps to Pierre, turns her back to the men. "The Denon crates are heavy, filled with paintings that will need to be aired. They require a room with the least humidity, with good light."

"The chapel, west facing, afternoon light, upstairs two flights."

She considers and nods her approval. "The archives are paper manuscripts and books, also heavy, and the ancient vases packed in straw are susceptible to mildew."

"Large hall on the right, one flight up, likely drafty, no toilets but the archives won't mind."

"The small ancient sculptures, highly valuable, Iberian, African, Etruscan?" she asks.

"Leave them in the reception hall here." He nods at the cavernous space with the mounted antlers.

"We're agreed, then?"

"Absolutely."

"Shall I give the instructions?" asks Mathilde.

"Absolutely."

There are now forty men gathered in front of her. Some are in military uniforms, others are local police, another dozen are in civilian clothes—volunteers from La Samaritaine, a department store in Paris.

"My name is Mathilde and"—Pierre nudges her to raise her voice—"I represent the Louvre museum, as does Pierre Schommer. We are living in an extraordinary time. An evacuation of the Louvre and all the museums of Paris has never been conducted at this scale. And yet, here we are, working to our utmost capacity to save these works from plunder by the enemy. We will do everything in our capacity to keep these works safe. We are here to save the beauty during this . . ." She searches for the right words. "During this ugly time."

She looks back at Pierre. He nods in agreement. They will make a fine partnership, she decides. Hands shoved in her pockets, she pushes down the wave of nausea and slows her breathing. She has never spoken to a crowd before. But she needs to show her strength and tell them the plan, because without a plan, this unimaginable catastrophe, the unbearable waiting, will make all of them go mad. The Nazis are preparing to occupy France. And when they do, they will steal and destroy. The plundering of cultural artifacts has accompanied every triumphant seizing of a foreign power. History is merely repeating itself. The Château de Chambord will become the largest depot for the art that must be protected from destruction or theft. Above all, the wooden case with three red circles under her bed must not be harmed. Mathilde will protect her. Whatever it takes.

She needs to tell the men gathered in front of her what they should do, and so she begins: "Here are your orders . . ."

CHAPTER SIX

Alsace, 1905

"Take the shot."

"Take the shot, Piggy, Jesus Christ."

Her brothers are wedged beside her in the hide, rubbing up against her in their wool coats, the smell of sausage dank in the air. There is a thin layer of snow on the ground, and the clearing in the forest glows with the dusting.

"Shut the fuck up," she hisses back. Her breath in the cold makes puffs of air. She can feel the space between her shoulder blades ice over. The hem of her pants has grown stiff with a coating of frost. "She's changing her mind."

"The only one changing her mind is you. Jesus Christ, she's right there, take the shot."

It's not that she is fond of them, the wild boars. They dig up the family garden and scare her with their raspy snarls when she has finished milking the cows at night. Lord knows, they're an ugly beast given to ugly sounds. The same goes for her brothers. But she does not want to kill the mother pig if there are babies. She would rather keep the mother alive in that case. So that the father does not have to raise the babies by himself.

She—Mathilde, or Piggy, as her brothers always call her—is only fourteen years old. Motherless. Her fate. She has never known anything different.

She is generally happy. Content to be alive. Her father tells her that the things we never want to happen are gifts from God. It seems an optimistic view of the world for a man who complains about the milking cows running dry, the rains that are too harsh, the sun that is too fierce, the Boche who are occupying Alsace. He has only once acknowledged that her mother died in childbirth by telling her, "Look at you, Mathilde, the cause of your mother's death, how you're growing up these days."

She is not a brooder like her big brother, not given to fits of rage like her other one. She is curious about the world, about people, specifically relationships between mothers and daughters. At school, her girlfriends complain about how much they hate their mothers: "She's so mean! She's a horrible witch." Then, the next day, Mathilde asks how everything is at home. Are they still fighting? Was the mother asked to leave? She's astonished when her friends say blithely, "What? What are you talking about? No. We're fine. We're going to have custards at the bakery today."

Mostly she is graced with a wisdom that sits quietly behind her pale blue eyes. She knows that her mother was thirty-four years old when she died, the mother of two school-going boys, Claude and Lucien, that she worked the land with a pair of geldings, and birthed foals and other women's children, that she scrubbed her nails and put a garland of flowers in her hair to dance at the annual spring festival in Haguenau. She knows her father was thirty-eight when his wife died. He must miss her, his partner on the land, the warmth of her body in the bed. Who could blame him for drinking himself to sleep at night or pounding beers at the village tavern with his boozy friends while his children were out in the cold hunting for their meat?

What were her mother's dreams? Did she tickle her children's feet or pick flowers and study the colour and shape of their petals? There is no one to tell her. Certainly not her father, certainly not Claude or Lucien. Mathilde would sit in the village church with its single stained-glass window and bask in its flickering light. She'd tell herself that her mother must have admired the rose window in the same way, because a neighbour, an upright, laconic woman, had told her about the magnificence of her mother's eyes, how they were cornflower blue flecked with crystal. This was on the steps of the church after mass one Sunday; the woman laid a kindly hand on the motherless child to impart the observation. Mathilde still clings to the telling, opening and reopening the woman's words like a gift wrapped in gold tissue, such was her yearning for a mother's tenderness.

In the confines of the hunting hide, she hears the boys muttering next to her, their disgust at her for being a girl. They are both well into their teens, their voices cracking, pimples on their chins. Soon they'll announce the hunt is over and it's time to go home.

"All right, then, that's enough," says Claude on cue. "That's enough entertainment for the night. Porcine, *allez*, hand me the gun."

"I will not," she says evenly.

They want her to be quiet and still, like a hank of wool twisted into a loop and secured with a knot.

"You're too much of a sissy," says Lucien.

"I am not."

"Piggy doesn't want to kill her kind. Piggy likes her piggies." Lucien laughs maniacally and the older one makes him stop, not because his comment is asinine but for fear of scaring the animals. Mathilde breathes in and out slowly. She sees the boar not merely as a mammal standing at the edge of a forest but as a composition of colour: greys upon blue and black. She sees the long, uneven bristles of its coat, the diagonal of its snout like the branches of the trees. She does not speak of any of this to her brothers, how she sees the depth and intricacy of the objects in the world, for this would be incomprehensible to them. She keeps her seeing as a secret. This is one of her skills, holding secrets, though it is lonely work, to be the keeper of things that have been lived but cannot be told.

"I could catch that boar with my hands. Look at her standing there glowing in the moonlight. The ugliest beast on earth."

"Be patient," says Mathilde.

"I'm done waiting. Give me the gun. Goddamn it, Porcine."

The shot goes off. And then a second one. Two big boars lie dead, the white snow suddenly stained red.

The boys are silent for a minute.

"Bloody hell, she did it," whoops Lucien.

"Well marked. Neat to the neck," says Claude, allowing a modicum of credit.

"That's dinner for next year. Wild boar pâté, sausage, salami, ragu, you name it. I feel full already," says Lucien, clapping his hands together loudly.

She wonders why her brothers always think of her as inadequate. Never good enough. Not good with her maths or fast enough running the hills. They tell her that she isn't as funny with the telling of stories or as clever with the making of stew. She is too pudgy, her pink little-girl cheeks wobble when she runs. According to their measurements, she is less of what they imagined but they never imagined what she did well. She decides to fix her fate in that hide as the snow falls: She will become a better hunter than her brothers. Rather than bend like the sunflowers in the hot sun she will stand upright. And so she does. She never misses a shot. She never complains about the cold. These are the rules. How hard work will help her overcome.

CHAPTER SEVEN

Château de Chambord, 1939

Inside Chambord, she throws back the curtains, and the silk moans and sighs, then drops into her hands. She opens doors, hundreds of doors, and walks into clouds of cobwebs that cling to her face. In the queen's bedchamber, a room that feels cold enough to freeze raw sides of beef, she finds swallows nesting within the chestnut rafters. It matters not at all that the canopied beds and furniture are draped in blue damask; the animals have taken over. The mice and rats have burrowed deep inside the pillows. She watches an owl circling the crystal chandelier in the governor's bedroom. When she unlatches the window, there is no glass, only a gaping hole. The birds screech and fly out.

She feels as if she is living inside *Sleeping Beauty*. She remembers reading the story in her village school, bent over the book in the springtime, eating her lunch of salami on rye bread, devouring the coloured pictures of the sumptuous château with its velvet chairs and cupids darting above the sultry maiden asleep for one hundred years. . . . *And there, on a bed with curtains drawn wide . . .*

Pierre hands Mathilde a white curator's smock. She looks at the coat, nods her thanks, and puts it on. It's just after sunrise; they've already had their coffee and some baguette with jam. He looks at her steadily.

"What is it? Tell me," says Mathilde.

"All right, then. Several thousand crates will be arriving over the next few weeks."

She was part of the team authorizing the packing of the crates in Paris. But now there is more, much more than the collection from the Louvre.

"That's not possible," she says. "We can't. There's not enough room."

"Orders from Paris." He shrugs. "All the works from the museums, the churches, from as far north as Normandy will arrive here."

"But where?"

Together they climb the massive stone stairs that wind through the centre of the château. Out of breath, peering into the uppermost rooms, some lined with crimson velvet, others with red-veined marble fireplaces, they look at all the possibilities for storing the crates. Finally, they reach some magnificent spaces pierced by ethereal light, with exposed timbers that curve magnificently to create vaulted ceilings, once bedrooms of invited members of French royalty. Mathilde cannot imagine a duchess negotiating all the steps in a corseted long gown and precarious heeled shoes. Perhaps this explains why the château was barely used except for a few months at a time: a revolt among the wives and consorts, refusal to occupy Chambord.

Pierre points to the heavy, timbered ceiling. "The fire risk is great but we need the room." She walks outside to the upper terrace, hundreds of metres above the ground, the corner towers and minarets pushing their mighty spires into the sky. Pierre hands her a cigarette and she takes it without saying a word.

"We start fire drills tomorrow," he says, surveying the terrace.

"We'll haul the hoses up here and practise taking aim." Her heart sinks at the news. More hard labour, part of the irony of living with her colleagues as bohemians, while guarding the world's priceless masterpieces.

The scale of the evacuation is too overwhelming to comprehend. She looks out to the thin gravel path and the expanse of forest beyond. The sky is banked with clouds the colour of slate and the winds are roaring, flailing the tree branches mercilessly. She notices that the ducks floating on the water of the moat have been replaced by a single white swan. Always, her mind clenches down on what is to come: the spectre of the Nazis, of when and how they will arrive.

They work flat out, no longer as curators but as labourers, forced to drag crates too heavy to carry, using old bedspreads that help to slide across the stone floors. They stack the large, unwieldy crates from the Louvre museum first, clearing space, but more boxes start to arrive sporadically from all over: from Versailles (sixty-seven crates), from the Musée Rodin (twenty-five crates), from the churches of Paris (sixty-nine crates and twenty-one paintings unwrapped), from towns in the north and the east, from Honfleur and Strasbourg, Reims and Grasse.

France waits, vulnerable and uneasy. Mathilde tries not to think of Philippe walking to class at the Faculty of Law and sleeping alone in their apartment on the Rue de la Seine.

To keep herself sane, she trains her mind to consider only what must be done. She hauls mattresses across the stone floor and up the winding staircase to a hall once designed as Louis XIV's theatre. The dormitory is hastily arranged to accommodate the guards and carpenters. Thirty men sleeping together in one stone-walled room is no joke. There has been some loud complaining. Cook does her best to serve plenty of coffee with sugar and a demi-baguette to each of them by 7 a.m. before the work begins. Then Pierre divides up the tasks. The Château de Chambord is his fiefdom, and Mathilde is happy to focus on the collections rather than the running of this ancient ruin of a place. Some of the men are sent outside to dig a canal to bring water from the nearby Cosson River directly into the courtyard of the château. Water is desperately needed for cooking and cleaning, but it is also paramount for fire prevention. Everybody works as if they are possessed, driven by the menace of the invading army, of what is to come, how their lives will be destroyed. A team of labourers are digging new latrines inside the château, while still others are fixing the leaks in the vast slate roof. Winter will arrive hard and fast. Pierre arranges for plumbers to be brought in from the local villages to run heating lines for new radiators. There are fences and gates built around the edges of the courtyards to the south and the north of the château, made from chestnut trees felled nearby. The barricades rise prettily four feet from the ground. Mathilde looks at them with narrowed, scornful eyes. Can they not see how this attempt to keep out the enemy is pathetic? A child could imagine something more sinister.

Not long ago, she wore fine leather gloves to walk to work along the Rue de la Seine and across the bridge to the Louvre, her heels tapping on the cobblestones. Now she wears thick gardening gloves to keep the splinters at bay from the rough crates piled three high. It requires all her strength and gymnastic flexibility to climb up to each one. She and Suzanne Kahn, a curator and assistant to Jacques Jaujard, the director of the national museums, work closely together. Ever since they had a drunken girls' night in Montparnasse a few years ago, they've addressed each other informally and always by their first names. They scramble up the crates like mountain climbers, setting their crowbars into place, working fast to release the nails. Now, only one month into "*le sadique*"—Mathilde's way of summing up the sadistic, senseless reality of war—her canvas pants are dirty and torn, a cotton scarf tied around her head, bangs in her eyes. She no longer cares.

In Paris, Jacques Jaujard had asked Mathilde to personally supervise packing the art into wooden crates, ensuring the careful wrapping of paintings into thick cotton blankets, the nailing shut of the wooden crates, and the bold type used for labelling. Next, he had asked her to commission hundreds of trucks that would be useless for the war effort. She'd hired taxis, private cars, ambulances, and even transport lorries from the department stores and the Comédie-Française.

The entire operation is given a code name: Maintenance. Of utmost importance is emptying out the Louvre without attracting the attention of local Parisians or German spies who might be circulating within the capital.

She failed to notice her bosses and the bosses of the bosses remarking on her high efficiency. But, in the end, she was called in to meet with Jacques Jaujard. "Your work has been impressive," he said to her, walking to his mahogany desk, offering her a cigarette, taking a long drag from his own. "Maintenance has gone impeccably because of people like you. How long have you worked here?"

"Seven years," she said, eyes flitting to the window and the magnificent view of the Seine River. She trembled in the leather office chair, gripping her toes in her oxford lace-up shoes, wondering how much information he wanted to know. "As an assistant in archives, cataloguing and such, but now I'm arranging the takedown of the collections." She looked back at him and managed to smile. "That's something I have taken to heart."

"That's all fine, very good." He leaned forward and lowered his voice. "The Nazis will invade Poland any day now. It will only be a matter of time before they march into Paris. Six months, maybe one year. God only knows. Above all, the art must be protected. Tell me, Madame Payer, what would you like to do? Stay here or go with the collections?" Mathilde looked at the handsome, intelligent director. He was quintessentially Parisian, his dark hair perfectly arranged, his hands moving elegantly every time he spoke.

She wasn't sure how to answer. Was he firing her or offering her a job? Her fingers were clenched together in her lap. "Well, I can't imagine being separated from the artworks. But the nature of my task is not up to me," she said, wondering what exactly he was asking.

"Madame Payer, I have a particular commission in mind for you, but it requires much time away from Paris."

She thought instantly of her son, Philippe. Enrolled to begin his studies in law, no longer a child.

"I see."

"What was your position before coming to the Louvre?"

At this question, she hesitated. Going into the details of her past was not something she would do. "I was at home with my son, and then I worked at a local museum in Chambéry."

He looked at her for a long time and, satisfied by her answer, nodded.

"If you are in agreement, I would like to put you in charge of transporting the collection to a new location." Her mind went immediately to the task of scheduling convoys and arranging for transport manifests. Yes, she could do that. "I see," she said.

"There is something else," he said. "Something of critical importance." She felt her back stiffen. "You would be tasked with protecting the museum's most significant painting, the *Mona Lisa*."

Panic shot through her chest. She suddenly felt flushed. The man was still speaking. She could not hear him. "I beg your pardon?" she asked.

"This assignment requires the utmost discretion and dedication."

Mathilde stared at the director, stunned by what he was asking.

"Monsieur, may I ask, why me?"

"Your superiors have reported to me that you do careful work and that you can be absolutely trusted. You are not high level and therefore—my apologies, please do not take offense—you will not attract attention."

She found his comment amusing, even baffling. At one time, as Picasso's muse, she was noticed and adored. Men orbited around her, raised her up on a pedestal. Now, she had changed her identity, her long blonde hair had been cut short and had darkened over the years. No longer known as Mathilde or Mathi, she had become Madame Payer. Like all other women in their forties: Middle-aged. Invisible.

"But I'm just a lowly assistant archivist," she blurted out. "I sort through donated collections, I read the histories of an artwork, answer people's questions about where our miniature paintings come from, or whether the *Winged Victory of Samothrace* has actual feathers on her wings, and—"

"I've been told you give the best tours of the museum to children's groups."

"Well, that's easy enough."

"It's easy if you are passionate about art, Madame Payer." He looks at her and nods decisively.

"They're like people, the artworks. They live inside of me."

He nodded thoughtfully at her. "I'm glad we have met. Thank you for your work."

"Not just me, monsieur," she said. "I thank all the students from the Louvre school and the clerks from La Samaritaine," she said, "all the curators and guards, everybody packing up the collection with such care and speed."

"Madame Payer, you have a very important decision to make. Let me know whether you are willing."

She wanted to stand up, go to the window to consider for a bit, weigh the pros and the cons. But instead she pressed her hands hard to her thighs. "I think so . . ."

"Madame Payer," he said, leaning forward on his desk, a slight smile on his lips. "I would need to have a total and absolute affirmation. A complete commitment. A sacrifice. *La Joconde* is considered the definitive masterwork by Leonardo da Vinci."

"The world's greatest portrait," said Mathilde, pulling herself together. Taking on this assignment would require much sacrifice. But surely that is the nature of war, stepping up, sacrificing, even if it means less time with Philippe. She looked directly at Jacques Jaujard and said, "It would be an honour."

At the château, she feels resigned to doing her job during a tragic time. Ever since the Visigoths sacked Rome, the world's most treasured artworks have been vulnerable during war. Napoleon's armies plundered the monasteries and churches of Italy and many other nations; that's the truth of how the Louvre amassed much of its glorious collection.

At Chambord, she frequently shakes her head, trying to clear the despair, wanting a cigarette, clawing at her gold chain. She has to slow her breathing to keep the black rage from overwhelming her. She walks along the corridors with it, she runs it up and down the helical staircase that twists and soars through the château, trying to outrun the horror. When she pries open nails with a crowbar, she feels some satisfaction. Easing oil paintings from the straw into the sunlight, she feels part of something honourable in the world.

At night, she and Suzanne join Pierre and other conservation curators to play cards or act out charades. It's best in those moments not to think of what they are doing, organizing the mass evacuation of the world's largest museum to a dusty ruin of a château, and why. In a village restaurant, they link arms and sing the chansons from the old wooden cabarets in Paris, and they laugh so hard they buckle over and stamp their feet. It seems that living at the precipice of war has heightened their enjoyment of life, making them feel strangely manic while the German tanks roll closer.

Later, lying by herself on her stiff horsehair mattress, she cannot ignore the fact that another world war is about to unleash its evil on all humanity. Darkness has taken hold again, eclipsed love and joy to favour all that is barbaric and unthinkable: the killing of young men, women, and children, the stealing of all that is most esteemed, most beautiful. She reads in the papers that in the first months of war, two hundred thousand Poles have died. And then she thinks, *This is insanity. Here I am in the land of Voltaire and Rousseau, of human freedom and liberty, and look at me now.* She wants cigarettes, yes, and more than that, she craves opium, to help soften the blows, to help her fall out of time.

She is counting down the hours before she is scheduled to take the train from Blois to Paris. She will surprise Philippe for his twenty-first birthday. Her sweet, brilliant boy. She needs to be with him, trade stories, hear his laugh. They will walk the Luxembourg Gardens arm in arm and go for hot chocolate at Le Grand Véfour at the Palais-Royal. Perhaps they will see Colette with her shaggy hair and heavily lined kohl eyes leaning out from her salon window. They will talk and maybe he will tell her about a girl he likes from the faculty. Or not talk at all; it will be enough to be next to each other feeling their tender love, which somehow makes the world feel good again.

What to bring him as a gift? The question distracts her for days, but especially when she sets to uncrating some of the ancient sculptures from the Louvre. The unpacking is long and physically exhausting. She pulls animal carvings and religious relics from the web of straw and sets them on a table. She digs deeper to discover small figures from southern Spain, heads of Iberian women with long, exaggerated ears and flat, broad noses. The eyes are wild with a desire to know or the fear that attends women wanting to know. They remind Mathilde of the ones Picasso kept in his cupboard. Long ago, during her other life, the one that nobody at the Louvre can ever learn about. She thinks, *I was wild and stupid.*

CHAPTER EIGHT

Paris, 1910

At Picasso's studio, Mathilde notices the tubes of paint and cigarette butts dropped onto the floor and a pile of coal heaped next to a wicker chair. She shakes out her umbrella and looks for hooks to hang up her coat. She had imagined that he would greet her at the door, but he has his back to her, engaged in lively conversation, hands gesturing, ears jutting from his perfectly shaped head. Such a short man, and yet he commands everybody's attention.

She gives up on hooks and drops her coat on the floor with the others. Georges Braque and Fernande Olivier are playing a game, waving rags at the timbered ceiling to set some colourful paper lanterns swinging through the air. She recognizes the artist Marie Laurencin, her head cocked to the side, lips pouting, glass raised. The energy in the studio feels unleashed, salty and sweet. The men in their rumpled suits look over Mathilde with hungry eyes.

How very unlike the sapping energy of weekends on the family farm in Alsace. When she was called Piggy, when her grandparents and the neighbour, a widow in black lace, drank beer and sat rigid in their fetid disdain for the Germans—reviled as the land-grabbing colonizers. Their bitterness infected her blood and grew tiny pointy teeth, attaching to her gut like a terrible unnamed growth. Hatred of the other sharpens the blade of her resolve to be selfish and chart her own path. This is the only advantage of being motherless. Her friends at school were all married by the time they were eighteen years old. That was considered an excellent option for a virtuous girl, a vision roundly rejected by Mathilde.

Mathilde took up her usual post on a wooden stool placed by the hearth, using folded newspapers as a cushion, her face a blank canvas, dreamless.

Porcine, *débarrasse la table.*

Porcine, *va chercher du bois.*

The genesis of the nickname Piggy, as relayed to her by her grandmother with a shrug, was because she drank her bottles of milk with a lusty appetite as a baby. "I'm sure, had she lived, God bless her, your mother wouldn't have been able to keep up. Even when you were four, you were still drinking gallons every week."

"But I'm sixteen now," Mathilde remembered saying to her. She felt an awareness of herself as a human being worthy of respect or occasional acts of kindness from her brothers and father. Maybe she ought to be able to speak of her dreams and aspirations as an artist without risking being humiliated at the dinner table. Instead, she would absorb their blows and smile along, sometimes excusing herself from the kitchen to run across the yard to scream her frustration in the pig barn.

Georges Braque removes his wool jacket and extends a hand to Mathilde. She likes his gentle, confident nature, a man from the north, a house painter from Le Havre, who can be trusted. Once, in his studio next to Picasso's, he explained to her that he no longer paints landscapes because he prefers objects such as vases or guitars that he can touch and celebrate for their original geometric shapes.

She likes the wool vest he is wearing over a white shirt, and the thin black ribbon tied around his neck. She likes the curl of his mouth and the way he is swinging her around in his arms to see if their movement will activate the lanterns. Their friends cheer them on. Max Jacob, ever kind and attentive, pours drinks and passes them around. He likes to recite the poetry of Verlaine, as he does now:

The sun, less hot, looks from a sky more clear;
The roses in their sleepy loveliness
Nod to the cradling wind. The atmosphere
Enfolds us with a sister's tenderness.

He recites, standing, while looking at Picasso, whom he loves as much as he can, for Max is a homosexual and his Spanish friend is not. The lines of their sexual preferences were drawn some years earlier when the men roomed together. Maybe this forced an existential crisis—to use an Apollinaire expression—so painful and difficult that it provoked both of them to contemplate suicide together. At least this is what Max had whispered to Mathilde at one of their parties, but she was never sure if it was true or a figment of his imagination, opium- or ether-induced. To her, Max is a kind soul whose own poetry is both bizarre and bleak, whose stories involve men attending mass while their wives are at the cabaret and children dying of croup or colic. Max and Picasso are not your typical work colleagues, she thinks. They have faced death together and now Picasso is illustrating one of Max's new books. Such is the way of artists. To prove themselves with the next brilliant work.

Braque heaves Mathilde effortlessly into the air and onto his shoulders. She gasps and laughs out loud. Everything about the atelier—the wooden easels, the guitars and mandolins propped against the walls—feels like liberation. She reaches her arms up toward the ceiling's wooden timbers and jostles the lanterns so that they move like scarecrows in cornfields. The artists in the studio stamp their feet and whistle. When Mathilde swings one leg around and slides her body down Braque's chest, he murmurs "You're fantastic" into her ear and she laughs and presses herself against him for a moment, enough to let him know that she is willing.

Picasso wolf whistles and signals for quiet. His eyes scan the room, and Mathilde notices how intensely watchful he is, chopping everybody up into pieces and reconstructing them again. She has never met a man like him. This Spaniard with bulls charging from his soul. The friends gather, out of breath, faces radiant with the dance of the lantern. Marie and Apollinaire stop kissing and drape their arms around each other to listen respectfully.

"*Biens, biens!*" Picasso calls in an accent that Mathilde thinks comical. He means to say *Viens, viens!* but his native Spanish often gets in the way. No matter. Everybody crowds around him. Picasso pulls open a drawer of an old wooden chest and reaches in. He is cradling something in his hand. "Snow White," he says, allowing everybody a turn to look at the wriggling tiny creature. He steps at last to Mathilde and lets her peek inside his cupped hands.

"Oh, a mouse," she says, disappointed.

"Eh, but, Mathi, you disapprove?" he asks, brown eyes startled wide.

"I used to kill them," she says with a shrug. "We didn't keep them as pets."

"You are not a nice girl," says Picasso, looking wounded. He puts the mouse quietly back into the drawer.

"Why did you say that, about the mouse?" asks Fernande, leaning over to Mathilde. "Now he'll go into a dark mood."

And she is right. The artists watch as Picasso storms out of the studio to the courtyard where another group of friends are laughing and shouting loudly. He tells them to shut up but this only provokes hoots of derision. One of them falls off the bench clutching his sides in laughter. But Picasso has produced a pistol and is firing shots into the air. The crowd goes silent, hands go up in surrender, and the friends slowly retreat to their studios. Fernande and Mathilde rush into the courtyard. Fernande tries to simultaneously soothe and reprimand her Pablo. "You shouldn't have done that, Pablo. They're not worth it."

But Mathilde interrupts: "I bet you are a lousy shot."

This gets Picasso's attention. "I am not."

"Show me."

"That apple tree over there." He takes aim and misses.

Mathilde reaches for the gun. He drops it in her open palm. "The wine bottle on the bench." She takes her time, aims well, and shatters the bottle with one bullet.

But by then, Picasso is already inside, commanding his friends to their next positions.

Easels have been moved to the edges of the room to make way for two straw mattresses and some wooden chairs. On the wall next to where she is standing, there is a very large painting that Picasso calls *Les Demoiselles d'Avignon*. Mathilde likes its violence, the jagged bodies, its truth. There is no softness in the faces of these women, no tenderness or redemption, just damage. These five whores exist to pleasure men. That is their lot in life, to sacrifice their worth. To put it differently would be a lie. A small oil lamp is lit by a friend of Picasso's—she doesn't know his name—and shadows from the flames are thrown against his canvases of sad-eyed acrobats and brothers walking side by side. A clay bowl filled with a tarry, amber-coloured paste is brought forward by Fernande. Picasso is holding a long, thin needle and a bamboo pipe adorned with metal inlay. He takes a pea-shaped ball of the opium and cooks it gently in the small bowl over the flame of the lamp. The ball grows elastic as it cooks, and then he tips the needle into the bowl and drops the liquid into his pipe. He reclines and pulls deeply on his pipe. Smoke rises into the room, sending a musky perfume into the air. "The most intelligent of all odours," he says, passing the pot and needle to others in the room. Mathilde has not brought her own pipe and so Picasso allows her to borrow his. "As a favour to you, Mathi, I share with you my friends and this substance for unlocking your mind. You will see, Montmartre is a world away from the Brasserie Lipp."

Smiling at him, enjoying the smell of oil paint on his tanned, burnished skin, she takes a deep pull on the pipe, deciding that she loves this life. How fluid and accepting everybody seems to be. She inhales again, stunned by the beautiful release, as if she is being baptised and given a new name. Mathi, so much freer than Mathilde. The room is cold but the air is perfumed by a tropical mix of nutmeg and sandalwood. These artists are penniless but they are not suffering; none of them seem to subscribe to the Catholic piling on of guilt and the need to seek forgiveness by climbing stairs on their knees until they bleed.

Suzanne Valadon has entered the studio. She stands at the door, smoking a cigarette, surveying the scene. Perhaps she will ask all of the men to take off their clothes so she can paint them. Mathilde wishes that she would. Her life in Alsace presents itself to her like an old sepia photograph with blurred faces. Only Franz made her believe that she could grow beyond Haguenau. She misses him desperately even while surrounded by all of these fabulous creatures. Together in Paris with him, what a dream. For Franz had a way of steadying her mind and inspiring her to move past some of the sadness of her childhood to get on with life.

Apollinaire stands up, brushes a lock of dark hair from his forehead, and holds his pipe aloft. The chain of his watch swings across his scruffy vest. After a few minutes, he begins to speak. Mathilde can't tell if he is reciting a poem he had written before, or inventing spontaneously:

Drunk on gin the Paris nights

"And opium!" Fernande shouts, interrupting.

Apollinaire goes on as though he hadn't heard:

Blaze with electricity
The trolleys flashing greenish lights
Warble along their staves of tracks
The folly of machinery

Apollinaire nods at the crowd and everybody applauds.

Picasso passes around a bowl of cherries and invites Mathilde to have some, emphasizing the soft *s* sounds: *cerises*. Far from being in a dark mood, he seems happy and needy around her. She takes his *béret basque* off a hook and angles the black hat over her long blonde hair. The rain pours down. Mathilde thinks it sounds like gentle splashes of laughter. She lies back on the straw mattress next to Picasso, staring up at the dancing lanterns. She likes the sound of Picasso breathing next to her, the way he turns to her and says: "When you know me, you will love me."

"We are all missing parts, but then we find them again," she says to Picasso. She smiles at her wisdom, at the colourful lanterns swaying gently overhead. The artists have drifted away, Fernande, as well, leaving Picasso and his young muse to lie in peace on a mattress on the floor. For a long time, they do not speak. Then, she can hear her voice:

"What scares you, Pablo?"

"Running out of ideas," he says, at last. She can see his eyes are wide open, blinking through new concepts.

"Anything else?"

"Of course, but you know already. Mice," he says, laughing. He reaches out and strokes a cheekbone high on her face. "But I must ask. How about you? Mathi, what scares you?"

"Who, me?" Mathilde grows serious. Inwardly, she thinks, *Trust.* Trusting other people. She cannot. She cannot bring herself to trust other people. Not entirely. Not deeply. Not in the way that makes true love possible.

Finally, she claps her hands and looks directly at Picasso: "Being a farm girl forever."

CHAPTER NINE

Paris, 1910

At the Louvre's building workshop, Vincenzo puts on a white smock and arranges his tools carefully on a thick oak table. Some carpenters pass by to say hello in a formal French way, others insult him, the Italian immigrant, bending close to call him "Macaroni" and sneer in his face. He steadies himself, arranging and rearranging his tools all over again. He opens a large wooden case and gazes down at the *Mona Lisa*. Four hundred years old and she is still magnificent. Her clothes have darkened but her face remains luminous. Lisa Gherardini of Florence, imprisoned by the French and given a distasteful nickname: *La Joconde.*

La macaroni.

Dirty Italian.

He stares at the Renaissance woman for a long time and the landscape behind her, the curl of the river, the undulating flood plain. If only he could show this Florentine woman to his younger brothers and sisters, they could gaze at this great painting and be proud of their Italian heritage. He sends whatever meagre income he earns to his family but knows they continue to live in grinding poverty like most other Italians. He wishes there was a way he could give his aging parents a comfortable life. They had worked long and hard as farmers with little to show for their back-breaking labour. Most of the men from his village have moved away, like Vincenzo, to find work in the big, modern cities of Europe. Others have crossed the Atlantic to make a better life in North America. Though their wages are slightly improved, they must endure taunts and barbs from locals who loathe people from away. He has heard this from a cousin who moved to Boston. In Paris, he knows about the opening of a new subway, has seen the Renault taxis powering through the streets, but he could never dream of such luxuries. He cooks his eggs over a candle.

Fingers trembling, sweat pricking his forehead, he places the shadow box on top of the painting and waits for calamity. A hairline crack through the poplar wood or a chip? He bends close and inspects every detail of da Vinci's masterwork. After a long minute, he breathes a sigh of relief. Everything seems to be fine. He secures the protective case with tiny golden nails.

A French worker in a white smock passes by and says, "Pasta face." Vincenzo grows cold at the insult but will not react, will not look up. He picks up the *Mona Lisa*, wraps the painting in a white blanket, and carries it like a swaddled child in both arms. "Hail Mary, mother of God, pray for us sinners, now and at the hour of our death." His lips are moving automatically—he began reciting the prayer at bedtime when he was three years old, with his mother kneeling by his side—and the words of the prayer are inaudible as he leaves the workshop, cradling the painting, treading along corridors and exhibition halls until finally arriving at the magnificent Salon Carré.

Below an ornate ceiling of gold and blue, with carved tributes to the arts and architecture, he steps directly to the empty square where the *Mona Lisa* will hang. He sets the portrait on the floor, leaning it gingerly against the wall, wishing he had arranged for a portable table. Thankfully, only a few people are visiting this morning. Keeping his head down, working carefully, he marks the identified spot with a level. He screws four iron bolts into the wall and steps back to evaluate. Feeling his own insignificance below the soaring heights of the gallery, he sets his level horizontally and vertically to ensure perfection. His eyes sweep across the wall to dozens of other paintings on exhibit, all plundered from Italy: Titian's *Allegory of Marriage* and Correggio's *Mystic Marriage of Saint Catherine*. A small, modest square pierced by four bolts hovers in front of him. It seems to him that to hang the *Mona Lisa* there is to make her asphyxiate. In Italy, she would be given a grand gallery of her own, room to be truly seen, to breathe.

Bending to the wooden floor, he unwraps the painting from its blanket and runs his fingers around the new protective frame and glass, checking for strength and integrity. The construction is solid and yet he feels bereft, as if he were a father dropping a daughter into the depths of the ocean without a life jacket. He looks at his calloused fingers, the hands of a labourer available for cheap hire. A wave of sadness crashes over him. He wonders whether the beautiful Mathilde will see him again. It seems unlikely, as she could have anybody, maybe even Picasso. Why waste her time with a penniless Italian? But he shakes free of such thoughts. His boss will be looking for him, wanting him to get on to the next painting. There will be more insults to endure from some of the French carpenters. The portrait hung in place, he gathers his tools, folds the blanket, and prepares to walk across the soaring gallery. Hesitating, he leans close to her stoic, legendary face, and whispers, "Signora, you don't belong here."

CHAPTER TEN

Alsace, 1899

After school, late in the afternoon, the sun vacates the sky, pulling blankets of warmth away from the day. They play hide-and-seek in the woods, below the farmhouse. Sometimes friends from down the dirt road join them, but today it is just Mathilde and her brothers. Leaves are thick on the ground, damp and mouldering. Winter hangs in the distance, ominous, crows cackling somewhere unseen in the bony trees.

Fifty. Fifty-one. Fifty-two. Fifty-three. Mathilde counts to one hundred, as she has been instructed, and now she is coming to get them. She scrambles to her feet and crashes through the underbrush, sure to find one of them behind the scratchy juniper bushes. But no, nobody there.

One. Two. Three. Four. Her brothers likely need more time and, obediently, she begins to count all over again. *Five. Six. Seven. Eight.* She turns in the opposite direction, feverish with anticipation, panting hard as she leaps down the hill toward the oak thicket and the dens favoured by deer and wild boar. She slices through the air with a bony stick, yelling, "I'll get you! I'll get you!" Nobody is there. She goes farther into the forest and, finding no one, races back up the hill, scratching her face badly on a branch that snaps back at her. "Where are you?" she cries into the shadows, for it is dusk now and she can't hear their voices. She hears nothing at all, not even the faintest whisper or conspiring giggles. She stumbles through the valley looking for her brothers for another hour. Her ears sting with the cold. She no longer feels her numb fingers. Still, it is her responsibility to play the game and find them because she is "it."

She fears failing at the game, that they will stop inviting her to play with them. She is also afraid that her father might be angry when he discovers his sons have disappeared and she did not recover them. She finally makes her way home, prepared to tell all to her father, only to discover her brothers hunched over their dinner at the kitchen table. When they see her, they point and laugh and call her an idiot for believing they were hiding.

"Eh, Porcine! That was two hours ago. We never even hid."

"You're so dumb. What have you been doing all this time, Porcine? Playing with your dolls?"

She stops her tears. Wipes the snot from her nose. Writes the experience down in her mind. At eight years old, this is when she understands that between black and white, there is something grey and viscous called duplicity.

CHAPTER ELEVEN

Paris, 1939

Mathilde abhors what is unseen and unknown, like a cyst on your liver, harmless until it strikes you dead. Being in limbo, waiting for the Nazis to march into France, is pushing her to the edge of insanity. Her skin crawls with invisible bugs; even on the train, she itches her legs and arms, convinced of bites that don't exist. The November skies of the Loire Valley are misted slate blue and the rain slides in silver tears down her window.

At last, from the far end of the car, a metal door slides open and a ticket agent appears.

"Monsieur," she acknowledges when he finally hovers by her side.

"Madame, *bonsoir*."

"When will dinner be served?"

"Dinner?" His uniform is rumpled and he looks to be unshaved. There is no chance of beating back the Nazis with this kind of recruit. "The dinner service was cancelled months ago."

She considers arguing with him but only allows a curt, dismissive nod. There are a few passengers in her car. Nobody notices, at least, nobody seems to care anymore. She uncorks a Sancerre from her bag and drinks unceremoniously from the bottle. The wine tastes of asparagus, grass, and wet stones. Very good, even if she looks like a sad alcoholic. She gazes outside dully at sheep grazing in the fields, the moss growing over some of the terracotta shingles of the little stone houses. She finds all of it, the shallow water, the bruised leaves of the chestnut trees, the people shuffling into the cheerless boulangerie, to be a warning. Nobody can say what or when. *But why?* A question asked by a child. An adult might answer: *Because the world creates tyrants and dictators with the certainty of the moon rising and falling. It's possible to set your stopwatch, such is the predictability of their rise. But how? By unleashing an evil appetite that can never be sated. And silencing anybody who doesn't kiss the ring.* Bending down, Mathilde starts to itch away a nasty bug.

When her train pulls into the station in Paris, the impending sense of dread suddenly lifts, to be replaced by the sounds of a crazed party. The sky has turned bright blue. An elephant is crossing the street with circus keepers dressed in top hats and white suits. A pretty woman dazzling in a trapeze tutu climbs effortlessly on top of the beast. Cars stop, pedestrians applaud, jesters turn cartwheels, and the elephant saunters away. She looks around, expecting Salvador Dalí to step next to her with a twinkle in his eye, twirling the tips of his moustache. The cafés and restaurants are packed and some of them are pounding with music coming across radio airwaves. She pushes her way to the zinc counter of a café and requests a double espresso. The barman looks away as if a little disappointed she didn't order champagne. He turns mechanically to the gleaming machine. Parisians seem oblivious to the impending war, and Mathilde thinks, with relief, *Let the party go on and on*. She walks directly to the Faculty of Law at the Place du Panthéon and waits by the monumental front entrance to surprise Philippe. The doors of the main lecture hall swing open exactly on time, but she must wait several minutes before he emerges, taller than his classmates, his hair carefully combed back, impossibly handsome, his cheeks blooming red. He is gazing sweetly at a dark-haired beauty walking next to him. Mathilde sees him grab her hand and draw her into an embrace. He kisses her and she smiles wide and kisses him back, and then they are out into the hallway, jostling with the rest of the class. She waits, enjoying this capture of him as a kind young man, watches the slight lift of shoulders, the way he bends his head toward his friends, his attempt to fit in and overcome his shy nature. She watches and feels incredible pride, for he has been alone in Paris without her. His father decamped to London a year ago. She waves at her son at last and sees his brow crease, his smile vanish. He turns to say goodbye to the woman. For a second she regrets her decision to simply show up, but he rushes toward her and lifts her up in a massive hug. He squeezes her tight and whispers, "Maman."

Now she is the one to be surprised. Philippe has never liked to hug, not even as a toddler when she wanted to read him a story cuddled under a blanket. He always preferred to sit side by side on the large rocking chair, twisting and jiggling, his fingers in his mouth.

They walk arm in arm down the hill from the Panthéon to cross into the Luxembourg Gardens. The trees are dressed in emerald greenery, the leaves shimmy and flutter. But, suddenly, the sun goes low and dusk descends. The familiar features of the park, the colours of the flowers and shrubs arranged in crescendos of yellow, pink, and purple, are snuffed out by the night, and they navigate the park by memory, bending and sloping their bodies around the circular fountains, trusting the sound of their shoes on the pebble path, guided by the intoxicating smell of hot chocolate wafting from a kiosk in the near distance. It isn't Le Grand Véfour but the cocoa is warm and thick, enough to propel them to Saint-Germain-des-Prés to change into fresh clothes. "We'll go to La Coupole for oysters and champagne. Then to one of the *bals-musettes*," she calls from her bedroom, thrilled to be back home with carpet underfoot and bold, colourful paintings by some of her friends on the walls. The kitchen sink needs a deep clean but she simply doesn't care. She is reunited with Philippe! It feels like receiving a beautiful gift, even with the knowledge that she must return to the icy confines of the Château de Chambord in two days.

"Maman, I am so happy you are home." He grips her again in his arms and holds her by the shoulders, looking suddenly serious: "If it's okay with you, I'd like to invite somebody else for tonight."

She has been expecting this and does her best to hide her disappointment that she must share her son on his twenty-first birthday.

"Wonderful," she says, turning away. "Of course. What is her name?"

"Rachel."

"Does she have a last name?"

She can hear his mind ticking over, as if debating whether or not to tell her.

"Rachel Reiman," he says, at last.

"Lovely. I look forward to meeting her."

She meets Rachel that night at a bohemian dance hall on the Left Bank. Inside, there are panels of faded red velvet on the wall and men in suits and ties drinking beer from frosted glasses. A waiter shows them to one of the little round tables with a checkered tablecloth. They order red wine with *steak frites*, clinking their glasses to celebrate Philippe's birthday. "A toast to Philippe, who makes me proud every single day. Here's to your brilliant legal career," says Mathilde, raising her glass to her son.

"*Santé*," says Rachel, smiling widely. "I'd also like to toast to

Philippe, who makes me so happy even when I have to memorize the Napoleonic Code." They laugh and clink glasses again. "And, if I may," adds Rachel, "to your mother, Philippe, who raised a fine, handsome son with qualities that matter so much to me: kindness, strength, and a clear, ethical mind."

The moment feels perfect, more real and authentic than anything lit up on the Champs-Élysées. Mathilde lights a cigarette and gazes at the young woman sitting across from her. The pearl earrings, the gold bracelets, everything glowing in the silky light of the table lamp.

Two musicians step forward and hoist their instruments. An accordion pressed against a man's chest, a violin to the crook of a woman's neck. Mathilde would give anything to let this night last forever. The steak, the wine, the music, everything done to perfection. The truth is that she dreads leaving her son and the glories of Paris all over again. But there is no time for melancholy. The waiters clear their plates and ask them kindly to get up so that they can move the tables to make way for a modest dance floor. Strangers in suits remove their fedoras and one after another ask Mathilde to dance. She laughs and twirls on the dance floor, catching glimpses of Rachel dancing the foxtrot with Philippe. He saves the waltzes for his mother. They swirl around and around, Mathilde's skirt flying, his one hand steady on her back, the other clutching hers in the air. They are singing along to the music and laughing when their voices stray badly from the actual melody. He leads her back to the table and she orders another round of champagne. After that, the evening unfolds like Josephine Baker singing some intoxicating jazz. Her fingers caress the tiny amber beads hanging from the fringe of the table lamp. A saxophonist and trombone player arrive to press in next to the other musicians. Waiters lift their drink trays high over their heads and squeeze through the crowd. Next a double bassist is waved through. Mathilde laughs at the comedy of it all, how he finds room to angle his gigantic instrument into a tiny performance space. Everybody applauds and the band starts up.

The next song is faster, more swing than foxtrot. Mathilde lights a cigarette and waves the young couple to the dance floor. She thinks back to the time when she first taught Philippe how to transition from quick step to lilting on dimly lit winter afternoons in their apartment on Rue de la Seine. She remembers his sweet, sweaty hands in hers, and his protests against learning dance when all he wanted was to go play soccer in the park with his school friends. But she held firm, insisted that dancing was what Parisians went out and did, even if her husband preferred the quiet of his study, reading the newspapers, analyzing the rise and fall of his financial stocks while the cat sprawled on his lap, purring loudly.

The three of them had moved to Paris from the town of Chambéry in the southern Alps, where people preferred mountain climbing to dancing. For Mathilde, it felt like seventeen very long years in exile. She looked after Philippe, found an insignificant job making some pin money at the local fine arts museum. With time, her hair grew dark and she cut it short. She craved friends but Chambéry was wary of outsiders. Winters, they skied as a family in the mountains, the snow blanketing the town with a white hush. Mostly, she shut out her years in Paris and her abrupt exit as a secret best kept under lock and key, and when some of it bubbled to the surface, she regarded it with alternating mirth and confusion. Being a mother required her to set aside her past delinquencies to model good behaviour for her son. Bending to Philippe, speaking to him kindly and firmly about how to cross the streets safely, how to address the neighbours politely, but also why he shouldn't steal the lemon candies from their local grocer. When she returns the candies to the shop with her chastised son in tow, her fingers twitch at the thought of pocketing a few sweets of her own. Old addictions, it turns out, are hard to break.

She sips her champagne, savours the bubbles, the delightful head rush. On her tongue, she tastes buttery croissants and green apples, but she also remembers the magic of Paris, of wandering through glass-roofed arcades at sunset, sitting on the grand steps of the Palais Garnier before watching *La Bohème*, children playing hoops in the courtyard of her apartment building. She watches Philippe dance with Rachel, marvelling at the way she arches her back elegantly to signal the start of the dance before following Philippe's confident lead. She moves beautifully, her long black hair floating through the air, her bright eyes looking up at him in a perpetual question. He looks down, head angled toward her face, and beams a smile at her. Their optimism for the future is palpable and she feels it, like the champagne, bubbling through her mind. Gone is her gloomy mood from earlier that day. The itching stopped the moment she got off the train. She sees Philippe and Rachel look over at her. She waves and blows them a kiss. Such a kitsch gesture, but why not? It's obvious they're in love. Mathilde finishes her glass, feeling the tiny, sugared bubbles waft through her head. She wants to be entirely happy for her son and let him revel in this first love, the way she did in Alsace so many years ago with Franz. But, without warning, she suddenly feels something crawling up the back of her neck. She has heard rumours that even now the Vichy government is rounding up artists, musicians, and academics—Jewish intellectuals—who escaped from Germany in the past year only to be handcuffed by French officials and sent to some kind of holding camp in Aix-en-Provence. She doesn't know the details. Surely this girl from the prestigious Faculty of Law will be safe from any harassment. The professors are among the most distinguished thinkers in Europe and could effortlessly denounce any crimes of humanity. She begins to itch her neck, scraping at her skin with her fingernails. *Relax*, she tells herself, *you're being overly dramatic*. The Nazis have yet to arrive, and maybe they never will. Damn the enemy. Long live the spectacle of love. She waves at the waiter, who bends close to her ear. "Another bottle, *s'il vous plaît*," she says, flirting back, happy with her decision to get properly drunk tonight. *Allons faire la fête!* It's Paris, she's in Paris! Her champagne brain wants the party to go on and on.

CHAPTER TWELVE

Paris, 1911

Picasso calls Mathilde at the restaurant and tells her to come to his studio in Montmartre.

"I have to work," she says.

"Ask somebody to take your shift."

"No, I can't." Mathilde is huddled next to a back alcove of the Brasserie Lipp where the restaurant's single telephone lives.

"*Biens, biens!* You peel potatoes instead of seeing me. You are not nice. I think you are a monster."

"But I like it here. They pay me."

"Come over. We'll have a good time. Are you going to make me say please? You are a monster of *indifférence*."

"No, I'm not going to make you say please. Speak however you like."

"I need the lines of your body. I need to put them down on paper. Your back. Your legs. Your hair."

His confidence is intoxicating. His arrogance. She has kept Picasso's advances at bay so far, but she realizes it'll be tricky to continue posing as his muse without having sex with him.

The cook in the kitchen appears in the alcove and rolls his eyes at Mathilde. Large meaty hands, white apron covering his enormous girth, his eyes glassy blue orbs. She puts up a finger to indicate one more minute. She can hear Picasso breathing at the end of the line. It would be easy to lose herself in the ego of this man, if she didn't come armed with experience about selfish men. She can thank her brothers for that.

"The end of my shift. Tonight, I might come see you."

"See you then." He hangs up first, and she steps out to the back courtyard to tilt her face up to the sunshine and bask in the thrill of being wanted by Picasso. She doesn't even mind when, back inside the kitchen, the cook sets three buckets of potatoes down on the floor beside her. "Peeled, and cut into quarters. Use a sharp knife." Mathilde nods quickly and reaches for a knife, admiring its honed steel and bone handle.

The Lipp is a classic brasserie on Boulevard Saint-Germain known for its French cuisine as well as its German dishes: Bismarck herring or sausage with cabbage called *choucroute garnie*. The owner, Monsieur Lipp, left Alsace after the Germans took over the region in eastern France some forty years ago. Monsieur Lipp introduced Mathilde to the kitchen staff as a painter and fellow Alsatian. To be an Alsatian is to come from a spirited, unique culture and rich land: the dry, languid autumns, Riesling wines with aromas of citrus and peach, plum and cherry fruit. The French have a nose for great grand cru wine and world-famous couture and perfume. Germans have a nose for promising returns on their investments. Under their stewardship, the Alsatian economy brightens, roads and railways are built, and locals have the right to speak French and learn German at schools.

Later that night, as she walks to Picasso's studio through the shanty town below the Sacré-Coeur Basilica, Mathilde's dark feelings come at her suddenly, dropping like a red velvet curtain at the end of a ballet. The shabby, small houses leading up the hill to the square look impossibly wretched. She does not wish to define herself against others, but she feels suddenly on edge. She should care about the poor but she doesn't, not really. Part of this has to do with her resolve to not end up poor, like her father on the farm. She won't be returning to her family at Christmas, such is her desire to make a clean break. Though her memories linger of some of what she experienced there—never daring to share any of her hopes to be an artist, hiding all of her sketches on rough brown paper from her brothers and her father, and Franz, always Franz.

There is a wet chill to the Paris air. *Another grey January day*, she thinks, feeling the cold stiffening her bones. She buttons up her coat and picks up her pace, willing herself to get warm, wishing her hands had not turned red before her arrival at the Bateau-Lavoir. Most of her art is kept on a lower shelf at Picasso's studio. He's generous with his studio space, always clearing plenty of room for her to work on an old warehouse table. She thinks her art might be inching toward something bold, that it could contain some provocations about the Industrial Age. She wishes that Picasso would ask about her own art projects, the collages she is assembling from wire and mesh found in construction sites. His interest, even if feigned, would help to boost her confidence.

Stepping into the Bateau-Lavoir, Mathilde hears the excitement of voices speaking in Spanish or French as painters prepare their canvases for the spring exhibition at the Grand Palais in Paris. She can see bare light bulbs illuminating the studios, smell the bitter scent of coal burners working overtime. Three easels stand in the middle of Picasso's studio, the straw mattresses from the recent opium party flung off to the side. He tells her to sit on a stool and turns to uncork a bottle of red wine. He takes a rag, wipes out two glasses, and pours a drink for himself and one for Mathilde. He stares at her while he drinks, a thick red scarf at his neck. She stares back at him evenly, relishing the heat between them.

"I don't trust blue eyes," he says, smiling a little. "Especially yours, like pieces of ice."

Most of what comes out of his mouth confuses her. But she is attracted to him. It's not like her sexual attraction to Vincenzo, necessary and delicious, like salt on your steak. Being around Picasso lights her brain on fire. His passion is infectious. In every work of art, he's telling a story about everyday objects, about a ceramic pot or a water jug, speaking their truth like Jesus and his parables. It's hard to know how much Picasso wants to have her. Mathilde thinks of Picasso's girlfriend, Fernande Olivier, and her wounded eyes at the party.

"Let us trade stories of our childhood," he says. "You go first." He looks at her intensely and drinks from his cup of wine.

She is sketching an underground subway tunnel, empty, except for a single dark figure. Looking up from her paper, holding the black conté between her fingers, she's not sure how much she can trust him. "I liked to visit the cows in the field next to us. In Alsace." He looks away from her and starts mixing some paints, refusing to give her advice on how to make art. "One day, I walked into the field with a pail of apples. The cows suddenly pressed around me. They were so close I could see the slobber dripping from their nostrils. I pushed their faces away, and when I ran, they came after me. Cows can run fast, did you know that?" She looks at him and he looks up and merely shrugs. "I dropped the pail and climbed up a tree. The cows kept me there for six hours, until nighttime."

"The cows kept you prisoner?" He laughs, short and scornful. "Well, that was an interesting choice."

Mathilde feels her cheeks burn hot with shame. She would like to return to her drawing. But she recovers and starts to laugh with him. "Spotted guards, chewing grass. It's an artwork. And you, Pablo?"

"I was raised by women." He looks at her, cocks his head to the side, and finally, stepping close, lowering his voice, says, "Don't think of me as a boar who hates women. I was raised by five of them. My mother, her two sisters, my grandmother, and our maid. They loved me. Too much, I suppose. They adored me, treated me like a little prince. I thought this was normal, do you see?" He looks at her with an amused expression. "I had to walk out of the city to get away sometimes. I would go to the little wooden shacks of the gypsies with the seabirds flying over our heads. They would grill sardines over open fires and give me some on coarse bread to eat."

"I could eat that right now."

"It was some of the best food I've ever eaten."

She reaches for her bag and pulls out a knife with a bone handle stuck into an apple, both lifted from the Brasserie Lipp. Cutting the apple neatly, she offers Picasso a piece and feeds herself the rest, proud of the pleasure her theft has brought to the Bateau-Lavoir. He watches her with interest but says nothing. Sighing contentedly, she asks him whether he will enter a painting for the upcoming exhibition. He shrugs and looks out the window. His hair is unwashed and messy but, with it parted expertly on the side, he always looks stylish.

"Mathilde, you are young so this may come as news, but the world is violent and mad." She loves this about Picasso, his passion to reveal all that is wrong with the world. Her understanding is thin and incomplete, but she wants to know more, about what motivates people, what gods they like to go after and celebrate. "There are people who are treated like animals. Like those women," he says, his voice thick with emotion, glancing at *Les Demoiselles d'Avignon* hanging on the studio wall. "They live like dogs. I have seen how they live in the brothels of Barcelona and nobody cares, not really."

"Is that why you painted them?"

"I painted them so people can see them through my eyes. Because the public doesn't see the truth by themselves."

She nods and stands quietly next to him, considering the *demoiselle* painting. After a long moment, she looks to the colour of his paints thrown on the table: burnt sienna, French ultramarine, yellow ochre, lapis blue, and titanium white. His brushes are flat-tipped and also round. She watches as he picks up a brush and approaches a canvas propped on an easel, leaning in to use the end of it to smear a detail around a bluntly staring eye on a distorted face. Satisfied,he steps away and paces around the studio, throwing her looks of yearning every now and then. He settles behind her and roughly pushes her composition aside. It falls to the floor. "That's mine," she says, and without thinking, adds, "pick it up." She watches with satisfaction as Picasso fetches her drawing.

Now he takes a wrapper from his cigarette package, a match, and a rough strip of cardboard ripped from a supply box. "Make something new out of these," he says, tossing the pieces on a sheet of white paper. "Make something interesting. Don't stop until you're absolutely satisfied."

She thinks he is joking but he moves away and leaves her to the task. An hour passes and she is still rearranging the parts, trying the cardboard in the upper right corner, allowing the match to pierce the rectangular wrapper like Cupid's arrow. She likes working with the textures of the found objects; colour is unimportant, just the force of the lines and commercial type made new for anybody interested. He steps over to her, inspecting her collage, and with a single nod gives the artwork his blessing.

“Take off your clothes, I want to see all of you.” His request, or rather his order, catches Mathilde off guard. She looks back at him and shakes her head, smiling a little. He really is unbelievable, but for his approval, she doesn’t mind posing for him.

The studio is cold and damp. There is never enough money to buy coal to keep it warm. He senses her reluctance so he throws his mackinaw jacket down on the floor and tells her to stand on it to keep her feet warm. She strips off her long woollen skirt, her red wool sweater and undershirt, and, looking at him hard, stands naked before him.

CHAPTER THIRTEEN

Paris, 1911

Later that week, Picasso seems softer, more confessional. The obstinate square of his shoulders has relaxed. It is late at night and there is coal in the stove. Gently, he takes Mathilde's hand and crosses the studio with her to a tall wooden cupboard. She peers inside at a mess of objects: a small mandolin, old eyeglasses, rusty nails, black smoking pipes. He tells Mathilde he is finding inspiration in ancient talismans. She looks puzzled. Rusty nails and wire for fixing fencing she can understand, but talismans? He says the word in Spanish—*talismanes*—but she can only shrug her shoulders. Smiling benevolently, he reaches into the farthest corner and pulls out a small stone sculpture of a primitive-looking face. He holds it up appreciatively, turning it to admire the long nose and sensuous mouth.

"What do you think?"

"It looks raw," she says. "Very strange."

"Pure, authentic form. Like the masks from Africa."

"An ancient piece, where did you get it?"

"From an old monastery, probably three BC. Iberian, from the barbarians who lived in the south of Spain, not far from where I grew up in Málaga."

"I see." She hesitates to ask more but her curiosity gets the better of her. "But how?"

"A friend gave it to me." She wonders how this friend might have discovered an ancient sculpture. Digging on a beach in the south of Spain? At a flea market in Paris? It seems unlikely. She bends to stare at the face with its hungry, devouring eyes. She can feel Picasso's hot breath on her neck. He caresses the head with his hands, kisses the face before putting it back and closing the door tightly. "Shouldn't this be in a museum?" Mathilde says.

"It is! In the museum of Picasso." Even in the subdued light of the studio, his face glows with rapture. "I'm like a cow constantly looking to chew and chew, and then I store all the good ideas in one of my stomachs."

Mathilde feels aroused by standing in the company of an ancient sculpture that seems to be stolen. Up until now she has always found a thrill in lifting small objects, but this Iberian piece takes her thieving mind to new heights.

Suddenly, the door of the studio bangs open. Fernande barges in, looking angry, her hair tangled and unbrushed, flowing wildly down her back. She stabs the air with her hands in exasperation and crosses the room to the table with the art supplies.

"These are mine. Not yours!"

She grabs a handful of paintbrushes. Her hands seem the size of a child's.

He shouts back at her, "*Mi via, mis reglas!*"

"You think everything and everybody belongs to you. Well, fuck you!" She glares at Mathilde. "Fuck you too!"

The door slams behind Fernande. Picasso shrugs and looks out the window for a long time. Then, abruptly, he charges back to his easel. He pins a large sheet of paper to a board, picks up a stick of charcoal, and orders gruffly, "Tilt your head and lift up your arms. Let me see your lines. I will blow them up and recompose them." It must be after 11 p.m., and she is tired from long hours chopping potatoes at the Lipp. She could force herself to pose for him, lift her arms high and do as she is told. She thinks back to the day when her brothers told her to count to one hundred and then try to find them. That was the day when she learned to never count on certainty. Eating porridge every morning was a certainty, although kindness within her family was not. For one year she had experienced love with Franz, but he had gone away on a train, and she was left with only a gold necklace and without the certainty of love.

What she learned from her childhood, eventually, was how to walk away.

"No," she says to Picasso. It takes him a moment to register what she has said. He looks dully at her, chagrined, lays down his charcoal, and pulls the opium pot from the cupboard. His fingers are black from sketching with conté. She goes outside for some fresh air, and when she returns, he has taped his drawing of her to the wall; she can see that she has been reduced to rectangles and triangles, geometric shapes outlined in black, with something curved, possibly her hip, and a single eye cast down like a sleeping Venus. He has been working on the picture for some of the week, often late into the night when nobody will bother him, and he seems content with it now.

Without asking, moving decisively, he takes her hands in his, draws her close, and kisses her passionately. She doesn't mind. He devours her mouth and licks her lips and the side of her neck before moving back to her mouth. The taste of cherries and vanilla from the red wine, mixed with tobacco, arouses her tongue. He lifts her up, her legs wrapping easily around his back, and they clutch at each other, sending an easel tumbling to the floor. She pushes him away when his hands seek her breasts. She wants to be a leader the way he is always a leader in the studio. He kisses her mouth again, and her resolve to keep him at bay, to honour his relationship with *la belle* Fernande, melts away. Then, angry with herself, she feels her temper rise and pushes him away again. He looks annoyed but stops. "When I know your soul, I will paint your eyes," he says, framing her head with his hands. She smiles then and stands to settle her clothes. He watches her pick up the drawing, pinning it back on the easel. They do not speak but she is pleased they have reached a tacit agreement.

Turning to the opium pot, he takes a long pull on the pipe. She leans forward and does the same. They settle back together on the straw mats and smoke some more. The room is perfumed with the smell of bitter cinnamon.

"*Hagas lo que hagas, hazlo con pasión*," he says, sighing loudly.

She thinks it comical and starts giggling. "Whatever you say, *el Rey*."

He looks over at her and smiles. "I, the King."

"I, the King!" she shouts, fist pumping into the air.

They erupt into belly laughter. It feels fantastic to laugh.

The borders between day and night fade and blur and then cease to exist. The smoke rises up to the wooden rafters. Mathilde is aware of her hair touching Picasso's shoulder and the Chinese lanterns shifting lightly on their strings. She imagines several Eiffel Towers growing tall from the top of her head.

CHAPTER FOURTEEN

Paris, 1911

It is well past dawn when Mathilde finds her jacket and steps out of the Bateau-Lavoir into the streets. She hurries down the slope, across Place Ravignan, below the trees gone spindly and shadowy in the winter, moving so fast she misses the corner bar with its crooked wooden shutters. The opium from the night before sent her on a multicoloured flight that took her across one thousand years and back again. Compared to the great breadth of time travel, the reality of her everyday life seems petty and insignificant. She stops in her tracks and looks around. Restaurant owners are sweeping up glass from the sidewalk and putting bowls of milk out for stray cats. A man with a two-wheeled cart pulled by a horse throws logs at the front steps of tin-plated buildings. She stands, marvelling at the white foam pulsing from the horse's mouth, and then remembers what she's about. Switching direction, she walks back and into the bar. "*Deux croissants et un grand crème*," she says, dragging her fingers through her hair and fashioning it into a loose bun.

"*Deux croissants. Un grand crème!*" shouts the barman, his hair slicked back, white shirt below a crisp black vest. The wood floor has been stained by decades of soot and gypsum being pounded over the threshold. Dark bottles of alcohol and aperitifs run up the glass wall, sparkling clean, but Mathilde judges the colourful liquids to be overwhelming. She thinks man is surely the only animal that craves more even while eating, drinking, and smoking to excess. She rubs her eyes, trying to clear her vision. Chills run up and down her spine but riding the opium was worth it. From somewhere in the back of her brain, she craves another hit of the pipe. For now, she gulps coffee, wolfing back the croissant in a few bites. Outside, her breath steams white in the cold air. She hands the extra croissant to a couple of kids dressed in thin jackets and mismatched shoes.

The walk downhill from Montmartre to the Seine takes almost an hour. Hugging her jacket to her body, she walks along deeply shadowed laneways, glad for bursts of sun brightening the boulevards and the warmth of the enclosed shopping arcades. Beneath a long glass roof, surrounded by luxury shops, her mind grows sombre and reflective. She lights a cigarette and leans against the glass front of a leather glove shop, watching the *grande dames* in their ribboned coats and fur muffs float by. Taking a drag, she wonders how poetry is born. She thinks her own life was written by her mother, and for that reason, her poem was born out of love and pain. Can paying the ultimate sacrifice transform darkness into light? Maybe it can, but nobody should be called to die while giving birth. Stamping out her cigarette on the mosaic floor, she goes out into the street, past an old couple bent over their ragpickers' hampers.

Midweek and only a few people linger in the vast courtyard of the Louvre. She is waved through at the entrance of the Denon wing and, as always, walks along the long corridors and up a grand stone staircase to eventually arrive at the Salon Carré. She stands one foot away and stares at the *Mona Lisa*. Her unadorned neck, right hand over left, arm resting on a chair, body in a slight twisting contrapposto. Eyes looking out into the world, declaring to anybody willing to listen, *Here I am, shattered but still whole.*

Vincenzo meets her there. She interlaces her fingers around his, loving the way he is a worker and vulnerable, even if she doesn't really love him. She likes being in his company, though. The hectic pace of the city seems to fade away when she is with him. She tells him about growing up on a farm in Alsace, shooting wild boar by the time she was twelve. He tells her he started working at that age as a house painter, first in Milan and then in Paris. "The paint was bad for me," he says, looking over at her.

"What do you mean?" She looks quietly at him.

"Lead poisoning. I couldn't think straight, the headaches, the muscle pain was bad."

"But are you better?"

"I guess so. I was hospitalized at different times. It's still hard to think straight."

She is utterly relieved that she does not need to hide her past from Vincenzo. His own is shot through with more daggers than hers. She feels a longing for him and asks him to take her to the storage closet. He hesitates; he only has a short work break, but she insists, grabbing at his hand, and they walk together out of the gallery, along the back corridors. He fumbles with the keys and she tells him to hurry. Inside, she removes her dress and her underclothes and pulls off his shirt. She unzips his pants and they drop to the floor. She kneels and takes him into her mouth until he tells her to stop and she climbs up onto him. He turns and holds her against the wall; her back is against a hanging tapestry and she can feel the smooth texture of lions and peacocks stitched in gold silk. She makes him kiss her harder, the way

Picasso kisses her. She thinks about how powerful Picasso is, about his boorish, domineering ways that she hates, how he keeps stolen artworks in his artist's cupboard, how soft and vulnerable he can be.

"Be wild," she says, opening her eyes wide, staring at Vincenzo. "Like Picasso." And he doesn't mind receiving her instructions.

He has sat her on a wooden crate and is about to put his tongue between her thighs. He is very good to her.

"What do you want me to do?"

She leans back, enjoying the pleasures of her body. It feels like she is flying through a kaleidoscope into a world of unexpected possibilities. She feels drenched in gold and silver, travelling fluidly through time, from Bacchus to the industrialists and to the Futurists.

"Steal something for me," she says, running her fingers through his dark Italian hair.

CHAPTER FIFTEEN

Château de Chambord, 1940

At night, sleepless, she wanders Chambord to check on the crates of artwork. She smells something delicate, old, sugared grapes left on the vine, snowflakes icing the air. The stone stairs twist in a spiral wide enough to hold a battalion of soldiers. Mesmerizing for Leonardo to draw in a sketchbook but, in reality, loathsome to climb. She plods up in her leather boots, arriving out of breath on the third floor, which feels like six floors, such are the exaggerated dimensions of the risers and the treads. Outside, a veil of moonlight shimmers through the windows of the great room. She is wearing wool pants, a thick cable sweater knitted by one of the locals, and her heavy duffle coat. The château is gripped by a freezing cold, and the stone walls built from two-foot-wide blocks of white tufa ensure that winter never leaves her bones.

Mathilde works and sleeps in the same layers of wool. To remove them would be to expose her flesh to sub-zero temperatures, and besides, her hands are bandaged and incapable of dealing with metal hooks of undergarments just now. The workmen stand around by day, smoking, cursing the weather; one of them calls it as cold as a frog's tits. Then he hands Mathilde a cigarette as a sort of apology for his language. Somebody else says it's bitter enough to split stones. She nods in agreement and grinds her cigarette butt into the pavers.

In Paris, while Mathilde worked for several years at the Louvre, it was her daily pleasure to lay out her lingerie on her bed and choose fresh, lacy bras by Lejaby or silk culottes that Josephine Baker had popularized. Mathilde spent loads of French francs on her underclothes—too much, complained her husband, who never bothered to look. There was a time when his ambivalence toward her provoked fits of rage. She would pound her fists against him in their bed when he turned away from her. There are memories she has buried deep, such is her shame and regret at having lived through them. She remembers leaping on top of him, naked, desperate for sex, a full year after delivering Philippe, her lithe body reclaimed, and—she is not proud of this moment—somehow humping her husband from on top, banging her vulva against his limp cock, demanding that it harden—"Come on, come on, we can do this"—and, desperate, spitting out any sexual titillations that he might find suitably arousing: "I'm going to put that cock in my mouth"—which she didn't want to do, such was the ugliness of his penis lying flaccid among his hairy balls; "I'm going to suck your balls"—clearly not an option; and, last resort, the only statement that was guaranteed to arouse him, "You want to fuck me from behind?" And that was when he would mount her doggie-style and she would know, through tears, that their marriage was uncertain, or simply over.

Her relationship with her husband went from marriage to boredom to full-blown dish-throwing anger, then to simmering acceptance of a broken union. They had met after she fled Paris, introduced by friends during a hike into the mountains. He was a young engineer with a canvas rucksack thrown over his shoulders. He extended a kind hand to help her climb up the scree. At night, he liked to gaze at the stars in the sky even while, as she was to discover, most of his dreams were about laying tracks to allow trains to connect all of France. By the time they moved back to Paris from Chambéry, they slept in separate bedrooms, explaining to Philippe that it was better to allow his mother to sleep rather than endure the earth-rattling snoring of his father. This arrangement facilitated the autonomy that each of them required. She thought of them as two ships sailing in choppy waters, trying to avoid ramming into each other.

Mathilde reflects on this without bitterness as she walks past the furniture and paintings of Chambord, their forms draped in white ghostly sheets, to climb the twisting stone steps, the stairs winding one above the other around a hollowed-out core as if trying to strangle each other. Leaving the staircase, she walks along the reception hall with deer antlers and taxidermy heads of wild boar peering over stacked crates. Raising her hands, using her forearms, she pushes open a double set of heavy wooden doors that lead into the chapel. This is where the most valuable paintings are stored, where the afternoon light from the west penetrates the large windows to heat the area better than the rest of the château. She likes to come here by herself at night. She unbuttons her coat and sits on a purple velvet chair by one of the windows. February 1940, the dead of winter, all is peaceful, snow as white as the stone face of Chambord; a feeling of serenity comes over her and because all is quiet, and because there is no word, no news that the Nazis will be invading France, it seems as though the world is still at peace.

She thinks back to sitting on the stump of a tree at the edge of the forest in Alsace, where she would cut loose from her family to listen for sounds. In the chapel, as in the forest, the sounds do not come immediately. She must wait without giving in to impatience or boredom. She thinks of the herons on the banks of the Loire, motionless for hours, their exquisite concentration, tuning into the subtlety of sound.

The moon sparkles against the shifting sepia tones of the winter sky. This is when the artworks start to speak to her. She can hear them creak and groan. The oil canvases taken from their frames shift like sandpaper. The marble statues tilt against each other, wheezing and gasping for oxygen. The paper drawings bleed ink. To hear the artworks speak terrifies her. It's as if the souls of the artists are rising into the air to be recognized at last. She hears it all and she wonders, as she did alone at the edge of the forest as an eight-year-old girl shaking with chills and fear, *What is it all for?*

CHAPTER SIXTEEN

Paris, 1911

Blessed with a day off from peeling potatoes at the Lipp, Mathilde walks into the Louvre's Salon Carré to start her copy of the *Mona Lisa*. She vibrates with excitement, carrying her easel under one arm, her box of pencils and paints in the other. She has rehearsed her approach countless times: how she will begin with a white ground of lime paint over her block of wood, then sketch the figure lightly with conté, heightening the pigmentation to show the bones of the woman's face, deepening shadows rather than lines. Next, she'll add the drapery of the garments, allowing ochre for the woman's sleeves, the right hand crossing over left as a symbol of virtue. And later, the ultimate act of bravery, adding layers of barely pigmented oils to approximate the sheen of Lisa's skin.

There is so much luminosity and mystery to any human being. She only wants to honour what Leonardo da Vinci accomplished four hundred years before.

But access to the portrait is impossible. Today, like every other day, there is a crush of men dominating the space in front of the *Mona Lisa*. They stand at easels blocking the view to the painting, black-suited, unmoving, like sleeping horses. In front of them, there are three or four men seated on chairs sketching her face, the slight twist of her body, the lines of the heavy chair, the rivers that run around her.

Her patience with the men in the Louvre is wearing thin. She wants to yell *FIRE!* Send them running out of the gallery while she sets up her easel.

"She gives me comfort," says one of the men, pointing his brush at the portrait. "As any woman should."

"As she surely did for Napoleon in his private bedchambers," says another, loosening his tie around his neck.

"When Josephine wasn't around." Another one smirks.

She thinks, *Men. Do they ever stop?* The conversation grates like chalk on her teeth. She hadn't known that the *Mona Lisa* once hung in Napoleon's bedroom. But why do men always relate everything to having their way with women? You have to be very fond of men, she thinks, because otherwise they are unbearable. Maybe someday her opinion will change. This is when her idea takes shape. For the first time, she sees the *Mona Lisa* and wants to have what she has. She wants her power, she wants to be something more than a motherless girl from Alsace. She wants to be grounded so that she can soar. She wants to trade in her clunky peasant name for something ripe for the future. Just as Picasso has. He was christened Pablo Diego José Francisco de Paula Juan Nepomuceno Crispín Crispiano María de los Remedios de la Santísima Trinidad Ruiz Picasso. He was known as Pablo Ruiz. But life chose his real name. The bastard. Of course it did. Picasso.

CHAPTER SEVENTEEN

Paris, 1911

Georges Braque strides into Picasso's studio holding a comb aloft and eating an apple. "This is the future," he says. "A simple hair tool." He has a ruffled, bemused look that Mathilde appreciates. "I'm going to drag this fine-toothed thing through some house paint and create the texture of a wood panel."

Picasso looks up from his worktable. "You mean, the artifice of a wood panel," he says, moving to the stove and heaping a shovel of coal into it.

"Exactly. The woodiness of wood," says Braque, beaming. "My father was a house painter." He kisses Mathilde on both her cheeks before embracing Picasso. "He taught me everything about how to paint." He hands Picasso his half-eaten apple and slides a glass bottle of milk from below his arm. "Café au lait?"

Picasso bites into the apple. "Stolen from the neighbours. Again?" He looks down at his worktable and over to his friend. "Your father was a house painter and mine was a painter of pigeons. If ever you are in need of a portrait of pigeons, take the train and do not get off until you reach Barcelona, Spain, and there you will find a perfect picture of birds. Entirely conventional. This is what he tried to teach me, to be traditional and rule-bound. *Merci, Papa.*"

He finishes the apple and throws the core on the floor. Mathilde watches cockroaches scatter. "There are very few artists who are doing important work these days." He angles his head to Braque. "You, for instance. But you are my best friend. We are roped together like mountaineers. Matisse is also important, but he is not a modern artist. Before him, Cézanne and Toulouse-Lautrec." Mathilde's cheeks burn at how she goes unnamed because she is clearly not an artist in Picasso's eyes. And why should her work matter? She has only just begun her career. Still, she is angry at him, the way he goes back to cutting out a stencil of letters with a sharp paring knife, oblivious.

Out of the need for comfort, Mathilde allows her mind to drift to Franz. Her art teacher, twenty years old to her seventeen, who not long ago visited her village in Alsace, opened her—to what?—to not just painting techniques but how to love. Tall and intelligent, with blue eyes that sometimes turned pale green in the late afternoon, he spoke a fine French, touched with a German accent. He made her feel for the first time in her life like she was a whole person, not a fraction.

During the summer, they hiked the trails, and he asked her to take the lead as if it were the most natural thing to request a girl to be in charge. They sketched the trees in the forest, sharing his thick white paper and beautiful pens from Germany. When Franz spoke about the land or the shape of a still life, or even how to sketch a naked figure modelling in the classroom, he did so with a face lit with curiosity and wonder. He taught Mathilde how to achieve the impression of mist by mixing watercolours, how to layer barely pigmented oils to create the dewy finish of a young woman's skin. As they painted, he asked her questions without taking his eyes off his canvas: "If you weren't an artist, who else would you want to be?" "Do you think there's an afterlife when we die?" "What part of your body do you like the best?" "What animal do you admire the most? For the patterns on their skin? Or, because of the way they move?"

To her, Franz belonged to a species previously unknown to Mathilde. She knew little about where he came from. Somewhere in northern Germany. Older than her by three years. Her first lover. She wondered what he was doing now in life. Was he already loving another, asking her the same thrilling questions?

Braque stands next to Picasso. "Are you planning to use a white ground layer over canvas?"

"Something like that."

"I'm doing a mix of linseed oil with barium sulfate, lead white, and gypsum." He taps his finger against his friend's shoulder.

Picasso nods in agreement. "It'll look like that woven paper."

"Exactly," says Braque. "There's a bottle, letters, movement."

"Movement and forms are fading." Picasso looks over at his friend, eyebrows lifted.

"Alive with their own energy. And Mathilde? What about you?"

She is surprised that Braque has turned the conversation away from Picasso.

"I'm trying to collage, the new, or, actually, the newly constructed Paris," she says, bending over a bowl, kneading sawdust into sand, glad to be working on her own art. "I'm gluing sawdust over my painting of the shanty towns."

"Sawdust?" says Picasso, looking over at her.

"The sawdust comes from a construction site close to Sacré-Coeur."

"Damn the bourgeois," says Braque, wrapping an arm around her shoulders.

"Damn their new bourgeois homes," she shoots back, adding a

drop of black paint, turning her hands ebony from the mixing. She draws a finger across a length of fallen blonde hair, leaving a muddy streak on her cheek. The declaration rolls off her tongue as if she has been chanting about human rights all her life. Fighting for the rights of the desperately poor working class never touched her existence in Alsace. Her family were head-down with hard work; they would have dismissed such discourse as nonsense dreamed up by privileged city intellectuals with nothing but time on their hands.

"I'm working with sheet metal after this. A little like you," says Picasso, glancing at Mathilde, "it's the industrial materials I'm curious about."

Mathilde looks intensely at her sawdust composition, but her heart is pounding. She is amazed that Picasso has acknowledged her work, possibly because of Braque's interest in her opinions. Her confidence lifted, she goes on: "Sheet and perforated metal interest me very much." She wants to explain that it was on her farm that she first encountered sheet metal, that it was used to patch barn doors, as ramps for animal feed, and for cinder screens on their fireplaces.

"For a series I'd like to do on guitars," says Picasso, interrupting. "An homage to the gypsies I knew. Outsiders, like us. They played their guitars around campfires like their lives depended on it."

Picasso and Mathilde had been working for hours in silence. When he works, it is obsessively. She has witnessed this before, the way he seems guided by an inner deity that he must obey without interruption. Mathilde dares not break the silence or even step away from her worktable for fear of upsetting Picasso. His moods can change dramatically without warning, from Spanish seducer to sullen oppressor. Braque's arrival has brought human warmth back into the studio, giving her permission to interrupt the deity and speak her mind.

"What will it be?" she asks, lighting a cigarette, flicking her eyes to

Picasso's paper assemblies. "A sculpture or a painting? Will it hang on a wall or rest on a pedestal? Do you even care anymore? I personally do not."

Picasso looks startled. He sets down his knife, looking fully at her, laughing softly. "It's nothing, it's *el guitare*!" He smooths a hand over her long blonde ponytail and down her back. "You carry something, Mathi, something fierce inside you." Taking his red scarf off and draping it around her neck, he says, "I decorate you with the colour of bravery."

The door of the studio bangs open and Juan Gris appears. "Does anybody have any milk?" Juan is a handsome engineer from Madrid. He and his wife, Lucie, live down the hall with their new baby, Georges. "Lucie's run out, and Georges is wailing."

"Only the stolen kind," says Picasso, tossing him the glass bottle. Juan Gris holds it triumphantly in the air. "Stealing it from you now, with thanks," he says, and disappears out the door. Suzanne Valadon walks in shortly after. Mathilde is impressed by the way she moves, slowly, brazenly, hips circling. "Darlings," she says, gazing at all of them. "You remember Erik Satie?" She raises a hand to indicate the man who has appeared behind her at the door. His hair flows beneath a tall black hat. In fact, Mathilde thinks of him as all hair, such is the abundance of his beard and his curly moustache, his narrow grey eyes shining out from wire-rimmed glasses.

"Master!" says Picasso, embracing Satie before kissing Suzanne on both her cheeks. "Your piano preludes, what do you call it?" His mood has suddenly lifted. "Mathilde, you will listen to them later. Lean as Spanish *jamón*, no musical fat."

"*True Flabby Preludes for a Dog*," says Suzanne, interrupting.

"We're going for an early dinner and cabaret at Le Lapin Agile," says Satie. "Stop working so much and join us."

Mathilde feels that Paris has allowed her to crack open her mind like the gaping mouth of a baby bird. *Feed me, feed me, let me taste your sunflower seeds one at a time.* In moments like this, she wonders why Picasso is wasting time on her, and yet he seems not to be bored by her. He has taught her so much and so has his entourage. She gazes longingly across the studio to Suzanne Valadon, admiring the freedom in the way she moves. *She's powerful*, thinks Mathilde. *I should be more like her.*

"We'll be there," says Picasso, sliding his eyes over to Mathilde. "But in a while."

"I've only just woken up," says Braque. "Hungry. Desperate for food. Let's go."

The moment the door closes, Picasso draws close to Mathilde. He presses his nose against her, inhaling the scent of her hair. "My god, you smell good." He moves his nose to the side of her neck and down her collarbone toward her breasts. "You smell so good. How is it possible?" She feels his tongue on her skin, but pushes him away. The memory of Franz still burns like a candle in a glass globe, something hallowed and protected.

"Let's smoke," he says, exhaling deeply, setting down his knife.

"But I have to work. My shift starts soon," says Mathilde, a hand on his chest pushing him lightly away again.

"Show me who you are," he says. "I want to take you apart so you can see yourself again."

He takes her hand and she tumbles with him to the straw mat. More time with him means more conversations, more time to make art together. Feeling unsettled but curious, she lies back on the mat and watches him arranging the ceramic pot and pipe, the long needle, and the opium paste.

It's a short session, but intense. Her body feels lifted by wings, and she allows the feeling of levitation, her feet suspended above the ground. When she finally leaves the Bateau-Lavoir, it is to float down the hill. She sees a collapsed building as a phoenix rising from the ashes; even the feet of children in rags seem burnished golden in the late afternoon sunshine.

She arrives, breathless, at the Brasserie Lipp, her cheeks on fire. She has no idea what time it is but Vincenzo is there to greet her with his steady presence, to reassure her that she has a half hour before work begins. They cut through the restaurant to the back lane and he arranges two metal chairs for them to sit on. She laughs, thinking that he is acting like her manservant. How lucky she has become! The air is cold and they can see their breath. She rubs her eyes to try to clear her vision. It feels like her eyelids are drooping and yet she can see Vincenzo more clearly than ever before. He has a tendency to look lost, she notices; his eyes have turned morose, but he always wants to please her. He kisses her neck, and she allows it. Her brain seems simultaneously bright and wonderfully slowed down. *Less control, more flow*, she thinks, as he massages her hands to help her in the upcoming hours cutting many pounds of potatoes. Her manservant, her sex servant! She looks in awe at the orange wrapped in rose-coloured tissue that he brings out of his bag for her to eat. "It's magical," she murmurs, rubbing the fruit up her neck and over her cheeks.

"What are you thinking, Mathilde?" he asks. "You seem far away."

"Really, I can't say," she says after a while. She is thinking she wants Vincenzo to be so much more of a man, more commanding, more daring. He leans forward and kisses her again on her neck.

"I need more than that. More and more and more." She smiles at him, aroused, and brings his face to hers. Inside his mouth, she explores deeply, wetting his lips generously with her tongue. She sits on his lap, pressing hard against him, goes in again with her tongue, does it all over, trying to fill the emptiness inside her. Sex can serve that need, sometimes creating art can. The fog of the opium has lifted and she feels a special level of clarity.

"I want you right now," he says.

"I know you do." She grips the side of his face, dizzy with the rush, what she has done to him. "Have you ever climbed the Eiffel Tower?" She taunts him, knowing exactly what the combination of kissing and words can do to a man.

"Do you want me to?" he asks, looking fully at her.

"Would you swim the length of the Seine?"

"Anything for you."

"Well then," she says, taking her time, daring the words, enjoying the way they sizzle on her tongue. "Would you steal something for me?"

He kisses her again and she pulls away, making him stop. "This again! And what would that be?" he says, his brow darkening.

"Show me just how powerful you are as a man," she whispers, pressing forward, licking his ear.

He does not say anything, but she sees a hint of a smile on his lips. A delivery buggy pulled by a mule rolls by. She can feel the rumble of the subway underneath the street. Past and present worlds are creating a symphony of friction. Mathilde feels a hunger to make up for lost time on the farm in Alsace. She wants to ride into the future on a beam of light.

If she were a bird, she would see herself floating in the sky above the dictates of the city, all of its rules, made to be followed or broken. Morphed into an animal, she would be a tiger of insatiable appetite, parading down the boulevard in orange fur with black stripes, ripping rabbits and chickens from meat hooks inside restaurant kitchens, sprinting to the forest to feast on deer and wild boar. Solitary. Powerful and lawless.

She leans back to Vincenzo and traces a wet finger around his mouth. "For me."

CHAPTER EIGHTEEN

Paris, 1911

A summer's night. Luxembourg Gardens. Mathilde lifts her face, kissing Vincenzo, caressing the callouses on his hands. The mist from a park fountain glazes their skin. It is one of their greatest pleasures, being together, absorbing the beauty of the city, all of this for free. Vincenzo passes a bottle of wine over to Mathilde, steps ahead, and bends down low to rip a dozen yellow tulips from a garden.

"To Marie Antoinette," he says, offering the flowers to Mathilde. Their roots are dripping with dirt.

"Merci beaucoup," she says, tipsy, curtseying down to the ground. She looks up and beams at him. "Although I was beheaded." She smells the flowers, flips them over, and smells the dirt.

"Although you deserved it."

"Yes, I did."

"Do you like my flowers?"

"I do very much. May I eat the dirt, and you, peasant boy, can eat cake?"

"I prefer the dirt, as I am a peasant, like you, my little French farmer." He bows, touching his nose to his knees. "We call it *terra*."

"*Enchantée*, Vincenzo."

"Yes, I am. I cook my love for you."

"Yes, you cook my love."

Vincenzo doubles over in laughter. "I said I cook my love!"

"You cook my love and you cook pasta," says Mathilde, flopping onto a metal chair next to a vast octagonal fountain. She smiles at a wooden toy boat left to float in the basin. How glorious to be alone in the park with her sweetheart. Vincenzo swigs from the bottle and crawls under her skirt, kissing the inside of her legs. She laughs hysterically. "Get out from there. Your tongue is so wet."

"No, your tongue is so wet!" he bellows from inside her skirt.

"Get out, get out, my little Italian peasant! STOP. You're tickling me. I will have you arrested for public spray." Mathilde cracks into giggles, feeling wonderfully drunk. "Vincenzo! I said public *spray* instead of public *display*!"

A month ago, he insisted that she move into his garret. Begged her. "With you, I'm the happiest I've been for years," he'd told her. "Paris is not kind. But now, everything feels different. I cannot see the hours for when you return. I need to touch you, have you beside me."

She is flattered by Vincenzo's adoration. He has his inner demons, but he is a survivor, as she is, trying desperately to make it in the rat-infested studios and dark garrets of the City of Light. While she does not love him, she likes him well enough, and besides, he likes to take care of her in an Italian, nurturing way. She agreed to move in. There is not much to shift, a wooden trunk with her clothes, her art supplies, and some photographs of her family: Mathilde and her grandmother sitting with shoulders pressed together, her father standing behind them, her brothers nearby, looking to the sides, avoiding the camera. Vincenzo insists that he carry all of her belongings up eight flights on his own. He has set the table with a scrap of red material and a single tallow in a beer bottle. Gentle breezes float in through their window, bringing the smell of pork cutlets being fried in garlic butter from an apartment down below. She buys a bottle of cheap red wine from the corner shop and they drink it down, eating a baguette with pâté for dinner. Then they make love as they do every evening.

Now, in the garden, Vincenzo comes up with a brilliant idea: "We have to ride the horses." He has slipped his head out of her skirt and now looks wild-eyed to the west flank of the park.

"Away to the horses," says Mathilde, standing up. "RUN!" She swoops a hand into the basin, grabs the toy boat, and races to catch up. She realizes one beat later that she is very loud and very drunk.

They half gallop, half skip like children along the lawns framed by double allées of plane trees. The stars are beginning to prick the night sky, the moon is beginning to rise; they run and stumble, holding hands, leaving a trail of stolen tulips and daffodils behind them. When they get to the fountain with the bronze horses, they open a second bottle of wine, drink half of it, strip naked, and hoist themselves into the churning water.

"*Cazzo*, it's cold!" Vincenzo shouts as he bounds through the waves. His hands grip the sculpted mane of his horse, his black hair runs slick across his forehead. He mounts the horse. Mathilde lies across the back of her horse, laughing uncontrollably, apparently unable to sit up.

"Onwards!" she shouts, raising a fist, clutching the toy boat to her chest.

"Onwards!" mimics Vincenzo.

"To Paris, forever!"

They slip off their horses, soaking wet. She is giddy on wine but keenly aware of the silver moonlight baptising her life at that moment. How smooth and untainted. She feels scrubbed clean. In the distance, she hears the shrill whistle of a park guard, anxious to clear the garden and lock the gates. *What a pity*, she thinks, looking up at the moon, *it would be lovely to stay, but off we go to the poor houses where they store all the artists, the intellectuals, and the immigrants.* They grab each other's hands and take off across the lawns, long before the guard arrives, to finish off their second bottle of wine in their garret below the eaves.

CHAPTER NINETEEN

Château de Chambord, 1940

At the village bakery, the locals stand around and talk, lulled and encouraged by the smell of warm yeast and buttery baguettes. The exodus from Paris of people crazed with fear grows to hundreds of thousands then balloons to millions. Rumours swirl about the Nazis, how they are cruel and rape anything with legs, how their brains are not their own, how they bludgeon babies to death. The lines have been drawn between the oppressor and the oppressed. Nothing is said of any cruelty and destruction the Allies might also inflict: The Canadians, the British, all their reputations sparkle bright. Her youngest brother, Lucien, is forced into service by the Greater German Reich, along with one hundred thousand men from Alsace and Lorraine. To refuse is to be shot in the head. She receives a telegram from her aged, withering grandmother telling her of this news. For the first time in decades, she remembers when Lucien would pack her into a sled and pull her, his happy passenger, over the snowy hills of their farm. She wants to travel to Alsace to offer some comfort, but mostly she wants to race to Paris to be with Philippe. At the Château de Chambord, Pierre tells her that none of that is possible.

"You can't leave," he tells her, looking to the floor, adjusting his bow tie. "The head office of the national museums will not risk the lives of its staff."

"But my son, Philippe. He lives alone in our apartment. What about him?" she asks, clutching at Pierre's sleeve.

"Mathilde, we have known this day would come. You can't go into the city when everybody is trying to get out."

"But he will be taken. He's a student. He's so young."

"Your son is a man now. This war will make all of us old beyond our years."

"He's studying law. Trying to fight for justice."

"He might be wise to abandon his studies for the moment. The Nazis do not take kindly to French law students."

Is any of this real, or merely a cruel joke? She cannot comprehend what Pierre has just said, thinks of it as something trotted out to test her mettle. She looks out a window to the moat. This awful body of water that is unknowable, unseemly, above all silent, never gurgling or fretting like the creeks that ran past with personality from her farmhouse in Alsace into the valley. Her entire body is shaking from fear. She expects that a battalion of German soldiers will goose-step out from the shadows of the trees any moment now.

"Surely the French army will defend Paris. They can't leave us stranded here."

"Unfortunately, our army surrendered after two hours," says Pierre.

"But they had a year to prepare," protests Mathilde, looking out the window at the Chambord forest, gone bright and green after the long, harsh winter.

"The Nazis are well armed beyond any of us. Their tanks are

lethal. The sandbag stations never even saw any action. The French government is in exile."

"What now? What do we do?"

"We protect the art."

"We can't simply wait."

"Fire drill in the morning. Same as ever."

At nightfall, she leaves the château, moving silently, barefoot. She walks across the courtyard and stands at the edge of the moat. The channel in front of her is a black snake. Removing her clothing, all of it, even her undergarments, she acknowledges the June breeze caressing her skin. Closing her mind, she steps over the wall of the moat, plunging into the lightless water, into the terror. Something unseen brushes a coarse tail against her and she does not flinch, refusing to allow herself the pleasure of self-pity in the oily pool. She does not cry out. She kicks her feet and slices her arms across the water, repeating a mantra with every stroke, that she will survive this lawless time in history. She submerges her head, wets her hair, makes it black and slick. When she lifts her body out of the moat, she is streaked with ribbons of grime and algae. She pulls two leeches from her legs, picks up her clothes, and walks naked across the courtyard. In this way, she allows the darkness to enter her body and the lightness to go out. She thinks, *What else do you want me to be?*

CHAPTER TWENTY

Alsace, 1908

Winter is coming to the mountains, yet Mathilde and Franz continue to paint, side by side in the community hall below the roof timbers and flaking plaster walls. He is by far the more experienced artist, with years of instruction, he admits shyly, from the tutors his parents had provided for him. But he invites Mathilde's opinion, and she suggests a deepening of red for the poppies in his landscapes or a dab of zinc white to enhance the action of ducks lifting off from a pond. Sometimes a local farmer's wife agrees to model for them and a handful of other students. She is ruddy-cheeked and irreverent. Her name is Pascale Fievre. Nobody else can know about the life-drawing classes. They would be laughed out of town, or possibly stoned to death, maybe both, thinks Mathilde. Pascale does not give a fuck; she once lived in Berlin and Paris, so she poses for them with no guilt and for pocket money. Mathilde knows this woman from lineups in the grocers and at church. She is known by locals as a wife, a mother, a keeper of a small apple orchard, and for her one signature outfit, a long, shapeless skirt and oversized wool shirt and sweater, everything the colour of oatmeal, or not caring. But, in the studio, stripped of her clothes, she is suddenly transformed from a sexless farmer to a woman with a long, beautiful neck and small, girlish breasts. After class, they sip sweet wine and share apple strudel. Mathilde gathers the paintbrushes, cleans them with solvent, and sets them to dry next to the pencils and inks that they are encouraged to try. At the end of the night, Pascale leaves abruptly, calling out with her head tilted to the moon, "Bats will be out soon. I must be getting on."

Franz and Mathilde exchange glances and smile at Pascale's lovely quirkiness. It feels as if they are actors playing on a stage, carving out an existence apart from the traditional farm town. Sometimes Franz speaks in riddles Mathilde does not always understand. "A Monet sunset. A Cézanne apple," he would say. Or, at dusk, he'll look out at the tall pine trees and recite a poem to her:

Oh, let mankind discover never
How true love fills with bliss our hearts.
They would crush our joy forever,
For joy to them no glow imparts.

Her grandmother has arranged to pay for the art classes, quietly, on the side, so that Mathilde's father never knows. The idea is to expose Mathilde to the technique of art, to plant a seed, so that she might paint some pretty flowers in vases or cows standing idle in a grassy field. But her time with Franz has opened up a new world. She isn't accustomed to poetry. His recitations stop her in her tracks, trying to make sense of it all. He merely laughs and squeezes her hand, and she squeezes back to let him know that she understood part of what he had spoken out loud. Franz is her first lover. With him, she develops a fondness for making love on the forest floor, her hands gripping his on the dirt, his shirt a soft cushion below her head, his tongue sending her into ecstasy. Then, laughing, he picks pine needles and leaves from her clothes before accompanying her out of the forest to the road leading to her family farmhouse. They tell each other stories of their families. How his mother celebrated his sixth birthday, sending a pair of messengers on horseback to his German boarding school, presenting packages of leather lederhosen and a felt hat with a long turkey feather stuck into it. How his tutor would allow him to race from the lunch table to feed an apple to his horse, Helios.

"What about you?" he asks, looking over at her with his eyes bright, showing flecks of green in the afternoon sun. "Tell me about your mother." They have climbed a large hill to stand within the thick confines of a peach orchard. The leaves on the trees have turned a deep ochre from the crisp autumn air, and the ground is littered with old peaches gone rock hard in the cold. She has never heard the sound before: two people walking slowly through the leaves in a trance of love. "What was she like?"

Eyes down, she says nothing for a long time. How to explain? Her answer rips through her mind, brutal and unkind. She thinks, *I am a motherless child. I have wandered alone for so long. I am a book without readers. The pages flapping in the wind, my story, my desires, all of them unseen and unread.*

He squeezes her hand as if to encourage her to go on. "She died giving birth to me." Is this the first time she has ever uttered these words to another person? It seems impossible, but true. "Without a mother," she says, faintly, "I felt half as valuable as the other kids, you know? Like a tin penny, instead of a silver coin. I'm sorry it sounds pathetic and selfish, but I was never given a hair ribbon. Nothing pretty to call my own. My father didn't know how."

He wraps his arms around her and buries his mouth against her neck. "Mathilde, I'm so sorry. I had no idea. Knowing this makes me so sad."

She looks up at him, and she sees his eyes shining with tears. Now it is her turn to make him feel better. Hands reaching up to touch his face, she comforts Franz: "But I talk to her all the time. I used to go out to the barn and, holding my doll, tell her all my secrets, things that scared me, what I was excited about."

"To your doll?"

Franz regards her gently, like she is a little bit crazy.

"I was looking at my doll, but I was talking to my mother."

Franz nods in his earnest way, looks at Mathilde as if she is a problem he is trying to solve. "Your father, widowed, was left to raise three children on his own. That must have been difficult," he says to her.

These words shift Mathilde's perception of her childhood, like she has been casting for fish with the wrong hook for many years. "He didn't talk much," she begins, reordering thoughts in her mind. "But he was decent. He's a decent man for raising me and my siblings without his wife by his side."

"Losing her must have ripped him apart."

Once again, Franz's words are a revelation to Mathilde. She has never thought about her father's suffering in that way. "Yes, I suppose . . ." She feels tears suddenly streaming down her cheeks. Once unleashed, her crying seems unstoppable. Her nose runs liquid into her mouth. She turns away, overcome, dragging a sleeve across her face. Finally, recovering enough to speak, she says, "I think it did."

After a long moment, Franz folds her in his arms. "Maybe he was only half the man without your mother. Maybe when she died, your brothers lost some of their kindness, like something had been cut away from them." She nods, and smiles a little. It is difficult for her to know what to do with him. He pulls out insights into human behaviour with such ease. It is a language she has never known. Much easier to scorn the boys, or resent her father, than to try to understand them.

"Tell me another story," he says, releasing her from their embrace and walking again hand in hand through the peach orchard, the pride of her local Alsatian community. She exhales loudly. She has suppressed so much. "Try," he says.

Before replying, she needs to cut through the scar tissue that has calcified around her heart. She winces as if somebody were slicing her open with a scalpel. At first, she speaks through her fingers pressed against her face. She tells Franz a story about her grandmother, the way she would yell "Life is short, eat well, there's no telling what'll be served in heaven" when pulling the *flammekueche*, the flaming pie, from her wood-burning oven in Alsace. And for this, telling that story to Franz and laughing together, she misses her grandmother, the painter of the land all around their farmhouse. She misses her warm, veiny hands, her desire to govern and never yield.

When June arrives, it is his turn to cry as he says goodbye to return to the north of Germany, his chest heaving against hers as they hold each other for the last time. They both know there is no hope for a future together. His family expects his return; a suitable young woman is waiting. Mathilde has new ideas fomenting beyond the farm to somewhere impossibly grand, built on the foundation of art and architecture where her dreams might have half a chance. He gives her the gold necklace, the one she will wear for the rest of her life, and she turns on the platform so he can attach the clasp beneath her long, messy hair. She takes note of the striped tie he is wearing, of his blue-green eyes, of the way she holds onto his shirtfront until the whistle blows and he is ordered to climb aboard. She lets go and watches him step into the first-class car, a straw hat pulled low over his blond hair, and she realizes too late that she should have asked more about his life in Germany, his family, and where to send him a letter.

She knows she will always carry this sadness for losing Franz. It might be that nobody else will know Mathilde or cherish her as well as he does. He discovered all of her dimensions, her curves and her angles, as if prying a pearl from an oyster with a tiny knife.

CHAPTER TWENTY-ONE

Château de Chambord, 1940

Yesterday, June 14, 1940, Pierre told her in confidence that the Nazis had crossed the French border and were marching toward Paris, that the government had surrendered and tanks were rolling across the country. Jacques Jaujard has told him the Nazis might arrive tonight at the demarcation zone, at the edge of the Chambord forest. There are no guarantees that they will stop at the trees. They might march to the castle, seize its contents, and take prisoners.

Her bedroom is windowless and dank, a box within a circle, held within the unscalable walls of a château corner tower. There is no telling how high the moon might be, whether it is midnight or nearly dawn. Wolves might be howling or larks trilling, she has no idea; the stone walls deaden all sounds. She will not hear the enemy lorries arrive, or their footsteps, boots crushing the gravel on the long path leading to the château. She will not hear the cries from the aged guards at the front entrance, locals recruited from the village who have not enlisted in this terrible battle because they are too old or maimed from the last world war. She will hear only the aggression of soldiers breaking the handle of her door. Swift and menacing, they will show their terrible faces. Thinking of her grandmother, thinking, too, of her father, Mathilde strengthens her resolve to face what is to come.

Backed against the wall, she points her old hunting rifle at the door and waits.

She despises herself for being weak, for wanting to set down the gun and give in to slumber. Time advances but she feels it as an iron weight, not something lightly ticking by. She slaps her face hard on one side, then the other. She will stay in control and protect the case lying below her bed.

Her thoughts wander. She weighs the fact that she is living in a barren château while some of her friends from Paris have decamped to their country houses to pick summer daisies and oranges. Others have found charming homes in Bretagne or near Spain along the Atlantic coast to play at being sea captains or beachcombers digging up mussels and clams with their children, making bread on old ironing tables. They send her telegrams, detailing the way they are waiting out this awful war, and kindly reserving one line to ask how she is doing, and where is she holidaying these days?

Her fatigue is profound and so she gives in to a light, fitful sleep. Something heavy slamming on the floor awakens her suddenly. Her rifle lies on the ground and she twists her body to grab at it. The door is closed, holding fast. But she feels a wave of cold panic rush through her body. Is the painting still safe within its case? Has it been destroyed by the freezing temperatures, or gone black with mildew? Her arms tremble and she fumbles to light the candle by her bed. There is something worse to consider: Might it be possible that in these long, languid months of waiting, somebody has stolen the masterpiece from its secret place?

Panicking, dropping to her knees, half asleep, she crawls along the stone floor, belly numb on the ground, and reaches for the large wooden box below her bed. She drags it out awkwardly, moving slowly to reduce the sound of wood scraping. The box is nailed shut, but she has arranged for a crowbar to be left in her room. "For safety," she said to Pierre. Working carefully, she pries open the edges of the double-walled wooden box. The work is hard and slow-going but eventually the lid releases with a reluctant sigh. She reaches inside and lifts the smaller wooden case out of the box onto the top of her bed. She examines the brass hardware on the side. Taking her time, she slides open the honed iron bolt and releases the brass latches. She sees a package wrapped in waterproof paper lined with fireproof asbestos-based sheets. The details of the protective wrapping she knows by heart. She supervised the shroud herself back at the Louvre. But the next moment is more difficult. She braces herself for the worst. There is nothing to assure her that the painting, on a wooden board, still exists.

Without warning, her mind flips back to that night at the Brasserie Lipp when she ran her tongue over Vincenzo's mouth and told him he should steal something for her. She tastes bitter coffee and swallows it back, putting a halt to the memory. It has no place here. She gives herself entirely to what is happening right now. With trembling fingers, she touches the protective paper and begins the unwrapping.

She is shaking uncontrollably but wills herself to lift away the paper sheets, removing the last one to reveal the top of the unframed painting. She recognizes the brooding sea-green landscape, the peaks of ancient mountains, the woman's hairline high on her forehead, her eyes staring out directly into the world.

At last, Mathilde allows herself to rest. She falls asleep again with the *Mona Lisa* tucked back in the wooden box and her rifle cradled in her arms, pointing at the door. Outside, summertime breezes gather momentum across the flats of the Loire Valley, building in strength, ripping oak leaves from their trees. A pair of tawny owls call rhythmically to each other, their quavering song connecting the hollows of the night. Such is the way that beauty exists, unexpectedly, beyond the château walls, beyond Mathilde's hearing. The Nazi trucks will roll into the Chambord courtyard. The soldiers will file outside to stand guard; if not tomorrow, then soon.

CHAPTER TWENTY-TWO

Château de Chambord, 1940

The village baker is a birdwatcher, and he offers to lend his binoculars to Mathilde. She runs as fast as she can up the da Vinci stairs, hauling herself up six storeys, and pushes open the thick wooden door to the rooftop terrace. Panting hard, she steadies herself to look out. She can see for miles with the binoculars. She trains her sights beyond the moat, beyond the courtyard, beyond its short, ridiculous fence, deep into the forest. There it is. What she had seen in her nightmare. A convoy of trucks covered in dark green tarps pulling up in neat formation. There are twelve of them. She cannot see the swastika, but she knows it is there, stitched onto the Nazis' uniforms.

Pierre joins her on the terrace. A cool wind lifts and pummels them, picking up speed as it travels across the flats of the Loire Valley. Mathilde's hair whips around her face. She listens to what Pierre has to say: "They have reached the demarcation zone. There, as you can see, beyond the forest. They're not allowed to come farther."

"But they will."

He shrugs. "Maybe."

"Tell me the truth," she says.

He shifts on his feet and looks evenly at her. "Yes, they will."

"They will reach the château."

"Yes, they will reach us in the château."

"What else should I know?"

"Jacques Jaujard tells me that the works of the national museums are protected. The Nazis cannot raid our collections."

"But what of the Jewish collections?"

Pierre looks off in the distance, then down at his feet. "They are at risk."

"But there are masterpieces in those collections. Renoir, Monet, Bonnard." She is still holding her hands to the side of her face. "They cannot just haul off and take them." She is screaming at Pierre, at the wind, at the Nazis with their trucks gathering in the forest. "They cannot fucking take them!"

"Mathilde, we are at war. This is what an invading army does. It steals and plunders. All of the Jewish collections in Vienna have already been confiscated by the Nazis. The same sweep has happened in Poland."

"But we must resist. Of course, we must!"

"No, you will not resist. Not even the French army is resisting."

"I will. I have a gun. I will shoot to defend these works of art. We must protect them."

Pierre looks over at Mathilde and shakes his head.

"You must not resist. If you do, they will kill you. My superiors in Paris have learned the details of the negotiation. These are their orders."

The ground tilts below her. She feels dizzy and finds it hard to breathe. "The paintings, the sculptures," she says, her voice barely audible over the buffeting winds. She reaches for the stone railing. "They are the best, the most noble offerings of humanity."

"I'm afraid that in this new world, Jews have been decreed as stateless. Their collections are in turn referred to as ownerless."

Mathilde's mind flashes to Philippe's girlfriend, Rachel. Rachel Reiman. The gold bracelets that graced her slender wrists. Not long ago, none of those details mattered. But now. A wave of panic courses through her. "Already?" She cannot find other words.

"The Rothschilds' collection has been seized, as has David Weill's. What the Nazis call degenerate artworks—some Van Goghs, Manets, the Picassos—are being held at the Jeu de Paume. Some of the canvases have already been burned in a bonfire in the Tuileries Garden. Others will be sold off at auction houses. But the Nazi elite will have their pick of the art to fill up their châteaux in Germany. Hermann Göring—"

"Who?

"One of the high-ranking Nazis. Close to Hitler. He visits Jeu de Paume often. Takes whatever art pleases him."

Mathilde studies Pierre, watches him straighten his bow tie, notices how his professional veneer cracks around his weary eyes. The Nazis are burning canvases? She thinks of her friend Rose Valland, the curator at the Jeu de Paume. A reserved, dedicated woman, full of knowledge and love of the art hanging in the Paris gallery. She speaks of the personalities of the artworks as if they were her children. What a hell she must be living through.

"What else?" She sets her shoulders and looks evenly at him.

Pierre flicks his eyes from the forest to Mathilde. "I'm told the Nazis have established a Kunstschutz, an art protection unit, to ensure that the wonders of art held in France will come to no harm. Hitler has ordered that this become a top priority. He envisions creating a monumental museum someday to showcase the world's greatest treasures. Jaujard is meeting with the director of the unit next week. He and I believe that you should attend this meeting."

"Me? Whatever for? What about you?" She feels like she's being thrown to the lions in an old Roman coliseum.

"Jaujard has asked for you, specifically. We believe you will convince the Nazis of the need to keep their hands off our art. You have a steady voice and a passion for art that is highly convincing. With any luck."

CHAPTER TWENTY-THREE

Paris, 1911

Vincenzo is acting strangely. Mathilde notices a nervousness in the way he moves, a reluctance to look directly into her eyes. When they make love, he is aggressive, holding her down on the splintered wood floor of his apartment, leaving bruises ringing her wrists. He smokes cigarettes while slouched on their bed rather than preparing his delectable pasta dripping in garlic and olive oil. His warm, gentle smile has gone from his face. He complains of headaches and stomach pains, of the August heat. But Mathilde is not a nurse. She feels the burden of Vincenzo, like he is becoming a ball and chain around her ankle. "I can't. I can't do this. Vincenzo, please."

Needing air, Mathilde slips away to spend time with Picasso and his entourage at the Bateau-Lavoir. She is gluing her art collages when Marie Laurencin surprises them with a visit. "I am at a complete standstill. Desperate am I for some fresh inspiration," she says, looking over at Mathilde. She steps closer. "Would you do me the honour of sitting for a little while?"

Picasso looks up from his worktable, no longer a bull in this moment but a vulnerable boy. He says nothing but his eyes seem to be begging Mathilde to stay. But why should she? Turns out she needs a break from this man as well. He is the jealous type and demands a woman's attention be heaped on him exclusively. If Marie distracts Mathilde, she may wander. The creative fires of Picasso will be extinguished and another muse will have to be found or his work will suffer.

Marie's studio looks like a rainforest, wooden easels propped against painted fig trees on the walls. She helps Mathilde to undress and sits her on a velvet wreck of a chair, complimenting her on her naked body, opening her legs a little more. Mathilde is aroused by Marie's gaze and soft touches. She looks around at paintings of women with kohl eyes, their hair cut into sharp angles, at terracotta pots filled with oranges and lemons, at baskets of dried lavender upturned on the old wooden floor. Marie leans forward and kisses her young model deeply on the mouth with her thick, pouting lips. When she pulls away, she breathes into Mathilde's ear. "I hope you like my style." The kiss tastes like chocolate. Mathilde wonders whether she means the style of her paintings or the way she likes men and women. The smell of oil paint punctuates the air as Marie prepares her palette of watery, dreamy colours.

After a few hours sitting in the chair for Marie, Mathilde returns to Picasso. He does not appear to be angry. Instead, he seems to be in a playful mood, so different from when she left. He asks her to hoist up her long dress, and when she does, he paints part of her legs with red and purple swirls. She laughs at the feeling of the cold, sticky paint. He smiles at her and says, "Now I will tattoo you." He takes one of his cut-outs and stencils *M & P* on her thigh. She thinks he is falling in love with her.

It seems that this is what it is to be intoxicated by life. Her head spins. The artists at the Bateau-Lavoir have made her trust the world. All around her, the possibilities are infinite, and she is free to do as she likes. Without restriction, without being contained. She agrees to spend the night at the studio. They smoke opium, laugh like a couple of schoolchildren, and eventually fall asleep, hands clasped like friends, not lovers.

The next morning, well rested and well fed, Mathilde strolls along the Boulevard Saint-Germain, her blonde hair knotted at the nape of her neck, her straw hat swinging from one of her hands. She finds she is smiling at the brand-new Saint-Germain-des-Prés subway stop with its red Métro sign welcoming Parisians to travel below the Seine and emerge on the Right Bank. She is glad for the striped awnings protecting café-goers from the sun and the round wooden tables and chairs where artists and shoppers are enjoying coffee after eating coq au vin for lunch. Life is best lived at this languorous pace, and besides, the heat of the day is oppressive. Her body is tingling with desire and delight at what she has experienced but also because of the exquisite textures of the city. The horizon is blushing pink but Mathilde knows that nightfall is hours away. She might have been a farmer's wife in Alsace, and yet here she is wandering through the streets of the city like a true Parisian. She buys an orange from a street merchant and bites into its delicious flesh. She steps close to a pair of grande dames to inhale their bright floral perfume, patting the head of a miniature poodle peeking out from one of the women's straw bags.

The newspapers have been released into the hands of the vendors and they are all shouting in husky, urgent tones. She pauses to make sense of their barking. Something has been stolen. Something from the Louvre. Her orange drops from her hand. She buys a newspaper and reads the front-page headlines: *Inimaginable! La Joconde volé du Louvre!* The theft of the century. Evil. Unimaginable! Police have confirmed, she reads, that the painting was stolen on Monday, August 21, when the museum was closed to the public. The *Mona*

Lisa had been missing for hours and the Louvre administration was oblivious until a French artist, Louis Béroud, complained to staff that it was missing and asked if it could be returned because he wanted to copy it. Monsieur Béroud, Mathilde knows him, knows that he and his artist friends always crowded around the *Mona Lisa*, preventing Mathilde and other women from getting a chance at copying her. But that was not observed by the police. According to their account, everybody had assumed that *La Joconde* was being photographed by another department or having its frame repaired. That evening, police confirmed the theft.

Shocked, unable to move, she leans against a light pole. But a newspaper boy is shouting the headlines next to her. She rushes, dazed, to the Italian ghetto and climbs the stairs to the garret. Out of breath, she calls for Vincenzo, looks everywhere. No sign and no trace that he has been there. She runs back to the street and eventually finds her way to the Brasserie Lipp. It seems normal to be among familiar faces. She trips over somebody's feet. The room spins. At the back of the restaurant, the staff are shouting the details of the theft across the kitchen.

"Says that every one of the two hundred and fifty-seven Louvre employees will be questioned and fingerprinted," says one of the sous-chefs, slamming the newspaper down on the counter. "The curators, the guards, even the plumbers and gardeners!"

"There's no security at the Louvre," says another, shrugging, then, seeing Mathilde coming into the kitchen, adds, "You should know. You go there often enough."

She stares at them and says nothing. The kitchen stinks with greasy heat and humidity. A deep feeling of dread is growing inside her. She feels time ticking by, one hour or two, she can't say for sure.

Two waiters in black tuxedos run into the kitchen. They set their trays down and weigh in:

"Police should post a reward."

"The thief will demand a ransom."

"It's worth more than this restaurant."

The suspense is too much. Without saying goodbye, she rushes back into the streets. She sees a crowd gathered outside the main entrance of the Louvre and flowers heaped up as if somebody has died. She races back to their apartment, runs up the eight flights, and opens the door with her key. He is still not there. The only thing that is unusual is a large white trunk newly installed in the salon. It looks ungainly in the tiny room. "Vincenzo?" she calls, opening its lid. She discovers a mess of his clothes piled inside. She leaves quickly, confused, desperate to find Vincenzo.

Plastered to every tall green information column are leaflets with the painting's image. A reward of forty thousand francs is offered. Posters litter the streets. She stumbles from the Left Bank to the Right Bank, negotiating shortcuts through back lanes and restaurant courtyards, getting lost, ending up at the Louvre. All the doors are bolted shut. She goes back to the kitchen at the Brasserie Lipp, as she doesn't know what else to do. She pulls out the basket of potatoes and starts peeling. The theft is still being debated by the staff. Nobody seems to have noticed that she has come and gone.

"It'll be copied by a forger, and put onto the market," says the head waiter, adjusting his bow tie, picking up two plates of sausage and choucroute. "Maybe a wealthy American arranged the heist?"

"I place my bets on the Germans. They want to start a war with the French," says a cook, speaking harshly, stirring cabbage over a hot grill.

“What’s his name?” offers the sous-chef, dumping sausages onto an iron skillet, grease and smoke flying into the air.

The head waiter sets the plates down and considers. “Carnegie. Rockefeller. J.P. Morgan. *Mona Lisa* is probably hanging in his mansion in New York right now. And here we are serving plates of fries and choucroute.” The staff nod in agreement, allowing the thought to linger in the air before it evaporates.

CHAPTER TWENTY-FOUR

Paris, 1911

The Louvre is a museum with more than a thousand rooms. Dozens of police are sent to search the old palace with scrupulous care, opening every broom closet, looking under stairwells and even in the storage cupboard where Vincenzo and Mathilde liked to make love. Police order all French borders to be closed. Newspapers offer rewards for information about the robbery, which is why Pablo Picasso becomes a suspect. Attracted by the cash reward, Honoré-Joseph Géry Pieret—once the secretary of Apollinaire—confessed to a local Paris newspaper that, in 1907, he had stolen small Iberian sculptures from the Louvre and sold them to Picasso.

Picasso closes the door of his studio and locks it. He stands still, frozen, his brain muddling through his actions. He realizes now how fucking stupid he has been. Storing the stolen statues in his studio cupboard. Keeping them there, close at hand, showing them off to people he wanted to impress. Recently, Mathilde. He recognizes it now, a boastful, macho act that is coming back to haunt him.

Those Iberian sculptures helped him to find a new art, leap through time and back, making a lean break with traditional art, the kind his father had tried to shove down his throat. Matisse loved the ancient forms too. That little African sculpture he found at a curio shop, from somewhere in the Congo. Picasso remembers seeing that magical figure a few years ago when Matisse brought it to Gertrude Stein's apartment. Face lifted to the heavens, eyes enormous and vacant, little childlike hands pressed up against the chin. *Dios*, it was loaded with wonder. He remembers saying to Matisse that when seeing the sculpture, he understood what painting means. "It's not aesthetic, it's a form of magic that stands between us and the hostile universe." Matisse let him hold it all night. There was something transformative about that sculpture, he and Matisse agreed on that, at least.

Picasso remembers how the African works ignited new creative fires for him. When he discovered that tens of thousands of African sculptures and ceremonial masks were kept at the Trocadéro museum, he went off to run his fingers over all the looted figures. There were so many objects taken from French Sudan, Senegal, Ivory Coast, and Niger, all the carvings piled up on tables in poorly lit rooms. Nobody else around, just Picasso grateful for the riches brought home to Paris.

Those ancient, raw forms gave him the confidence to leap into something raw. Eventually, he painted the gaping, hollowed-out faces, the angular bodies of *Les Demoiselles d'Avignon*. That was obvious. But he had never thought to hide the evidence. Why? He cannot explain his lack of judgment to himself, let alone to a court of law.

But he has accomplices. Apollinaire, he might as well blame the whole mess on him. The poet had insisted that the little sculptures not be returned to the Louvre because their radical forms held the key to unlock the future of art. Picasso had channelled their power in his work, but now his own power has disappeared. He looks to the large painting on the far side of his studio, picks up a hunk of clay from his table, and hurls it, narrowly missing the canvas. He picks up a bigger chunk and throws it harder at the cupboard. It is not only the charges from police; he feels he is at the centre of a crisis. Weighing down on him is the hanging suicide of his young German friend Karl-Heinz Wiegels, after a raunchy night mixing opium with hashish and ether. Women are also overwhelming him. Fernande is on her way out and so is Mathilde. His resentment toward Fernande has been growing. He slapped her the other day when she surprised him at the cabaret down the hill rather than staying in the studio. He apologized and bought her flowers and perfume. They made love in the studio and their bond felt washed over, cleansed, until the next day when she confessed to having sex with the new Russian artist who had moved into the Bateau-Lavoir.

He pulls open the doors of his wooden studio cupboard and bends low to recover the small sculptures from the back recesses, capturing them in his hands. He can't help himself, his hands find comfort holding the corpulent figures, examining the elongated faces, the heavily lidded eyes and exaggerated ears. The Iberians believed that having outsized features allowed special access to the gods. And maybe they do. He prays for truth, sketches these figures often, marvels at how simple and powerful their forms.

Apollinaire shows up, slamming the studio door. They shout at each other, the way they never have before, growing hysterical, hurling insults in French and Spanish.

"Imbécile. Va te faire foutre!"

"¡Vete a la mierde!"

Then they fall to the ground, holding each other, breathing heavily, not speaking for a long time. Finally, Picasso draws Apollinaire close to him and whispers an urgent message in his ear. He will pack the sculptures into a small leather suitcase. He will walk to the Seine at midnight, when the sky is cloudy and the moon is merely a shard, and he will drop the bag into the river. That's it. "Nothing complicated. It is what I must do. If there is a god," he says, wringing his hands, lifting them skyward.

Apollinaire looks wide-eyed at Picasso. "*Mais, non, mais non, non, non, non!*"

"*Sí, sí, sí!* It's obvious. I must hide the evidence. We are both aliens in this country. You're Italian. I'm Spanish. They'll kick us out on our asses."

"You are completely insane. Think of all the people you have shown the Iberian sculptures to. You have shown them to all of us, Suzanne, Max, Georges, Fernande, of course. I bet you have shown them to Mathilde. You pull those ugly creatures out of that goddamned cupboard every time you want to bed another woman. You want to throw these ancient works into the river? They're one thousand years old! Your ego knows no limits."

They debate for hours. They smoke their pipes. They smoke opium. Wrestle each other, push their tormented selves outdoors. They walk down the big hill of Montmartre, past the bars and the prostitutes who shout at them to come back. They are carrying a bag. It is heavy and they share the load, one of their hands on each of the handles. They make a wide girth around the Louvre and walk west to the Pont Alexandre. Down the steps that hug the embankment, cursing the reek of urine. Nobody is around. Apollinaire has a firm grip on the leather case. He has no intention of allowing Picasso to throw the artifacts into the river. But he needs his friend to get close to the river, see its devouring depths, imagine what it is to banish the works of a previous culture. They look to the moon for answers and find none.

At dawn, exhausted and resigned to imprisonment, the men

climb back up the steps and walk to the *Paris-Journal* newspaper office, hoisting the bag onto the front counter. Outside, the sky turns away from the black night and unveils a weeping grey dawn. The artists wait to be charged as suspects in the theft of the *Mona Lisa*.

Meanwhile, the Louvre museum opens its doors again to the public.

CHAPTER TWENTY-FIVE

Paris, 1911

Mathilde is turning circles in their tiny garret, clutching her hair, weaving from the bedroom to the living room and back again. She cannot be sure. She convinces herself that this is where her mind needs to go, to find a measure of comfort in the state of not knowing.

When Vincenzo arrives at the garret later that night, he goes to her and she wants to beat her hands against his chest and his face, but she holds back. She cannot assume. She must be patient to slowly tease out the truth. She takes off his clothes, his painter's smock, the belt at his waist, the canvas pants reinforced with patches at the knee, his undershirt damp with sweat from the hot August day. He wraps his naked body around hers, feels her polished skin with his hands, apologizes, as he always does, for his rough hands on her silky thighs. She inhales his armpits, licks the salty sweat from his neck.

The excitement of the theft hits her like an opium rush. She holds him, kisses his mouth, draws her fingers around the semicircle of his ears, lets her breasts graze his chest, reassures him, tells him everything is going to be all right. She moves against him, soothes him with her voice, and all the while, her head is exploding with wanting to know and yet holding back so she won't expose her distrust of him and, worse, his distrust of her.

They cling to each other during the night. The room is hot—even the rats stay away—and she rises to open the window, allowing thin breezes to float in. When he is finally asleep, the white sheets knotted around him in a pile, she looks under the bed, in the cupboard, in the pine chest, and does not turn up the painting.

"Can I trust you, Mathilde?"

Vincenzo is sitting up, looking directly, sadly, at her.

"What makes you say that?" She stands naked in the doorway, casts her pale blue eyes his way.

"One day with me. Another day with Picasso. Sometimes with women. You say a German from your past is the most important man. And so I ask you again: Can I trust you?"

"It's none of your business what I do with my life," she says, turning rigid.

"But I love you. Many times I have said I love you."

She wants then to curl her body around him and reassure him. She wants to tell him that she loves him back. She takes one step toward him, lifts a hand up but drops it. Something inside tells her to step back and scrape away the frivolous talk of love.

And now she knows for certain what he has done, and she hates him for it. "Vincenzo, what have you done? Tell me."

"Can I trust you?"

"Yes, you can trust me," she says, her voice low in her throat.

"I don't believe you trust anybody."

Now, instead of feeling titillated by the theft, she feels trapped. She wants to get away from him, senses he is unwell; all of his headaches and stomach aches, maybe his brain is not fully functioning.

She begins to get dressed. Her long, blue skirt, a blouse, stockings and shoes.

She moves to the door but he blocks her way. "You can't leave," he says, his soft brown eyes turning black.

"What do you mean I can't leave?"

"You know the secret. I need to trust you with the secret."

"What are you talking about? Get out of my way."

He puts an arm up to bar her from the door.

"You have to understand that this painting belongs to both of us."

"Both of us? I didn't steal it."

"I did what you wanted. You kept telling me to steal something, to be like Picasso."

She can't deny feeling the thrill of the steal. But the consequences are too great this time. She tries to push him away. But he is much stronger and impossible to budge. He crosses his arms over his chest and flattens his back against the door. Finally, she goes to the window, considers escaping that way, but it is a drop of eight floors. Lunacy, of course. She falls onto the bed, sobbing loudly, hugging her knees to her chest. They do not speak for the rest of the day. At night, he sleeps sitting against the door.

In the early morning hours, they are woken by newspaper boys shouting news about the stolen *Mona Lisa*. "*Chef d'œuvre par Léonard de Vinci. Volé!*" "Masterwork by Leonardo da Vinci stolen. Massive police hunt!"

"They will hunt you down," she says, rising unsteadily to her feet.

"You and me together."

"I am not guilty!" she screams. "You alone are responsible for this, for this . . ." She grabs his shoulders, starts to shake him. "You did something very, very wrong. I don't know why, what possessed you." She bangs the window shut and screams into her hands.

She feels sick to her stomach.

"You asked me to steal for you," he shouts back at her. "You were very specific. Remember, Mathilde? Are you stupid, or you just don't want to remember?"

"How dare you drag me into this? Of course I didn't tell you to actually steal something."

"You're always stealing stuff. Stealing from people who never hurt you. Those wineglasses from La Rotonde. The owner gives artists free coffee. Why steal from him?"

"Those are little things."

"Little things become big things. You are a thief and a liar."

"I am not."

"You said if I stole something, it would make you happy."

"In what way could a painting stolen from the Louvre make me happy? Your brain isn't working," she shouts at him.

"You said it," he says, shouting back at her. "This is what you wanted and I did it for you."

"For me?" She points a finger at him, jabbing at his chest. "You did it for your country. Remember? All your speeches about your nation, your Italy being plundered, your rage at the Louvre?"

She lies down on the bed, exhausted, aware of an intense need for opium. Picasso can provide that, make her feel better, the way he takes charge, creates a world of his making inside his studio. Everything with Vincenzo is a mess. If she goes to the police and confesses, she might be imprisoned for collaborating. They need to get rid of the painting; somehow, it needs to disappear.

Mathilde sits up and wipes her eyes. She will figure out what to do. She speaks slowly to Vincenzo. "We need to carry on with our lives, like nothing happened. I need to go to work at the brasserie. You need to go back to your work at the Louvre or back to painting apartments. It will be too suspicious otherwise."

He looks over at her and nods slowly. She likes him when he looks like this. Sweet, tender, gullible Vincenzo. A simple mind. A lost soul in search of a cause célèbre. Somebody put salt in his wine at a café one night. Maybe that tipped him over. Or being called a dirty macaroni too many times at the Louvre. Or being poisoned by lead. Mathilde knows what motivates Vincenzo. He is not a bad person, he is not dirty or mean; he is merely a man born penniless, powerless, living on the wrong side of privilege and fortune, like her, scraping together an existence.

"Don't attract attention. Go to work and come home. I'll do the same. Back to the brasserie." She is saying the words even while she is thinking of visiting Picasso.

CHAPTER TWENTY-SIX

Paris, 1911

Later, exhausted from their argument and the poison spilled between them, they lie on the bed, the moon streaming silver across them. They are holding hands, looking up at the ceiling. His confession comes easily, blithely.

"How peaceful the Louvre was early on Monday morning, the museum closed to the public, maybe twelve guards on security," he begins.

"But how did you get it out of its frame?"

"Easy. Ripped off the paper at the back and rotated the four metal clips holding the poplar board in the frame. The whole thing weighed less than ten pounds. I took off the protective frame in one of the service stairs. Not hard. I built that frame myself less than a year ago."

He tells her how he hesitated about which painting to take because there were so many works by great Italian painters to choose from. "Titian, Raphael, Giorgione. But I made it on the spot. The *Mona Lisa* was the smallest and it wasn't hard to lift the painting off the four iron bolts in the gallery. Now you can copy her without having to fight for access, all those men who used to crowd around."

"Vincenzo, I don't know about copying her."

"What do you mean? You've complained for months about not having your chance."

"But I'm not sure we should hide her here."

"Too late for second thoughts. *Veni, vidi, vici.*"

"I don't know what that means."

"I came, I saw, I conquered."

She does not know where he has hidden the portrait and he does not tell her. She searches the entire apartment, looking for it below their mattress, even in the stinking WC down the hall. She opens again the new white chest he has moved into their apartment but only finds a mess of his clothing inside, his stained shirts, his dirty underwear.

He works another month at the Louvre but, overwhelmed, sure to be questioned, he quits, citing a better-paying job elsewhere. Making his own art is abandoned. Instead, he resorts to house painting, travelling on bicycle or the Métro to grand apartments overlooking the Seine. Evenings, he comes home to their garret, a baguette under his arm, carrots and onions to make some soup, headachy and moody; his resentment toward the wealthy who can afford to hire him seems to grow and fester. "I thought we would be happier after the Louvre," he says to her one night, his back resting against the chest, popping some chestnuts into his mouth, roasted by an Italian friend. "I did something big for you to make you smile, but honestly, I don't think it made a difference. You're not so nice."

"After the Louvre"—this is code, Mathilde comes to understand, for *after stealing the Mona Lisa from the Louvre*, the moment when life became complicated for both of them. She serves him a German lager and some pork cutlet taken from the brasserie, and looks at him cautiously; he is both dumb and volatile, and she realizes, watching him chew on chestnuts, that he might turn both of them in to the police the next morning or the morning after. "The fumes must be getting to you," she says steadily. "Get some sleep. You'll feel better in the morning." And he does. He behaves. He does not go to the police.

Left alone in their garret, Mathilde studies the white pine box, convinced that it is hiding the treasure. She checks all of its mortise and tenon connections, its underside. Finally, she sees a tiny gap running around the base of its interior. She pries it up with a knife. The painting, wrapped in a white blanket, lies below the fake bottom.

She pities those who give themselves over entirely to love. It's the ultimate betrayal of one's self. She does not want to be rescued. Or rehabilitated. Now she begins to sketch her escape.

Later that night, she hears Vincenzo turning over in the bedsheets and moves her body next to his. In her mind, she already believes in her story that Vincenzo is the thief, that he acted on his own, that she only made his acquaintance at a party in Paris. Should the police ever question her, she will simply say that she knew Vincenzo briefly. That she is ready to betray her boyfriend does not figure in her mind. She has known a crowd of sorrows, witnessed her own despair, observed the malice of others. She has been betrayed many times in her life, beginning with her mother, who wronged her most of all, by dying rather than living. What a piece of unfortunate timing because, in the end, nobody wants to die, everybody wants to live.

CHAPTER TWENTY-SEVEN

Paris, 1911

Early in the morning of September 7, police arrest Guillaume Apollinaire on suspicion of some involvement in the theft of *La Joconde*. His assistant has implicated him in the theft of the ancient Iberian statuettes from the Louvre. The cops find his journals, his art criticism for prestigious art magazines and handwritten notes for the twenty-six historic erotic texts he has been commissioned to translate and edit, an assignment he has taken to help pay the bills. Police also bang on the door of Picasso's studio, their boots heavy on the splintered wooden floors of the Bateau-Lavoir. Eyes wide, protesting his innocence loudly, he is handcuffed, shoved outside into the cobblestoned square, and taken away in a police van. Panicked by the commotion, a flock of pigeons take off noisily into the sky.

Feeling exposed and vulnerable, Picasso is emotional at his trial. The power that he wields in Montmartre goes up in smoke. Instead, the judge meets a man who is crying and pleading for his life. He seems unhinged, given to condemning himself out loud. At a certain point, when asked about the poet Apollinaire, Picasso shouts that he does not know such a man! The judge absorbs it all and shakes his head at the confused artist. The man likely needs hospitalization or time away in an asylum. He releases him without sentencing.

Apollinaire is jailed for six days at La Santé prison, wrongly accused of stealing the *Mona Lisa*. The police question him and slap him around, treating him roughly because he's a foreigner, born in Italy, and because their records show he has been writing some kind of pathetic pornography. They threaten him with deportation. Feeling a hint of guilt, Mathilde walks to the eastern edge of Montparnasse on the Left Bank, past the walled courtyard of the prison, where Apollinaire is being held along with a thousand other men. She shoulders her way through a crowd that is dispersing after gathering to watch the early morning execution of an inmate. She waits patiently for two hours before the guards allow her to see the poet. "How are you doing?" she asks kindly. Apollinaire looks defeated, his eyes dark and haunted. "I'm sorry," she says, gesturing to his face, the lips split open, a cheek shining with an ugly red bruise. "The guards have been unkind."

"French-style interrogation. They like to use their fists."

"Has Picasso come to visit?" she asks. The poet shakes his big head sadly; his lips, usually bright red and primed for prose, are drawn in a grim line. "Marie?" The moment she mentions the artist, Mathilde regrets it.

"Marie Laurencin fancies women these days, not her ex in jail," he murmurs. "Pansexual, she calls it, and I'm no longer suitable."

It seems impossible to Mathilde that their glorious party in Paris has come to a crashing halt. She thinks of the first time she met Apollinaire at La Rotonde, when the poet and Vincenzo almost came to blows before discovering their Italian roots and toasting each other with absinthe. She thinks of the many nights making collages with Picasso and carousing at the Bateau-Lavoir below the

Chinese lanterns. Time frayed and ripped with misery but also sacred and golden.

"Drunk on gin the Paris nights," she says, remembering a line from one of his poems. How sad to see the brilliant Apollinaire in jail without his pipe and journal of poems. He is the kindest soul holed up in a prison cell because of Vincenzo's demented heist, and now the Louvre and its artifacts, including the previously stolen ones, are under careful scrutiny. Apollinaire looks up at her, surprised. A guard is approaching. Visiting is over. He stands, looming large in the room. "Blaze with electricity," she says, standing up, her voice rising. "The trolleys flashing greenish lights. Warble along their staves of tracks."

He half smiles and shouts back, "The folly of machinery!"

CHAPTER TWENTY-EIGHT

Paris, 1940

Mathilde has grown accustomed to living at Chambord, accepting the hardships, even the vinegar smell of mildew filling her nostrils. She simply copes with the fact that there is one toilet for thirty other curators and guards. In the morning, she squats like a cat in her bedroom over her wooden bucket and empties her pail across the courtyard next to piles of horse manure.

At Chambord, there is a poetry to the banality: daily checking on the wooden crates with the other curators, the routine, rhythmic airing of some of the canvases, fire drills, playing cards at night with Pierre and his wife. She feels like she's living inside a surrealist play that Apollinaire might have written had he not died from the Spanish flu. She misses him, misses Picasso, so many from the golden years in Paris, and Franz before that. But there, just beyond where Mathilde sits laughing at cards, evil is banking on the horizon. The Nazis stand at the ready along the demarcation line. For now, the château is in the free zone. She has stopped looking out, has set the panic aside, performs her tasks with alacrity. Only rarely does she manage to visit Philippe, with formally arranged permits from the Louvre. She and Philippe plan every moment meticulously, setting aside time for tea breaks when he flops on the couch to study the Napoleonic Code, and Saturday nights are reserved for dancing with friends at the *bals-musettes*. Sometimes if they are in a serious mood, they go to see a classic play at the Comédie-Française, her son by her side, his girlfriend, Rachel, with her head on his shoulder, basking in the clever words of Racine, his comedy about the judicial system, everybody arguing and quibbling, culminating by putting a dog on trial for his doggy behaviour.

This weekend she will see her son. But that's not the only reason she is travelling to Paris. Mathilde has been summoned to the Louvre to meet with the Nazi officials who have taken up position there. Her body trembles all over, such is the unrest she feels at the thought of the enemy trampling her city. Mathilde dresses herself in a tightly fitted navy suit, skirt falling to just below her knees, leather pumps, and stockings, effectively a cloak of armour. She calls up her power in this way, repels the enemy, keeps herself safe from the harm all around.

She feels herself go inward, as she did when she left Paris for Chambéry to escape her past delinquencies. Outside, the earth has gone pale and melted like streaks of butter as the train rumbles by. She stares out, unable to recognize her own country. France.

From her seat on the train, she sees enemy troops with the swastika emblazoned on their truck doors. She sees a few German soldiers standing on each of the arrival platforms, their rifles lifted and pointed at the train, like they want to kill locomotion. There are no commanders around, and yet the soldiers are performing their tasks with expert precision. She feels a terrible pressure in her mind, snake-coiled, ready to explode.

In Paris, at the central Gare d'Austerlitz, dozens of soldiers in face helmets are on guard, controlling behaviour, looking around for anybody dumb enough to defy them. They look young and fit, blue-eyed, remarkably tall. One of them raises his hand in front of her like a stop sign. He lifts his chin, indicating a passport check, takes his time looking at her and her passport. He asks in a heavy accent what her business is.

"I have been summoned to the Louvre museum to meet with—" She is at a loss for words, of how to say their names in the same breath. "French officials. German officials."

"Yes?" He looks her over for a long time and finally hands back her passport, smiling. "The Louvre is beautiful. I toured it yesterday with my battalion."

In the taxi, she looks out at the streets, harmonious and peaceful, the chestnut and plane trees glistening with lush greenery. German soldiers occupy the rattan chairs outside of the cafés, drinking grand crèmes, laughing among themselves. She sees small groups of perfectly coiffed Parisians in their heels and hose, looking shyly at the soldiers, swaying their hips as they walk by. Mathilde stops to stare, watching the streetscape with disbelief, the characters Parisians and Nazis bowing to each other, testing each other's chemistry, imagining what the other is capable of. The French Vichy government has declared Paris an open city, meaning open for occupation, and moved south to get out of the way. How lovely for Hitler, she thinks, a delightful walk in the park. Who knows, maybe, with luck, the occupation will be over by Christmas.

Philippe has already told her he fears for the worst, how he has never walked so fast to class and only when the professor closes the doors of the lecture hall does he feel that he can fully breathe. He tells her that the Nazis are imposing new rules and breaking into Jewish homes, stealing their art and jewellery. While she issues a mother's tone of shock and disapproval, she cannot bring herself to believe this, thinking that Rachel must be heightening his outrage.

Trucks are parked in the sprawling courtyard next to the Denon wing, their tires sinking ever so slightly into the pea gravel. Trucks have always been banished from the public space, but now the Louvre's courtyard has become a parking lot. The air smells of diesel where once it carried the perfume of civic freedom. She narrows her eyes, presses a hand against her nose, and walks steadily toward the entrance, toward the guards, their eyes turned on her. They look rosy-cheeked and dumbstruck that their first assignment since occupying Paris is to guard the world's most famous museum. The Louvre, after all, might be worth more than all the rest of France.

A hand goes up in front of her, and there is a passport check. Slender white fingers flip through the pages; time seems to slow, the flipping forward, the flipping back. Finally the doors are heaved open by two soldiers and she is motioned down the hall, relieved to find her own way. A half-dozen statues from the medieval era grace the front hall, strategically left because they are not so valuable, and yet their presence gives the impression that the French have gifted the invaders some spoils to enjoy. Her heels knock loudly on the wooden floors. She notices a nasty new sign propped on top of a marble column, about the height of her hip. It declares, in German, *Rauchen . . . verboten*. No smoking.

Alone, she walks up the monumental staircase and stares at the space where the *Winged Victory of Samothrace* no longer resides. She had personally supervised its elaborate, exhausting move, steadying some of the wooden slats that workmen made to fit the ancient Greek sculpture with a protective corset. She attended to all the details of transport but could not bear to watch the sculpture's precarious journey down one ramp, then another, before it travelled away in a lorry.

Mathilde turns right and looks down the empty Grande Galerie. She wants to sink to her knees and cry like a child, for the devastation in front of her feels like a punch to her gut. Once, this existed as one of the world's greatest treasures. Lit by an elegant series of skylights, running for hundreds of metres along the Seine River, the gallery was devoted to works by Italian geniuses. Now it is a ruin. On the ground, ornate gilded frames lie askew where canvases were hastily removed from them in advance of the Nazi march on Paris. The names of the works are scrawled on the wall and nails have been left where once the masterworks hung. Mathilde was part of the ruin. The panic to evacuate, to save whatever they could from the occupiers. She can recognize her handwriting on the walls: Leonardo da Vinci. Ghirlandaio. Raphael. Caravaggio.

When she was young, an artist in Paris, she thought beauty could only belong to one person. That great heights achieved in a studio could only be fully understood by the maker. Now she understands that beauty, if it is a powerful beauty, belongs to the masses; they want to see it, hold it in their eyes and their ears. "Ave Maria" is not a song but a universal anthem, Beethoven's Fifth invigorates all minds. The *Great Sphinx of Giza* is a lioness that belongs to every Crusader. These works infiltrate the collective like critical exaltation. Without them, humanity would be less of a grace worth aspiring to and more of a chronology grinding along through time.

Her cloak of black grime from swimming in the Chambord moat has helped to strengthen her against the tragic consequences of war. Beauty is truth. She understands this, has read John Keats. She walks along the Grande Galerie, eyes lifted to the skylights, and repeats his words in her mind: *Beauty is truth, truth beauty—that is all ye know on earth, and all ye need to know.*

Mathilde turns a corner, gains a flight of stairs, and notices that a temporary wall has been constructed. A drop cloth hangs over a gallery entrance. She pushes it aside and freezes at the sight of hundreds of wooden cases, many stacked three high; in the distance, Germans in plain clothes. Stepping into the space, she bends and finds the same name stamped on every one of the wooden boxes. *Rothschild*. On the far side, she sees German curators inside the exhibition hall, the paintings being hung on the wall with meticulous care. "*Sadique*," she says out loud. "Have you no shame?"

Somebody looks over at her. Mathilde disappears down the hallway to the room where her meeting is to take place.

The person in the Nazi uniform has his back to her when she enters: a tall, thin man dressed in military grey, tight belt, tall black boots, army cap on his head. He is not a man, thinks Mathilde, but a Nazi monster. This is the man she and her fellow French citizens have been primed to hate. She looks at the back of the monster's cleanly shaved neck, his blond hair barely visible below his cap.

Jacques Jaujard, the French director of the Louvre, welcomes her like a long-lost friend. "Madame Payer, a pleasure to see you again," he says, shaking her hand warmly and kissing her on each cheek. She looks out the window as he embraces her, sees the morning light flickering silver on the Seine, and wishes she could be strolling along the banks of the river rather than in this museum she no longer recognizes. She admires Jaujard; his work as the head of the Louvre and all of the national museums is legendary. Since meeting him that first time in his office a year ago, she has learned that he also orchestrated the transport of the artworks from the Prado in Madrid to Switzerland during the Spanish Civil War. Dark circles ring Jaujard's eyes. He holds Mathilde's hand a moment longer and she squeezes back.

"Let me introduce myself," says the Nazi, turning abruptly on his heels. "I am an artist and art historian from Rhineland. My mission is to protect the artworks and archives of France. As I have said to your director, Monsieur Jaujard, I am most impressed by the clearing of all the artworks from the Louvre to safe refuge in the châteaux of France."

Mathilde bristles at the mention of the efficient removal of the art. She and her team did what they needed to in response to a desperate situation. With every artwork taken out of its frame, every artwork rolled into a truck or held upright in wooden armature—some masterworks measuring five metres high, *The Raft of the Medusa* by Théodore Géricault strapped into a set-design truck, blowing out the electric tram lines in Versailles—there was a collective mourning. She assesses the Nazi, this monster, as he looks down at some documents clipped to his dossier. "I myself spent last year clearing the art from the Cologne cathedral. Now it is my pleasure and honour to meet with you as director of the Kunstschutz."

But Mathilde has stopped listening to his words. She is thinking about how things least expected can turn up, like the water of a château moat seeping into the veins of limestone. She is staring at this man's face. He bows politely and states his name: "Franz von Wolff-Metternich. A pleasure to meet you." He lifts up his eyes and looks evenly at her.

She feels displaced, dislocated. She can no longer recognize the place she stands in. Slowly, she meets his outstretched hand and shakes it. "Madame Payer." His eyes flicker and then rest on her face. The Nazi standing in front of her is Franz. Her art teacher in Alsace. Her first love. The last time they touched was thirty-one years ago.

CHAPTER TWENTY-NINE

Château de Chambord, 1940

Her son, Philippe. He has not always been a passionate, articulate law student. Far from it. More like a restless child, darting from his puzzles to his trucks to booting his soccer ball down the stairs of their apartment building in Chambéry. Up three times after being put to bed, to check on his wooden tower, to peer from his bedroom window to see if the gleaming moon had come out from behind the clouds. He obsessed over maps of towns, connecting lines from his school to the park with the elephant fountain, and from Grenoble to the Alps. It didn't matter if they were in a boulangerie or a shoe shop, Philippe had a compulsion to touch everything with his hands. Mathilde found it annoying to shop with him. Most days she tried to do her errands after work at the small fine arts museum before picking him up at the lycée. In the playground, Philippe would always be the one leading a pack of boys in soccer. They kicked rocks at one another if a ball had been forgotten. His other favourite was *poulet, renard, vipere,* in which the kids called chickens could eat the snakes, snakes could eat the foxes, and the foxes could eat chickens. Nobody wanted to be a chicken. Who would?

On the big issues, on what was right and what was wrong, he was always decisive. Very clear. It was unacceptable to walk by a man huddled in an alcove near their apartment. Food and water must always be offered every day before the start of school. If Mathilde forgot, and against her protests, he would dig into his satchel and pull out something from his lunch. Giving something daily to the homeless man was non-negotiable. She felt sometimes that had he lived during medieval times, Philippe might have joined Saint Francis in Assisi, handing out food to the poor, finding crutches for the crippled. Big-hearted, her son. But then he would drive her crazy by touching all the croissants in the bakery and jumping on his bed so high, his bony knees would whack his chin.

At ten, Philippe insisted that they do a family hike to an old stone hut at the edge of a mountain lake. His geography teacher had told his class about the beauty of the area, where shepherds would run hundreds of sheep during the summer months, where the trails of the Belledonne mountains travelled through dense pine forests and along steep, rocky cliffs. They packed rucksacks with wool blankets, baguettes and cheese, chocolate brioche and apples. At the last moment, Mathilde's husband begged off, saying he had some work that needed his urgent attention. This was before she understood that his sudden disappearances were to meet with one of his lovers. Mathilde and Philippe drove south on their own, parked, and started to scramble up. His hands touched every tree trunk that they passed until the trail took a sharp turn across a creek and up along exposed rocky terrain. She was amazed by her son's strength, his manic energy propelling him easily up the mountain until he quickly outpaced her. When she caught up to him, he was curled against a boulder clutching a lamb on his lap. "He's lame. His leg is broken. He can't walk. We'll have to camp here."

Now that they were beyond the treeline, the winds had turned fierce and relentless. She looked from Philippe and the lamb to the darkening sky. A spring storm would soon thrash them. She remembers how her problem-solving mind went into high gear. There must be a quick and easy way to solve this, using the same cool logic she applied to cataloguing paintings or engravings according to their provenance or condition. She had seen a shepherd an hour earlier, but he was descending with his flock, the bells on their necks clanging loudly across the rocky valley. "Philippe, we have to keep moving," she said, trying to stay calm. "We need to get to the stone hut before the rain starts."

"No, we can't," he said blithely, not bothering to look at his mother for her opinion. "We need to feed this lamb and keep it warm for the night or it might die. For sure, it will die. For sure it will."

She remembers thinking that her son was wise beyond his years, that his moral compass was perfectly intact, whereas hers had been a mess when she lived in Paris. He convinced her to make camp there, in the leeward side of the wind, behind a couple of big boulders. They wrapped one blanket around the lamb and another around themselves, and they dined on crackers and cheese, feeding morsels mixed with hot chocolate into the pink, anxious mouth of the animal. The nighttime cold of the mountains stayed in Mathilde's bones for two days in Chambéry. But they kept the lamb alive and delivered it to the ascending shepherd, who did not speak but nodded his thanks and held it in his arms. He motioned to them that the animal's leg would be treated and braced. Maybe it was kindness, mused Philippe to his parents at bedtime that night, but probably just the right thing to do, obviously.

Not long ago, the Nazis hovered beyond Chambord in the fringes of the forest. Now the free zone has shifted to the south. The soldiers have marched across the moat and entered the castle gates. At

Chambord, Mathilde is starting to understand that the enemy are a bunch of crazy bastards that she hates. She is helpless when two dozen Nazis march into the château, their captain barking orders at her in German, demanding to know where the Jewish crates are kept. Her desire to claw his eyes out with her bare hands is so strong, she ends up cutting her own palms with her nails. He raps a bunch of documents against her chest, and she takes a step back, afraid that she will punch him. Staring at him, her eyes icy with defiance, she places her fingers against her tongue and wolf whistles. Her alarm pierces the hall, where the soldiers suddenly freeze and stand automatically at attention. To her great inner delight, she catches a look of surprise on the face of the Nazi captain. Satisfied, speaking in her childhood German, she informs him that her staff can show him the crates. "We hold the collections of the following families," she says, reciting the names of Jewish families by memory. "Jacobson, Leven, Levy, Loewe, Reichenbach, Reinach, and Rouff." She plucks the captain's documents from his hands and reviews the paper. Her heart is pounding. "Yes, that's what I thought. You do not have the authority to seize any of these works."

"And you are a powerless French bitch," he says to her, muttering between his teeth.

"Come back when you have the stamp of the Nazi Art Protection Unit. Good day, monsieur." Saying this, Mathilde turns her back and walks up the staircase, away from the bad air in the lobby.

It takes her the rest of the day to cool down. The Nazis leave without any art, no doubt to return to try again. Meanwhile, she wanders outside into the courtyard, where some Nazis stand guard. What a contradiction they are. One of the soldiers, she discovered, has completed a Ph.D. on Molière. Another studied Renaissance art at an academy in Florence. They look to be about the same age as her son. They are tall and milky-eyed, their uniforms draped awkwardly around their slim bodies. Underneath their leather gloves with the cuffs extending to their elbows, she imagines their hands resemble Philippe's, soft and childlike, marked only by the ink of fountain pens. Looking at them from the rooftop of the château, she imagines what they might have worn before the war started. Light cotton shirts and tweed vests, sandals in the summer. Now they are forced into double-breasted army coats that fall below their knees and utility boots heavy as concrete. What do they think about while standing on guard for hours every day? Girlfriends left behind in Bonn or Heidelberg? Or living on lattes and pasta in Italy, like the poets and musicians who came before them? The only difference between these helmeted soldiers and Mathilde has nothing to do with their devotion to beauty, it's that some of them are armed with freshly oiled guns.

To honour the moral code. To honour beauty. To abide by the legal system. Those principles can even operate according to rules imposed by democratic leaders or, indeed, oppressors. But, for those who are interested, there are also loopholes. Ways to get around the totalitarian regime in order to operate for the good. The war she is fighting resides in her mind. How can beauty be truth when there is so much evil in the world?

Mathilde thought of this the day before at Chambord. The Nazis were expanding throughout France, pushing south. She had been handed a telegram: *Bats will be out soon. You must be getting on.*

She can almost hear Pascale Fievre, a farm woman in her village, shout to the others after drawing class in Alsace, before adjusting her crown of flowers and walking home in the dark. "Bats will be out soon. I must be getting on."

She speaks to Pierre Schommer and announces that she must leave the château the next day with the most valuable pieces in the collection. He looks at the telegram she is gripping in her hand and back to her face. He does not speak for a long time, and his eyes fill with resignation and sorrow. Finally, he lifts his chin and nods in agreement. This is the nature of their communication; words no longer need to be wasted, they mostly get in the way, except words like *fuck*, which soldiers used so often during World War I that it became commonplace during peacetime. Mathilde telegrams Philippe a simple message designed to placate, not alarm.

She wants to scribble *FUCK!* but writes that she is fine and adores him, reminds him to eat fresh vegetables. *Love, Maman*—no period at the end.

Two hundred staff members will travel with her, a large entourage of curators, custodians, security guards, cooks, and cleaners, along with two dozen refugees, young Jews who escaped from Poland. About three thousand works—masterworks, every one—will be transported with them. The château is thrown into a flurry of activity.

The medieval abbey at Loc-Dieu had been notified months earlier of the possibility of incoming artworks. The Nazis have pushed the zone of occupation farther south and much of France is now in the control of enemy troops. Perhaps her brain is playing tricks on her. She feels dirty and horribly guilty. But also somewhat hopeful because Franz, her first lover, might still be the man she remembered.

CHAPTER THIRTY

Château de Valençay, 1940

Pre-dawn, the sky is grainy, the colour of silt. Mathilde approaches the soaring archways of the château toward the fading night. She is pushing a handcart laden with two large wooden cases. Chambord guards follow closely. Behind them, dozens of men are pulling dollies loaded with crates and draped art objects. They emerge from the chapel and the oversized royal bedrooms, talking to their cargo as if it were alive, scolding the metal wheels if they flinch and turn the wrong way. For a moment, everything is calm. The procession is as silent and elegant as swans floating on a lake.

Mathilde stands at the arched portico of the château, wringing out last moments of levity before having to say her goodbyes. She jokes with Pierre Schommer about who plays the meanest poker game, and his wife expresses the hope that Mathilde will find fresh churned butter in the south as it has disappeared from the shelves in the Loire Valley.

They embrace warmly. Nobody mentions that the abbey where Mathilde and a procession of lorries are destined was once called the Devil's Place, where the dark woods harboured bandits during medieval times. What's important to know is that the zone of occupation has been moved to well south of Chambord and the artworks need to find a safer harbour. She believes in the telegram absolutely, and though Pierre knows nothing about the exact message of the telegram, he trusts her.

A year ago Mathilde arrived with the *Mona Lisa* pressed against her body. Now she has also been charged with protecting the stunning portrait of Isabella d'Este, a drawing by Leonardo da Vinci, along with three thousand paintings from the Louvre and other national museums. She will not cry. Rather, she lifts her chin, nods at her friends, and tells them to be brave.

Mathilde allows a soldier to push the handcart forward. She walks quickly across the courtyard to a waiting ambulance. Two guards have opened the back doors for her. Stepping in, crouching down, she places both boxes on a cushioned stretcher. On the floor there is a machine to keep the air in the vehicle at a constant humidity. Her assistant and then her friend Suzanne argue with her that it would be best if she travelled in front, but she refuses. The other drivers have started the engines of the old, beaten-up lorries. They spit and lurch, and some of the engines sound like glass is being churned out the exhaust pipes. The best trucks have been claimed by the French government or taken by the Nazis to be repainted with swastikas.

Finally, braced inside, she feels the ambulance move, its wheels crunching on the gravel road. She imagines the vast forest that they must be travelling through and, feeling hot, removes a scarf from around her neck, opens a button on her blouse. The ambulance turns onto another minor road with heavier gravel and potholes. She hangs on to the sides of the vehicle and knows that they are cutting south, away from the Loire River. Travelling in the back reminds her of riding low to the ground in the apple cart she and her brothers had built to amuse themselves one summer in Alsace. The wheels were mostly metal with a thin cover of rubber, left over from some tractor wheels, and the floor was made of tin siding from an old shed. They would tie the cart to their cat and their dog, but eventually the animals were dismissed and Claude and Lucien took turns pulling her in dizzying circles around the fields. She can still hear their roars of delight at their show of strength. It brings a smile to her lips every time.

She feels every nuance of the road. When the ambulance angles down a steep, curving road, she slides along the corrugated floor and her hips hit the front partition wall. It takes a full minute before she can finally find balance enough to scramble to her feet and grab the ceiling straps. Her eyes never leave the wooden cases tied firmly to the stretcher. When the road becomes bumpy, her head bounces against the metal ceiling, and she hovers a protective hand over the cases to ensure they do not fall.

The entourage stops an hour later at the Château de Valençay. Mathilde raps on the double doors and is immediately waved inside by the owners, an elegant and resolute couple, the duke sporting a paisley cravat, the duchess wrapped in an Hermès scarf decorated with nautical images. The entrance lobby is ornately painted with scenes of men and hunting dogs bounding through leafy forests in search of grouse. Mathilde takes in the view. There are apparently one hundred rooms here, the entirety owned by the duke, whose family had some nominal governance over a small German-held province. As such, Valençay has been granted immunity from the horrors of war. Bombs cannot fall on the château. Two monumental works are stored here and Mathilde asks to see them: the *Venus de Milo* and the *Winged Victory of Samothrace*, ancient Greek sculptures, so magnificent as to be considered guardians of the Louvre, now gathering dust while bombs fall around them. Mathilde walks first to Venus, the goddess of love and beauty, and touches a hand through a tiny opening in the thick wooden box where she is restrained. She feels the woman's bent knee and the drapery of her Greek toga, poetically carved from a block of marble some two thousand years ago. She looks across the hall to the *Winged Victory of Samothrace*. Once her wings spread wide to soar. Now they are obscured behind the wood strapping and protective blankets roped around her.

She leaves the staff in charge of accommodation and dinner to consult with the château manager. Most will find a place to lay their heads down in one of the magnificent rooms. Others will sleep in their trucks or on the stone floors of the reception halls. Ten guards are posted outside to watch over the artworks parked in the courtyard. Many of the men have brought rucksacks full of sausage and bread from Chambord. But a dozen cooks converge in the stone-vaulted kitchen with its four hearths to prepare potato and leek soup, make bread and egg tarts.

Bombardments wake them at dawn. They seem to be coming from about twenty kilometres away. Everybody is suddenly out of their beds, standing bleary-eyed in the courtyard. Some of the men are debating whether the bombs sound like they belong to the Germans or Italians. Mathilde had hoped they might take the *Winged Victory of Samothrace* and the *Venus de Milo* farther south to the unoccupied zone, but no longer. Not under such conditions.

"Does it matter?" says a barrel-chested man with hair standing on end. "They're bombing our homes. We'll be going back to destroyed villages if we're lucky enough to make it home."

The entourage prepares to leave quickly after coffee and bites of baguette, warm from the oven and thick with local berry jam. The owners of the château, grim-faced, hand out more bread from golden plates. They pull Mathilde aside to tell her that the German advance is coming fast and the road to Loc-Dieu is said to be long and difficult. She nods, expresses her thanks, and meets with each of the truck drivers, impressing upon them the significance of their loads, the need to be cautious. To avoid panic, she does not translate the warning about the fast approach of the Nazis. The conversation turns instead to truck mechanics. One of the drivers says gruffly, "The brakes are bad on this lorry."

"How bad?"

"If we come to steep hills, the brakes could burn and spark. Engine fire is what I fear."

"Engine fire?"

The thought has never occurred to Mathilde.

"Can you repair the brakes?"

The driver looks around the vast parkland, grass manicured and perfectly kept, then forest, no village in sight.

"Nobody around to fix them. Everything is shut down."

It's true what the man is saying. The roads have been clogged with refugees heading south, abandoning villages, their homes, and their jobs. People are crowded into cars, with suitcases and bags of food heaped onto their laps and in wagons pulled by horses with chickens flying about, and men and women ride bicycles hunched over with the weight of their bags strapped to their backs.

"We'll have to risk it," says Mathilde.

Two hours later, the ambulance travels up a steep hill and she holds tight to the straps dangling from the ceiling. She can hear the ambulance driver gearing down, and she prays for the vehicle to advance and not slip backward into the other trucks. In the distance, she hears all of the engines screeching in unison, trying to gain purchase as gears fail, brakes thrown hard down to their metal plates. Her eyes narrow, anticipating that the door of the ambulance is about to swing open and she will come tumbling out to be crushed by the truck wheels, along with the paintings. This is not what Franz wanted—to send her to a dirty car-crash ending—when he was trying to keep the treasures in her care safe. She sets the soles of her shoes on the floor and pulls herself up on the braces of the stretcher. "Help me to get through this," she says to herself, to Franz. But now a feeling of dread comes over her. Can Franz be trusted? For once he was a young teacher in Alsace showing her the art of painting and the art of love. Now he turns up in a Nazi uniform, and who can say that he hasn't turned from something radiant to something monstrous? In that tin ambulance, hanging on to the straps, she feels frightened of being made a fool. That's what the enemy likes to do, after all. Plunder and pillage when their victims are crying for mercy.

Eventually, at the top, because it seems that they must have reached the top of the terrible hill, there is a lull, a teetering; her shirt is soaked in sweat, and she tries to prepare herself for the ambulance going over a cliff. She does not dare move. There is no more oxygen in the van. She wonders if this is true. Now the ignition is clicked off and the engine lurches before going quiet. She does not acknowledge the stains of sweat that are blossoming under her arms and on her back. Years as a teenager running through the mountain foothills, racing over roots of trees in the rain, slogging through the mud, have disciplined her. Her older brothers taught her how to set pain aside. They ran past her, shouting, "Come on, Piggy! *Allez*, Porcine!" never stopping to check on her when she fell, negligence that she found to be strangely encouraging. She learned back then in Alsace that if she lost focus, she would trip, she would fall on the track, she would rip the skin on her knees, and that is how she knows to stay quiet and endure.

She imagines a roadblock of Nazi soldiers with rifles pointed at the convoy. She wants to hide the paintings behind the medical case and electric machinery, but she also feels a need to lie down in search of air. It is better for the paintings if she is flat on the floor.

She does not exactly remember the doors being unlatched and the driver and his assistant hauling her out of the ambulance. They place her on the side of the road, give her sips of water to drink. When she blinks open her eyes, she is not met by Nazis but by the men and women she is meant to lead. After several minutes, she stands up and surveys the scene. Most of the trucks have made it to the top of the monumental hill, but three have not. They have been parked precariously across the hill, angled in this way by their drivers to ease off the brakes and stop them from crashing backward. A large wooden crate sits off the road. Mathilde presses her hands against the headache that is pounding in her forehead. She strains her eyes to look again. It does not contain the usual red or black circles from the national museum art collections.

"Is that ours?" she asks her assistant.

"Not ours," he says, shaking his head. But he looks distraught and does not elaborate.

"Tell me," she orders.

"It has the Rothschild stamp."

"The Rothschilds? You mean the bankers?"

"*Oui*, madame."

"Open it." She turns from the young assistant to another driver, older, with eyes wary and watchful. He does not question but nods in agreement, retrieving a crowbar from his truck in quick time.

She drinks more water and walks halfway down the hill to the wooden crate. The side bears the same Rothschild label that she had seen on the crates in the Nazi-occupied Louvre. Gold letters against a black background. She is considering possibilities in her head but another driver walks over to her, toothless, from the Chambord area, a war veteran with a bad leg. "Likely had to dump it to make the hill, must have been in a hurry."

Mathilde calculates that the port of Bordeaux is only three hours away by road. But if the Nazis were in pursuit and keen to intercept the shipping of even a fraction of the Rothschilds' extraordinary art collection, there would be no time to waste on trucks slowed down by weighty cargo. The drivers might have made the decision to drive fast to the Atlantic ships rather than risk being arrested by German soldiers.

Now she is getting a clear picture of the hideous nature of this war, the *sadique*. People fleeing for their lives, dumping extraordinary valuables on the side of the road.

Two other men have joined the lead assistant. They pull from the crate a large landscape flowing with afternoon light that is still in its gold frame. Mathilde tilts her head and examines the painting. "Monet," she says.

They slide the work back carefully into its hold and produce another, slightly smaller painting.

"Watteau," she says.

They produce ten other masterworks by French impressionists, one Cézanne, a Matisse, a Toulouse-Lautrec. Then her heart stops. A painting of two pastel-soft women by Marie Laurencin is pulled from the crate. Mathilde blinks at it for a moment, remembering her friend, her artistry, their brief fling. That time when she visited Apollinaire in jail. Marie Laurencin, the girlfriend who left him. Finally, she says, "Pack everything up." She turns to the older man. "Monsieur, how do you propose getting this crate up the hill?"

"Ropes, pulleys, muscles."

"That's fine. We'll add it to one of our trucks."

"The trucks are heavily loaded, madame."

"I understand, but we can't leave this behind. It's now under our protection."

She takes a water canteen offered by her friend Suzanne and drinks again heartily.

"And we thought Montmartre was a big hill," says Suzanne, taking back the bottle, shaking her head.

"I'll never complain about walking up to Sacré-Coeur again," says Mathilde, smiling wryly. Her head is still throbbing.

"You doing all right, Mathilde?" asks Suzanne.

"I'll ride up front for the rest of the journey." Mathilde wishes she could wrap an arm around Suzanne and reassure her with a hug. She wishes they could sit down in the forest and talk about the sad, mesmerizing songs of Edith Piaf and Al Jolson's jazz hands and wake up in the morning to discover all of this to be a horrible dream. But she knows the men are watching her, and what they need now is her strength, not her softness.

Stepping away from Suzanne, Mathilde lifts two fingers to her mouth and wolf whistles. Two hundred men and women stop to look at her. "Time to drive on. Let's be quick, safe, and efficient. The Nazis are right behind us."

By nightfall, after five long hours travelling through dense forest and rough, potholed roads, the convoy pulls into Loc-Dieu. The mountains have ceded to plains. All is still. Not even a bird cries out in evening song. It feels like the end of the world. In this strange place, far from the war, they lay their bodies down and sleep.

CHAPTER THIRTY-ONE

Loc-Dieu Abbey, 1940

The next day, the convoy members do as the Cistercian monks have done for centuries: They do not speak. They wander the parkland, sit mute by the edge of the pond; they eat sausage and bread gone stale from the journey. Some of them lie back in the sun and allow the trauma from the previous day to swirl in their minds. They had survived the bombardment by being asleep at the Château de Valençay. Had they not opened the doors of the ambulance, Mathilde might have died from asphyxiation. The tires threatened to blow but did not catch fire. The Rothschild treasures had been dumped on the road and recovered by the museum convoy. Disaster had been pushed back. They were lucky. Blessed, in fact, compared to the tidal wave of refugees on the roads travelling south in panic. Survival is not about your money or status. It is pure luck. War makes no distinction. It is the great leveller.

Mathilde staggers through the abbey's interior courtyard, overgrown with thistles and coneflowers, the smell of wet clay rising from the ground. She climbs the stone stairs that sweep up to the grand salon. A secret passage is opened within a bookshelf and she rushes inside, and into her small, monastic bedroom.

What now? she thinks.

She finds herself thinking of Franz again. Their meeting at the Louvre was brief, mere minutes, but she believes, in thinking through every second, that he showed signs of recognition, that his formal Nazi persona disappeared with a long exhale. Thinking back on their meeting, she struggles to recognize her Franz of the art studio in Alsace, the one in the light blue cotton shirt rolled up at the sleeves, in the older one, a middle-aged man with less hair, more jowls, still broad-shouldered but thinner and cinched within the confines of the Nazi uniform. She is not sure what or who to trust. Her country is at war with Germany. It could be that Franz has changed, that he has become an Aryan-obsessed soldier dedicated to Hitler.

She has never stopped thinking about Franz. All these years, his tenderness has always been with her, his hand gently at her back. He helped her to believe in herself as an artist, to see and hear and touch the world with acute attention. To smell it! He taught her how to inhale the perfume of wine. Pulling a bottle from his rucksack, what she had considered to be the plonk of Alsace, he invited her to detect all the delicate notes of the local Gewürztraminer. "Do you smell it? Peaches, apricots?"

"I smell roses." They smiled at each other and took turns drinking from the bottle. She was seventeen years old and surprised herself with the revelation. But discovering roses in wine always lifted her spirits in the years that followed no matter how dark the times. She had not tried to find him, had no idea where he lived in Germany. She had never told him where her family lived in Haguenau. Inviting him over for dinner would have been an impossibility because, even then, he was a German, one of the invaders, or a Boche, as her family would call them. Once, he insisted they go to her home so he could meet her family and win them over. Her beautiful, naive lover boy was convinced of his success. He grabbed her hand and started loping happily down the country road where he guessed she lived. A part of her wanted desperately to show him off, Franz, who knew so much about the world. The other part knew that he would be pummelled by her brothers, possibly shot by her grandfather. Naturally, she wrenched free of his hand about halfway down the track and refused to take another step with him. After that, he never tried to go to her family farm again.

She had thought of him over the years, imagining what he would say about Picasso, about the way he made her feel desirable and also inadequate. Or Vincenzo, how they shared much in common, how he dared to steal the *Mona Lisa* to please his countrymen, possibly to please her. She glossed over the ugly truths, that Picasso had dumped her for another muse, that she had been an accomplice to the theft of Leonardo's portrait. Even later, while living in Chambéry with her husband and son, she wondered what he would think of her decision to allow her husband the freedom to leave her, so that he might be true to himself as a gay man. Life had thrown daggers at her, and she had learned to resist. But having seen Franz again, she realized that she had never stopped missing him and who she was with him. How sweet it would be if she could lay her head against his chest for even one moment. To be carefree. To be vulnerable. To be young. Were they to see each other now, would they walk through the forest and sit on a log and paint watercolours together? They would not discuss the war or politics or who ended up on either side but only find stillness listening to the guinea fowl scratching in the leaves, the woodpeckers knocking on trees far above. Who would say that they did not deserve this peace? Is there a law that forbids her from loving an enemy? Of course there is. It comes by various names: collaborator, traitor, turncoat.

It is dusk by the time she awakens. She has been kneeling on the floor, her hands pressed together in prayer. Leonardo's portraits of the *Mona Lisa* and Isabella d'Este lie under her bed.

She goes to the small window, presses her hands on the deep stone sill, and looks out. She sees the quiet of the people lying on the banks of the pond, wandering in silence through the parkland. Tomorrow they will unload the trucks, and she and Suzanne and the other curators will begin the arduous process of cataloguing the works that have been brought to Loc-Dieu. Jacques Jaujard has already sent a telegram ordering this to be a top priority.

She wishes she could divine the future. But her thoughts are interrupted by something strange happening in the sky. An epic swirling of birds. They look to be black starlings, and they seem to be arriving from many miles away, from across the country, to perform a miraculous flocking and flying in perfect formation. She pushes open her window and listens to the whooshing murmur sound they make. There must be a thousand birds doing a dance in front of her. They are swarming in currents of air that allow them to fly in perfect figure eights. A murmuration. It is dark and frightening to see. But also intoxicating. The absurdity of life in motion, birds and human beings, have a look to where the heavens are stained. The past will never change. History is unflinching in its lessons.

CHAPTER THIRTY-TWO

Loc-Dieu Abbey, 1940

She gets up at sunrise, flings the blankets off her lumpy straw cot. Dressing quickly, she catches the view of the mist rising off the pond in front of the abbey. It takes her breath away, the outline of the oak and pine trees barely visible in the distance and the grey cats curled around the stone urns in the garden. All the sharp edges of the world have disappeared into the soft forgiveness of the fog. The beauty in front of her is mystical and serene. If it were only up to what she can see, the war might seem tolerable during these times.

Three times a week, she and Suzanne ride battered bikes along a narrow country road, the grinding of their rusty chains a raw soundtrack that accompanies their cycling. Finally, pedalling hard to get up the short but steep hill, they arrive at the sober, walled medieval town of Villefranche-de-Rouergue. The market vendors are neither warm nor icy, their reception to the women from Paris merely laced with suspicion. Mathilde is careful not to mention that she works for the Louvre, for this is a museum the locals will never visit because it is too far or because it was dreamed up to house the collections of royals. The locals are happy to sell to the Parisians, though, whoever they might be, these two women in canvas pants who arrive at the market sweaty and panting, they notice, from travelling on ruinous bikes, to purchase all their links of pork sausage, a dozen baguettes, and fill their bicycle baskets with zucchini, potatoes, and carrots. Sometimes they buy extra lengths of sausage to dry for the winter stores. There are two hundred mouths to feed and Mathilde and Suzanne are delighted to find supplies, and especially to race downhill on the way back to the abbey. The merchants nod at the women when they wave their light Parisian goodbyes, these curious refugees, pretty enough but wearing dirty clothes, who have suddenly interrupted their lives. Nobody smiles and possibly none of them will smile fully until the war is over. When they bike away, Mathilde turns and sees the vendors sweeping the stone plaza clean.

At the abbey there is morning coffee and bread without jam, the summertime preserves depleted a month ago. Occasionally, the serving women put out Cantal, a creamy local cheese, on wooden boards, and the entire dining hall erupts in cheers. After breakfast, Suzanne and Mathilde climb onto the crates, pry out the nails, and eventually pull out the artworks tenderly but firmly, as though they are midwives birthing babies. It is punishing work but must be done to allow the paintings to bathe in some natural light, or turn black and sooty over time. Nobody thinks to complain. Other curators are doing the same, climbing over the wooden boxes, taking down notes in other rooms and reception halls stacked with the art collections. Everybody is talking about how the autumn winds are rising and the oak trees are beginning to turn orange. Mathilde thinks of the colour as bike chain rust. A chill penetrates deep into the abbey. It feels suddenly cold, colder than even she can remember from Chambord. The brittle leaves fall wasted to the ground.

"I feel it in all of my bones, from my toes to my vagina to the back of my neck," says Suzanne, who is wearing two sweaters and a third wrapped around her head.

"Since when is a vagina a bone? I thought it was all flesh." Mathilde flicks her eyes to her friend but does not smile. "Obviously, I've been away from men for too long."

Suzanne shakes her head, lifting her pen from the clipboard, where she has been recording all the works for their archival records.

"It smells very wet, like a river is running directly beneath this old abbey," says Mathilde. "But it doesn't flow away, it's flowing up into the air we're breathing." She is reaching with both hands into a crate with objects tightly packed in straw. Suddenly, she shouts, "My god, no!"

"What is it?"

Mathilde pulls out a handful of discoloured straw to show Suzanne. The smell is pure vinegar. "Black mould," she says with a lowered voice. She reaches back into the crate and pulls out a vase with elegant Roman lines. It's impossible to make out the painting on the jug because of the dark, sickly patches.

"This can't be happening," says Suzanne. "I've never seen this before."

"I need to tell Jacques Jaujard," says Mathilde. "But we must keep this quiet from the rest."

She and Suzanne replace the straw and nail back the lid. Temporary measures until they decide what to do next. In the dining hall, the hearth is heaped with logs and the bright fire crackles. She is thankful for the woodsmoke and its earthy, musky smell. Mathilde leans across the dining table that night, speaks in whispers, not wanting to alarm the other curators or send a rumour whistling through the ranks of the custodians and guards. "We've only been here two months," says Suzanne. "It's impossible to think about another move.

But it might be dangerous for the artworks, the canvases might crack, the sculptures might break."

"You know my word for this war, right?"

"Your word and mine too. *Sadique*."

"Exactly. And the sadist is capable of inflicting all kinds of pain. But black mould on these priceless artworks? We can't risk that."

Suzanne sits back on her chair in the dining hall, its grey gothic archways soaring above her. "Funny. All of our work. What we're doing, breaking our backs to protect the collections. None of the locals could care less about art. They care about whether their cows are making enough milk and whether their daughters are fertile or barren."

"We're at war with Germany and Italy. They care about that. Especially if their husbands and sons are joining the resistance." says Mathilde. "I'll send a telegram to Jacques." She excuses herself to write a message out by candlelight that night.

In her room, she paces and flings herself down on her mean narrow cot, hating its horsehair filling a little more. She lies on her back and lifts her feet overhead, trying to bring some fresh clarity to her head. She does not want to frighten Jacques Jaujard, but she also has a responsibility to not hide the danger from him. The collections could be ruined by the damp at this place. She picks up her hard little pillow and roars her anger into it. There are no bombs going off in this hidden kingdom, no snipers, no marching of helmeted soldiers. The devastation she feels is insidious and darkly cruel. Her relocation farther and farther away from her son in Paris. The vulnerability of the masterworks. The absurdity of having to remove all the art from the national museums in the first place. She feels angry at being banished and wonders if Dante Alighieri, exiled from Florence, felt the same, or Ovid before him, for writing *The Art of Love*.

Finally, she rolls off the bed, drops her boots to the ground, and writes: *Loc-Dieu Abbey bad for art. Collections at risk. Black mould in some crates. Do we stay?*

Within twenty-four hours, Mathilde receives a reply from Jacques Jaujard. *German analysts on their way.*

She feels the breath go out of her. Clutching the telegram, she sits down where she was standing, on the stone floor in a chapel where the monumental canvases and tapestries are rolled up below the windows. Jaujard's telegram unnerves her. Could it be that this great cultural leader is no longer in control? It feels as if, even from this remote part of southern France, the Nazis have unleashed oppressive control over France's greatest institutions, kicking their finest, most esteemed leaders out of play. On their way? The zone of occupation seems merely a formality on paper. The reality is that the Nazis want all of France. Her mind goes immediately to the dozen of refugees from Poland who are staying with them at the abbey. They will have to go into hiding within the homes of the local villagers. Negotiating that might be harder than she expected. The locals like to keep to themselves and want no trouble. She thinks of the precious masterworks in the crates, and naturally, she thinks of the two portraits in their wooden cases she keeps under her bed. Is it only a matter of days before they will be torn away from her arms?

She knocks on Suzanne's door, and wordlessly, they descend into the dank, mouse-furred cellar of the abbey. They each hold a candle, but they have travelled this path often and know the way by heart, down tightly spiralled stairs, boots sliding on wet clay floors, along a passage into a low, vaulted space. They stop at whitewashed niches carved into the cellar walls. Once, they were designated for senior monks and patrons of the church to store wine specially produced to mark the birth of a baby or the ordination of a priest. During cataclysmic events, thinks Mathilde, such as the abandonment of a church, or war, these wine cupboards lose their prestige. There are dozens of them, every one of their iron padlocks broken. Suzanne is standing right behind her.

"Survival of the fittest," says Mathilde, creaking open one of the gates and lifting out two bottles. *Syrah,* she sees by the light of the candle, *Grand Cru. 1930. Languedoc-Roussillon.* The bottles are coated in dust so the women rub them like rolling pins along their canvas pants. One each. Uncorked in quick time. They lean their tall, thin bodies against the stone walls and devour the aged wine with lusty thirst. Deep and robust, full of tannins that alarm their mouths. "The Cistercian monks knew how to pick their wine," says Mathilde, then, raising a bottle, "Here's to the end of the war."

"May it come."

She looks at her friend, at her narrowed and joyless eyes.

"May we go home with a crate of this wine."

They walk to the end of the cave, and Mathilde suddenly hurls the empty bottle against the wall.

"Cigarette?" Suzanne lights one for Mathilde and another for herself.

The flame of the match goes out and they smoke in the dark, enjoying a private moment outside of the war. And then Mathilde starts to sing. Badly, she recognizes that, but she gives in to a desire to sing and warble Edith Piaf's newest song, released a few months ago, "J'ai dansé avec l'amour." Her memory is sharp, honed over years of keeping archival records at the Louvre, and she can remember lyrics easily, about blue eyes and a wondrous night. She swings and sways, clutching her hands around her body.

Now Suzanne takes over. She sings on pitch with throaty desire. The women move and sway side by side and the song fills every corner of the low stone cellar. Mathilde does not smile; she feels no joy, but she sings with Suzanne the grand finale: that there is so much love.

CHAPTER THIRTY-THREE

Alsace, 1909

That splendid day in June, Mathilde is teaching Franz the names of the local flowers with blooms that prick through the thick, leafy undergrowth of the oak forest. His French is excellent but there are gaps in his vocabulary. "*Campanules, crépides*," she says, pointing out the flowers as they hike. "*Campanules, crépides*," he would repeat.

"*Impatiens, épervières, myosotis*." They are ducking along the forest floor, shielding their eyes from the dogwood and gorse. A few butterflies are opening and closing their wings on a bush of thistles.

"*Impatiens, épervières, myosotis, papillons!*" he says, bringing her in for a kiss.

Summer has suddenly arrived, and they throw off their wool sweaters to bask in the sun and touch each other's skin. She wants to show him the old tree fort she built by herself when she was a child. Hauling branches, walking for a few miles, nails in her pockets. Years later, her haven from her family is still intact, even the walls that she painted with flowers and birds. But Franz is distracted by the solar eclipse predicted for that day. He wants to experience the event with Mathilde, for she said she had never seen an eclipse or known about them; somehow this phenomenon that Franz is raving on about has been left out of her education.

They emerge from the forest and look to the fields in the distance, dazzling green against the gathering dusk and, beyond, a line of trees standing up like the fur of a beast.

"There's a hill over there," says Mathilde, pointing.

"How far?"

"Ten kilometres, I guess."

"If we hurry, we should make it in time," he says, holding her hand and pulling her along the road. She likes the way his German accent sounds strong when he is excited and trying to get something he wants. But she doesn't like to be pulled, so she takes her hand back and starts to run beside him. He looks at her, nods, and falls into step. They are on the outskirts of Haguenau, the gravel road cutting between large rolling farmland with stone houses set back. The hills are heavy with purple vetch, the fields planted with barley and einkorn wheat. Some farmers are outside working the land with their horses, others are gathered around their threshers to talk about the day. She can see a group of people assembled for some kind of celebration, hear the wheezing, shrill sound of a violin and an accordion grinding out notes somewhere in the back fields. She is enjoying the sound of the music accompanying their leather shoes crunching along the road.

"Hey, over there . . ." says Franz, taking off before she can understand his meaning or stop him. Running faster, he tears down a dirt driveway toward a pair of bicycles resting against a shed. Mathilde knows this farm and whom the bikes belong to. A sister and brother, Bleuette and Boniface, who went to her school, one or two years below her. They are quiet, with fleshy pink faces, and she knows they will be thrashed for the thefts. She does not mention this to Franz;

he looks so pleased with himself, holding the bicycles aloft like hard-won trophies.

"With these, we'll make the eclipse in time," he says, his eyes bright and shining.

They take off, and even though the bicycles are too small for them, they make the hill in less than an hour. He holds her by the shoulders and points to the sky like an excited child. "Yes, okay, this is the moment, the moon is coming between the sun and Earth. You see that? It's happening now, the moon is blocking the face of the sun."

She's mesmerized by the dark figure spreading over the sun. "Looks like an invasion," she says, wanting to add to Franz's child-like excitement for the eclipse.

"Exactly right! Some people in ancient times thought the eclipse was a bad thing. Like demons were trying to take over the sun."

Along the flats, a handful of marmots are standing up to bask in the last light of the day. The sky shimmers and then falls into darkness. "It won't be dark for long. The sun will return," says Franz, looking at Mathilde, asking for permission. She clutches his shirt, holds his head with her hands, and they kiss passionately as if they're new lovers touching each other for the first time. "I love experiencing this with you," he says, looking around at the darkened sky. "It's a good sign, like an omen." He removes her clothes, eases her to the ground, warming her naked body with his own. There's no wind, only darkness and the sound of crickets chirping through the strange, suddenly dark sky. He slides his shirt below her so she can stay warm in darkness while he kisses her everywhere, the inside of her arms, her kneecaps, each one of her toes. He caresses all of her skin before finally sliding his tongue up between her thighs.

Opening her eyes, looking up to the sky darkened to a silvery-grey hue, she sees an outline of a nearby pine waving at her, beckoning with its squirrel-tailed branches. *Walk away from judgment and shame, for they are lonely places.* It seems the tree is talking to her. *Walk toward empathy and grace, this is where we can meet.*

She allows herself to be still and enjoy the angel bringing her body into full, outrageous ecstasy. "Close your eyes," he says, rising to lie over her, his fingers pressing lightly over her eyelids.

In fact, she is incredulous, moaning loudly despite herself. Her orgasm tips her over into new consciousness about how human beings should harness this extraordinary feeling. She smiles to think that her grandmother would surely chide her for being loud and vulgar. That is a sacrilege for any decent woman. Mathilde no longer cares. She likes being loud, moans again as a second orgasm courses and feathers through her. She's never felt anything like it, as if she has finally realized that the world is not flat but stupendously round. Everything seems extra-dimensional. Because she is experiencing it all with Franz and giving herself over entirely to their lovemaking. When he lifts away his fingers, she witnesses the erasure of the dark above her, the sun showing its face again.

Afterward, sitting cross-legged around each other, foreheads pressed against each other, she asks him what he wants to do with his life.

"Just what we are doing. Exactly this. You and me."

"But this will come to an end, there's nothing certain about us."

"Ah, a bit heavy just now? Can't we just enjoy? Enjoy this, all of this, it's gemütlich." He kisses her gently.

"It's strange. I saw it but I also felt the darkness, did you not?"

"The moon became a tiny dot against the sun."

"It doesn't come around often, as you yourself said."

He rolls onto his back, humouring her. "I want to do good in the world, I do. But sometimes my parents—their plans for me—get in the way of my own. They want the best for me, they do. I mean, they took me to the Louvre to see all the masterworks for my sixteenth birthday."

This admission washes over Mathilde. The reality of Franz's childhood sounds entirely unreal to her.

"What is your dream?" she asks.

"You. You are my dream."

They kiss again, deeply. Mathilde is surprised and thrilled by her appetite. She leans toward him, rising from the ground to push her tongue deeper into his mouth. Now she straddles him and pulses against his hips, her hands pressing hard on his shoulders. The feeling of climax is heightened with her previous orgasms, and yet she is shocked into the fabulous possibility that climaxing is available to her at any time with this man.

Later, she wakes to hear a sweet whistling breath coming from his mouth, and her body lifts and falls on his chest. He wakes and wraps both arms around her.

"I think time does not matter during sex. It disappears. It's irrelevant," she says.

"The calendar should be rewritten with this in mind," he says.

"The calendar of sex," she says, laughing.

"Goodbye, solar calendar. Ours is much better."

Mathilde runs her fingers along his face, down his arms, to hold his hands. They do not speak for a long time.

"But tell me, Franz, seriously, what do you want to be?"

"To be an artist, to study art, protect what has been created, the beautiful masterpieces."

"Can't you do that?"

"I hope so, it's what I want. But my parents, they want me to study law, or just look after our property."

"But, so, why come here? Did they make you come here?"

"To Alsace?" He hesitates, looks out over the outline of the hill. "Yes, they did. It was their idea. You know, they said it would complete my education, culturally, I guess."

"So, I'm part of your education. Me, the farmers, Haguenau, Alsace?"

"They just wanted me to experience how other people live. And I'm glad I travelled to your city, to teach art, and to share our love of beauty. You know what I mean?"

She knows she is about to ruin their perfect evening, but her temper gets the best of her. She stands and hauls on her shirt and pants.

"Well, thanks for climbing down from your castle to experience the little people."

"No, stop, Mathilde, it's not like that, *scheisse*," he says, pulling on his pants, running after her. It is the first time she has heard him swear.

She runs ahead of him, furious and regretful that he had insisted on seeing the eclipse and they had cycled to the hill on stolen bikes.

CHAPTER THIRTY-FOUR

Loc-Dieu Abbey, 1940

The Cistercian monks who built the abbey at the bottom of the valley forbade any art or decorative stonework, but out of their reverence for music, they punched holes into the gothic vaults to enhance the sound of choral performance. So it is only natural that the sound of the Nazis goose-stepping along the cloister reached Mathilde's ears well before their boots march into the dining hall. She rises slowly from her place at the ancient oak table and surveys the two hundred people scooping rabbit stew diligently from their tin bowls. They are in her charge and she loves them fiercely, will do anything to protect them, but she is also embarrassed by their whiskered rodent smell. Human sweat trapped in wool sweaters as if they have been spending their days crawling through wet clay tunnels. Such is the subtle indignity of war. But these people are not marmots, she thinks. They are villagers with families they love back home near the Château de Chambord. They are curators and archivists, conservationists and logisticians from the Louvre, the Musée Rodin, and the Carnavalet. They are elegant, professional Parisians who once visited their favourite cafés for morning espresso daily and bought flowers after having their hair washed and set at the *coiffeuse* every week. Now they are people on the run. They look old and tired, their eyes sullen and watchful. They have been forced into impossible housing. Mathilde wonders, setting her old silver spoon down next to her bowl, whether the Nazis will find cause to punish them because of the rodent smell.

Six men in Nazi uniforms march without hesitation toward her because she is the only one standing up and therefore must be the leader to be singled out. The rest of the diners set their spoons down and rise in a single movement of solidarity. Other soldiers back themselves against the far wall and point their rifles at the diners. A unified populace is to be feared and destroyed.

"SIT!"

The diners continue to stand.

"SIT!"

Another soldier, about twenty years old, full-lipped with acne on his chin, waves his rifle at those assembled and adds for good cheer, "SIT, or we will SHOOT!"

There is another pair of boots that Mathilde can detect in the distance. Supple leather, soft tread, thoughtful pace, as if somebody is taking the time to appreciate the architectural lines of the old abbey.

She sees him, Franz, arrive at the entrance to the dining hall, waving down the rifles of his soldiers, who lower their weapons immediately. He walks to the front of the room, his face turned to the stone-mullioned windows and the pleasant view of the arcaded courtyard. She studies his profile below his army fatigue cap, the fine structure of his nose and jaw, and meets his gaze directly when he turns to look at her. The shock of seeing him again roars through her. He has entered her territory. It is an outrageous move on his part, and yet she is overwhelmed with joy to see him stand before her. Her forehead goes damp with sweat.

"Very impressive, a fine example of medieval architecture," he says to her, looking around at the dining hall. Then, turning to face the crowd, he speaks in impeccable French, "*S'il vous plaît*, continue with your dinner. *Bon appétit.*" He turns to Mathilde and says, "Madame Payer, when you are able, please do me the favour of meeting with me. I will wait in the foyer with my men." Only when he has left do the French sit on their chairs. The hall sizzles with low-burning outrage. Nobody takes their eyes off the invaders.

Mathilde sinks to her seat, exchanging glances with Suzanne. Mechanically, she scoops the stew into her mouth though she wants to vomit it all back into the bowl. The sharp smell of her vinegar sweat rises from below her clothes to assault her nose. She feels trapped, paralyzed. Suzanne mouths something at Mathilde, communicating something like *Liberté, Egalité, Fraternité*, or maybe just *Bon courage*. She pushes away her bowl and walks down the hall to the foyer with chin lifted.

When she reaches Franz, he extends a hand and she looks closely to check that he is truly the man she thinks he is, and finally shakes it. His soldiers drift away to the courtyard, leaving them alone.

"*Bonsoir*," she begins cautiously. Is it true that most people are liars? She believes this to be true. Only rarely do people speak the truth, and if they do, it is likely only a partial truth.

"*Bonsoir*," he returns, his voice tight in his throat.

They are miles and decades away from admitting their shared past.

She watches his eyes, the way they flit to her left hand, the absence of a wedding ring.

"Tell me clearly," she says, feeling the anger rise. "What is the purpose of this visit? Will you take all of our collections now or will you extend this cat-and-mouse game for many months, or years?"

He looks at her. She sees the fatigue around his blue eyes, a hollowing of his cheeks. Strangely, she feels sorry for him, the forces that have changed him from the gentle, spirited artist she once knew to a military man. She is angry but she also wants to apologize for the strangeness of everything that is happening, of the impossibility that he is now here with her at the end of the world.

"I'm sorry, this war is very difficult for us," she says.

"For all of us," he answers, nodding.

"I would have preferred a visit from Jacques Jaujard, not the director of the Kunstschutz."

"Yes."

"Is he well?" She wants to be sure that nothing untoward has happened to her esteemed colleague. His decision to stay as a figurehead of the Louvre makes him a highly visible target.

"Yes, Monsieur Jaujard is well. Keeping regular hours in that lovely office, the view of the Seine. We are attempting to collaborate as best we can." She hears his French, even more elegantly turned out than before, but she hates the German accent, its brusqueness.

"But it seemed only right that I should make a personal visit."

She blushes deeply at this last sentence and turns away to hide her face. How dare he presume? Why should it be right that the head of the Art Protection Unit make an eight-hour trip over difficult roads to check on humidity levels in an old, forgotten abbey? She walks briskly down the hallway. "I will show you the collections, how they are being stored."

He follows her in silence. She is keenly aware that he is looking at her. They turn first into the chapel, where wooden boxes are stacked. Some of them have been opened, with mounds of tainted straw sequestered in a corner as evidence of the black mould.

He bends to the straw, grabs a handful, and smells it. His military cap slips forward and she catches sight of his hair, still remarkably corn yellow. He leaps easily to the boxes that are open and peers in, pulling out two Renaissance portraits on wood, gazing at them tenderly, sliding them back carefully into the box.

"We will set up our hygrometers to measure the humidity levels," he says, articulating his words carefully, looking seriously at her. "You were right to travel south away from the zone of occupation, but I fear that this old abbey is not the best depot for these precious artworks."

"What you are suggesting is very difficult to hear," says Mathilde. She feels a need to respond to his formality with some of her own. "To move three thousand artworks is not without its challenges. We only have old trucks and risk much every time we change position."

"It is difficult for me as well. I am only trying to do what is best for this collection." He steps toward Mathilde and lowers his voice. "There are some highly placed officials in the Nazi regime who want all of these masterworks to be moved immediately to Germany."

"They cannot. They can't do that," she says, half shouting, before looking around, lowering her voice. "It's against international law."

"I know. But it is the reality."

"Give us better heating, something to lower the humidity, surely that is a solution to consider?" She sees him lift a hand to place on her arm in a reassuring gesture, but he lowers it in the next instance.

"This is a large space surrounded by water. We could not solve the problem that way." He looks away from her, shifting his eyes to the courtyard and back again. She watches for a hint that he is softening, as she will not be the first to trade away any of her emotions. "I will tour the abbey tonight," he says stiffly. "In the morning, I would like to see the surrounding area."

"There are bicycles." She looks at him to see if his eyes will flicker with remembrance of that ride on stolen bicycles. "We can visit the surrounding area together." She wonders if he will react to the ironic tone in her voice.

He nods. "Very good. I look forward to it." He bows to her and steps away. His body looks imprisoned by his uniform, the double-breasted wool coat pulled in tightly at the waist with a thick leather belt. Once, she pressed her breasts over his smooth naked chest as the sun went dark. Once, he placed his shirt beneath her head and lay down on top of her in the forest. Kissing her face and neck, the arch of her back, his cheeks flushed, their breathing hoarse and desperate. She remembers his eyes, his serious mouth, his slender hands. But it seems that he does not remember hers, how she saw, how she smelled, how she felt. She looks at Franz as he walks away, every detail of his uniform absorbed like brutal punches to her gut.

CHAPTER THIRTY-FIVE

Loc-Dieu Abbey, 1940

The next morning, she bathes in cold water and dabs some perfume on her body. She finds her pink blush and brushes it over her cheeks, then rummages through a drawer to find her only red lipstick. But instead of applying it, she hesitates, then throws it across the room. It clatters and ricochets against the stone floor. What is she thinking? Franz is not a lover to seduce all over again, but a Nazi, the enemy. She needs to banish all thoughts about what he meant to her. She performs a mental trick; she places the forbidden memory into an iron box. All of him, everything he meant to her all those years ago, sealed and locked.

He is waiting for her in the courtyard, bending over some apricot-coloured roses blooming luxuriously despite the cold, damp air. "These are a sight for sore eyes," he says, standing up to his full height. "Especially now, late in the season."

"I suppose they benefit from the southern light." She assumes the voice of a schoolmarmish official, hating its prudish tone. Two cooks carrying baskets of eggs pass through the courtyard on their way to the kitchen. They nod at Mathilde, being careful to avert their eyes from the Nazi.

"I'll show you the bicycles," she says, desperate for a cigarette. They walk stiffly to the barn beyond the gardens. The smell of apples, stored in baskets, perfumes the air. She wants to offer him one, to watch him smile wide while eating sweet fruit as he once did, but catches herself.

"This one should do," she says, pointing at a large bike and stepping away from him, glad that it has a large woven basket at the front, so the Nazi will look ridiculous on a girlish bike. He nods to her and they cycle across the vast garden in front of the abbey and onto the dirt road. They pedal through the wild, savage land, rocks and boulders heaving out of the clay earth. A westerly wind is blowing steadily against them. The area is poor for agriculture and most of the farmers devote themselves to raising sheep or pigs. Franz rides slightly ahead and she watches his back. Tall, broad-shouldered, she watches the way he moves slightly from side to side, detects a yearning, a lonely man.

When they first met in Alsace, she found him sitting on a wooden fence, sketching a horse that stood still in the field, the mare batting flies away with its tail. Mathilde remembers feeling sorry for him then, the stranger in front of her, for his ready eagerness to discover the goodness in the world, the beautiful lines of a horse that eventually trotted away.

Now Franz slows his pedalling so that he rides next to Mathilde. "Riding into this remote countryside, seeing the frost," he begins, looking out to the silver hills. "It feels impossible that our countries are at war." His voice has softened, sounds more hopeful than his officious talk from the previous day. She knows he is looking over at her but she does not acknowledge what he has said. "Is this real? Or are we riding through a dream?"

She lets out a gasp. Tears fill her eyes as she thinks of what the war has done to her life, how it is ripping apart families, and the absurdity of riding a bike with an old lover, pretending, both of them, that he was never a beautiful boy from Germany but a Nazi wearing a swastika on the shoulder of his uniform.

"You think this is a dream?" she spits out, looking angrily at Franz. "I think of this as a nightmare. Every day I fear for my son, keeping his head down, trying to survive in Paris. I fear for all the French whose homes will be destroyed, all our cathedrals and town squares. Oh, and let's not forget, I fear for the artworks that may soon enough be stolen, burned, or blackened by mildew."

He looks steadily at her and then forward, his eyes on the road. At last, he says, "Like you, I fear all those things. And protecting these masterworks is crucial beyond any greedy dreams of autocrats and kings. But right now, we are riding bicycles again, you and I, reunited after all these years."

She inhales sharply, unable to set aside her anger just yet. "Take that hideous helmet off. I hate it."

They ride farther, the wind picking up. He unbuckles the chin strap of his helmet and throws it into the bike's basket. She looks over, unwilling to smile, but glad to see his hair, thick blond laced through with grey. She does not see the rock on the road or realize how fast she is pedalling. Her wheel hits and twists, sending her flying over the handlebars and into the ditch. "*Merde!*" she shouts, grimacing from a dizzying pain in her shoulder. "*Merde!*" She wipes her eyes with her good arm, refusing to let Franz see her cry.

"Mathilde, let me help you." Her shoulder sears red-hot but the moment feels suspended. Hearing him call her Mathilde brings her an unexpected joy. She wonders how he would paint her portrait but stops herself. He already did, thirty-one years ago, a sketch he created when she and the students were labouring over a still life of fruit tumbling around a pot of pink primroses, applying lustrous oils to conjure up the personality of the apple as Paul Cézanne once used to. Only now, lying in a ditch, does the scene from the art class come hurtling back to her. Franz sat to her side and sketched her profile in soft grey conté, her eyes larger than she had imagined, full of childlike wonder, her neck long and emerging from naked, swan-white shoulders. He did not show her the portrait but she glimpsed it before he hurried it away into his portfolio. She remembered the revelation that came from it: feeling beautiful for the first time.

"No. I don't need help." She tries to get up but her arm is hanging limply beside her. The skin on the palm of her hand is scraped raw. She looks at the blood and is annoyed by the thought of all the bandages to come. Her inspection of the artworks will suffer because of her stupidity.

"Wait here. I'll go for a doctor. You've broken your shoulder, I think."

The wind is howling and she shivers from the cold. He unbuckles his belt, takes off his uniform jacket, and wraps it carefully around her. "I'll bike back to the abbey. It won't be long."

"There are no doctors around here. Do you see any hospitals? There's nothing here, just us and the dirt, and mildew creeping over the paintings." She feels hysterical with pain and rage. The wind whistles in her ear, accusing her of something she is not yet sure of. "That's what we have. We have a war that's between my people and yours. Doctors? They're trying to put back together the French boys who have been blown to pieces by Nazi guns and bombs. Your Nazis. You're one of them. So, no, thank you, I will walk."

"Mathilde, I'm not a Nazi. You know me better than that." He has crouched down beside her. His eyes, like his voice, are soft and mournful. His fingers graze her stomach and she remembers something she had forgotten about Franz, that he was always the first to reach across space to touch her lightly on her hand, on her back, on her thigh. When she was with him in Alsace, she was at first startled by his touch and would step away, unaccustomed to such a gesture. It was foreign to her; her father rarely hugged her, her brothers wrestled her. Tenderness was not a language any of them spoke. But after being with Franz, she came to trust his touch and crave it. She was the one who would stand beside him during an art class and secretly graze her fingers against his.

She sets her head down in the ditch, trying to make sense of her feelings for the Franz of the past and the man before her now. Her head throbs and she sees only an outline of Franz in the light, shadowy and grey, impossible to know who he really is. In the distance, she hears the engine of a vehicle rumbling down the road. Franz crawls out of the ditch and waves down the truck. It glides past slowly and stops well ahead of them. Finally, a man steps out. He is carrying a rifle. A woman follows. Pig farmers, thinks Mathilde. She recognizes them from the market, silent types, leathery hands, sunken brown eyes. They are not old, not young, strong people, coming toward them.

"A bike accident," begins Franz. His French is excellent but there is no hiding his German accent. "She needs a doctor. For her shoulder?" He gestures at Mathilde in the ditch, throwing off his Nazi coat, struggling to get up. The couple shift their eyes to her and back to Franz. The man points his rifle directly at the German doing the talking. The Nazi.

"Did he violate you, this Boche?" Eyes scanning the ditch with the woman lying in it.

She turns her head and looks out to the rolling scruff of the hills. A wooden wagon, the bright red dogwood, the milkweed puffing white silk onto the road. When might the bombs reduce this place to ash? The land cannot be described as poetic and yet it does not warrant being scorched by enemy fire. All the time spent on this earth accusing one another, fighting to possess what others have, she thinks.

Mathilde lies very still and hesitates. She can feel Franz's eyes on her. This is what war is about, picking sides, a game invented not by adults but by schoolchildren choosing teams for jumping rope or playing soccer in the fields. *Stand over here if you are with me; the rest of you, stand over there.* But where does one's humanity lie in this choosing of sides, when the past and present collide, stranded on a country road?

Finally, she manages to raise herself up awkwardly on one side. "No, no, he did not. I fell off my bike is all." She feels compelled to speak fast or risk the shooting of Franz in this godforsaken place where nobody will ever know who did the killing. Maybe, she thinks, they will also shoot her dead for consorting with a Nazi. She sees the rifle is freshly oiled, a classic long gun, much like the one she used to shoulder and aim with while hunting boar in Alsace. The one she hides under her bed at the abbey. "I have bought many of your sausages at the market, do you remember me?"

The wife steps closer to get a better look at Mathilde. She slides her eyes from her and back to Franz. "*Collaboratrice*," she accuses, the soft *c* of the word sounding like the hiss of a snake.

"Not a collaborator," says Mathilde, getting to her feet, cradling her bad arm against her. "I work to save art during the war. Like him." She nods to Franz. She thinks of the painting of people on a raft trying desperately to survive a storm raging all around: *The Raft of the Medusa*, sky ominous and ocean waves devouring corpses grey and twisted. She stands up. If she had a white flag, she would wave it. *Is there anything sadder than lines tattooed over geography?* she wants to say, but the woman interrupts her thought.

"We hate the Germans."

"We come from the abbey," says Mathilde, ignoring the accusation. "Loc-Dieu." She feels faint and desperate to lie down. The pain in her arm, she would cut it off to end the agony. "He leaves tomorrow, and then only us, the French—we will be left in peace."

The man and woman exchange some words that are impossible to hear. Finally, the man motions with his rifle. "You can get in the truck," he says to Mathilde. She climbs awkwardly onto the road, leaving the Nazi uniform in the ditch. "We'll drive you to the abbey." They help her to walk down the road to the truck. The woman lifts Mathilde's broken bike into the back.

The man steps to Franz. "Nazis are the enemy," he says, gazing out to the empty fields. "I should shoot you." He shoulders the rifle and curls his finger around the trigger. Mathilde turns to see Franz in his white shirt, hands in the air. The wind howls across the hills, grasses and tumbleweeds jostle and bend. She has always had a good nose, for wine, for the heat of guns cocked and primed for violence. She puts a hand, the bloodied one, against her mouth. She cannot speak. If she does, she betrays her country.

"Norbert, *arrêtes*," the man's wife says, shouting so she can be heard above the howling wind. "*Allez*. It's time to go." She is calling from the truck, hands on her hips. Mathilde watches the farmer slowly lower his gun and spit on the ground. She sees Franz as a vulnerable shape of a man against the frosted hills.

CHAPTER THIRTY-SIX

Paris, 1913

After the Louvre, as Vincenzo would say, meaning *after stealing the Mona Lisa,* Mathilde no longer walks or strolls through Paris but tiptoes. She takes her shoes off after crossing the interior courtyard to the back of the apartment building, walking soundlessly in her stocking feet up the eight flights of stairs to their garret. She and Vincenzo live here but are disciples of discretion, *after the Louvre.* She tiptoes across his narrow room, sets her basket down, plugs in a table light that glows a sickly yellow. Her hands hover over the white pine chest, and she looks to the door, expecting police to burst through, accuse her of terrible things, incarcerate her, march her to the guillotine in the grainy shadows of the dawn. But there is only the banging of metal window shutters several floors down, the fluttering of bedsheets being hung out to dry for the day. She rummages through Vincenzo's clothes, his socks and underwear, his tie and white soiled shirt, finding the edge of the trunk's fake bottom with a thin knife, takes the portrait out, holding the heft of the wood on which it is painted, unwrapping its thin white blanket. Lisa—she calls her by her real name these days, not by the names cooked up by the museum—deserves more than a modest shroud. But Lisa does not carry a superior air. She has never been haughty. Rather, she looks out through the craquelure of the oil painting, older than the rocks that rise behind her, at peace with herself. Mathilde sits with her, staring back, caught in her spell. She keeps Lisa Gherardini company. Every woman needs to. To belong. To push back loneliness.

She wants to know about Lisa. What were her dreams? Did she have children? Did she lose them to disease or war? Was her husband kind to her?

Did she die alone in an unmarked grave?

The police plaster all the streets with thousands of copies of the portrait. For months, the mug shot of the *Mona Lisa* eclipses the Eiffel Tower, eclipses Paris itself. The secret is almost too much to bear. Mathilde worries constantly that Vincenzo will crack.

The theft is covered in all the newspapers across Europe. The painting is reproduced and examined, the public grows accustomed to seeing her daily, and her face is variously described as a dinosaur, a relic, an Egyptian mummy, a silk merchant's wife, a woman for the ages, the Virgin Mary, a wife, a mother. Mathilde remembers how the people loved to gossip about Lisa, the woman they called *La Joconde*, and her painter, Leonardo da Vinci. "He must have been in love with her," the waitress from Alsace whispers to her in the back kitchen. As if somebody overhearing will relay the details to Lisa Gherardini and scandal will unfold. Parisians want to let other Parisians know that they saw the painting for themselves at the Louvre. "Just earlier this summer," or "I remember her, lower row, surrounded by maybe twenty other paintings. She seemed to glow with something unseen, an inner light."

But that was nearly two years ago. The press has moved on to other news events. And still, Vincenzo has refused to find a buyer.

Mathilde is suffocated by his inaction. Having the portrait in their tiny garret is a constant reminder of Leonardo's genius, and her own incompetence as an artist. The truth is she had duped herself into thinking she had talent. Yes, she was clever and inventive, she made some interesting collages standing next to Picasso, but their relationship—not exactly as lovers, more as friends who admired each other—ended unceremoniously. They had started arguing; he was angry at her indulgence with Marie, and in the end, he locked her out of the studio at the Bateau-Lavoir. What clinched the separation was his decision to move to a grand apartment with Fernande far from the dusty gypsum air of Montmartre.

The lessons Franz had given her in Alsace had moved her past basic techniques, but hardly gave her the skills and intuition required to reach the heights of the *Mona Lisa*. She attempted to copy her, to draw the woman sitting contrapposto on a chair with the Tuscan landscape resonating behind her. She'd hashed out forty rough copies. Each time, she found her sketches to be juvenile in form, without depth, certainly without anything approaching the luminosity of Leonardo's portrait. Humiliated, she burned them all.

No more gallivanting in the Paris fountains for her and Vincenzo. They do nothing but wait to be found.

Her intuition tells her that the police are closing in. She cannot help imagining a future with Vincenzo going to the police, confessing all, and the inside of a prison. She must stop waiting, it's killing her; she'd rather sit in a prison than wait any longer in this cell of a garret. Without thinking, moving automatically, she strips the bed of a white sheet and wraps the *Mona Lisa* with the cotton. Standing up, she slides the painting into her basket. The Germans have been accused of stealing the portrait. And the Jews as well. Every day that the painting has been kept confined to the airless trunk has been a torment. She will find a way to return it. To leave this masterpiece somewhere to be found.

With the straw handles of her basket hitched over her shoulders, she walks quickly from Vincenzo's apartment, down eight flights of narrow back stairs, across the courtyard with the children's tricycles idle in the shadows, and out into the streets. She passes the fruit and vegetable vendors at the corner, the café with people sitting outside under the striped awning, past the newspaper kiosks, toward the glittering river. Crossing the Pont Alexandre, a group of school children prance toward her and her basket bumps against a teacher, who shoots daggers at her. *Get out of my way.* Mathilde glares back, feeling emboldened by the power of the painting. *Get out of* my *way. I am not a poor girl from Alsace. I have something the entire nation wants.*

At the Louvre courtyard, she dares herself to set the basket down to pull the portrait out. She feels royal, a privileged handmaiden carrying the image of a great woman through the city. She suddenly finds that she cares not a whit about consequences. She unwraps the painting entirely and shines *La Joconde* up to the sky and toward the Denon wing, where once she was exhibited. She sets the *Mona Lisa* on a bench by the arched entrance to the museum. She turns a pirouette, tempting fate, feeling stronger than ever, the need for opium no longer scratching at her belly. Guards walk carefree across the vast courtyard of the museum and turn nonchalantly toward her. They walk on. Several American women with enormous, feathered hats rush into the museum, chatting loudly among themselves, carrying bags from Dior and Hermès. The idea that a gaggle of American tourists discover the *Mona Lisa* on a bench and dine out on the tale for decades to come convinces Mathilde to reverse her decision. She turns back to the bench and returns the painting to the basket.

She crosses Rue de Rivoli, walking past the Comédie-Française and through the Palais Royale courtyard, its arcaded gardens faded like an old bourgeois woman past her prime. Ahead, Place Vendôme glitters with its jewellery boutiques. She sees a woman accompanied by two cheetahs ascending the stairs of the Ritz Hotel. Smiling, half skipping, she travels north to the foothills of Sacré-Coeur, her basket swinging by her side.

When she arrives outside the ramshackle workshop of the Bateau-Lavoir, sweating and out of breath, she feels suddenly overcome with exhaustion, and staggers into a familiar bar at the corner of Place Ravignan. The barman sees her, leans suggestively across the zinc. His lips are unattractively wet. He slides a glass of water and an espresso across the counter, watching her. She tosses her coffee back and walks out without paying.

Picasso is *persona non grata*. He owes her an apology, must have been mistaken about bolting his door and refusing to see her. She walks up the slope of the square and sits on a bench beside a public fountain gurgling with clear, drinkable water. Her arm is draped around her basket and she feels the power of the painting pulsing with its own heartbeat. The city feels lush with optimism. She is convinced that *Mona Lisa* is as alive as the trees growing beside her. She looks at their glossy leaves and thinks of the luminous skin of her face, the brightness of her almond eyes, the strength of her hands. Do not think poorly of this woman, do not imagine some kind of sorrowing curse within her smiling lips. Let her be many things, all things, let her be perfect in herself and as flawed as humanity. Picasso could learn from *Mona Lisa*, could he not? She will take the portrait to him and make him learn from da Vinci's masterpiece. This is what painting is about. Communicating something magnificent to travel across time. She will show Picasso the painting as a peace offering.

He can study it for the night. She can rest by his side as he copies the work in his own time, first in pencil, then ink, but also a loose version in oil. And she is thinking these thoughts as a group of artists emerge from the Bateau-Lavoir. Her vision blurs and finally she can see through the glare of the sunlight that a group of men are approaching, two tall, one short. Her friends! She sees Georges Braque in his rumpled suit and Apollinaire wearing a straw boater perched on his head, giving him a jovial, clownish appearance. She rises to greet them, embrace, and kiss cheeks the way they always have, but Picasso steps slightly ahead of them, blocking their view of her. She floats a hand up, thinking he will grip it and kiss her fingers, as he liked to, and yet he does not slow his step. He walks past her, unsmiling, and does not look at her when she says his name. Inside her stomach a dagger twists her guts. She thinks she might vomit. She looks at the Bateau-Lavoir, at the scuffed green panelling, how difficult it is to discern the outline of the main door, the way to get in. It seems she is a fool and has lost her way.

CHAPTER THIRTY-SEVEN

Paris, 1913

She is done with Paris and the men she has come to know here. When she climbs the stairs to the garret, she is prepared for Vincenzo and his anger.

"How could you?" he begins, hands pressed to his forehead. "This is unbelievable! Taking her out into the city in your goddamned basket?"

He refers to *Mona Lisa* only as *her*. Never by her name.

Next come the personal attacks.

"You stupid French farmer."

She places a protective arm around her basket, where *Mona Lisa* is swaddled like a baby.

"Give me that basket."

He removes the painting delicately and, with the other hand, hurls her basket against the hearth. She looks on with amusement. Though it is often freezing in their apartment, she has never been allowed to light a fire because Vincenzo fears the smoke could alter the canvas.

When he is finished raging, he slaps the wall and starts crying.

She also anticipated his apology. And how it would go after that. How she will conduct the future. She has come to her own decisions. She unbuttons his shirt, removes his vest and suspenders, and slips her hands against his chest.

"The press has gone quiet. There is no more talk of her." She kisses him tenderly on the mouth, strokes his handlebar moustache with her fingers.

He looks mournfully at her and kisses her back. "What do you mean?"

She has been alert to the mood in the city, buys the newspapers and devours them, goes without lunch to afford them. "They hung a portrait by Raphael in her place at the Louvre. The word is that the *Mona Lisa* will never be recovered. The public has lost interest. The new obsession is the sinking of the *Titanic*."

"Yes, that ship. Many died?" It seems that Vincenzo has dropped out of daily events so as to keep his head down. He is not the sharpest stick, but his innocence is one of his endearing qualities. And it makes what happens next easier. She needs to leave Paris, get on with her life.

Their makeup sex, as always, is fantastic. The absolute fulfillment of human desire, animal grunts, thrusting and pounding, without anything formed like words.

Afterward, they smoke propped next to each other and he picks up his mandolin and starts playing. She loves this part. They might as well be stars inside a film lying in a beautiful bed and not on a lumpy mattress with a single torn sheet and a depressing view to the rooftops, which is all their salaries can afford.

"Vincenzo, it's time to sell the portrait." She keeps her voice low and sultry, the one he cannot resist. "I found an antiques dealer in the *Paris-Journal*. He deals in old master painters." Vincenzo's eyes shine and darken. She sees exhaustion in his face, a lifetime of poverty, the eldest of a large family who left his crumbling village to find work in Milan as a twelve-year-old. She decides to slow down her appeal.

She is half singing, half talking, her voice a mix of charm and wobble, like the cabaret singer Mistinguett. She saw her one night at Le Chat Noir cabaret with Picasso and Marie Laurencin before everything turned sour. She lost her friends but never forgot Mistinguett's enormous eyes, her lacy gowns, her seductive voice singing about life, and *la vie est belle*.

Mathilde rubs her hands over Vincenzo's torso, caressing the black curls of his chest, kissing his arm. He looks straight ahead to the dirty wall at the foot of the bed.

"Go on," he says, setting his mandolin down on the bed.

"His name is Alfredo Geri. He has his offices in Florence."

"Alfredo Geri."

"Would you like to sell the painting to him? Perhaps, if you are willing, it might be time."

"It might be."

She lies back in the bed and lights another cigarette. "How much will you ask?" she says nonchalantly, exhaling.

He answers without hesitating. "Five hundred thousand soldi."

"Or you could turn it over to a French newspaper and receive a reward. They're all offering forty thousand francs."

"No. The *Mona Lisa* needs to go home."

"Alfredo Geri in Florence is your man," she says, inhaling deeply and blowing out a trail of smoke. She looks over at Vincenzo. His eyes are placid and fixed.

She sits up slowly, wraps the sheet around her shoulders; the autumn wind blows in from the broken window. "He'll know all the people. The director at the Uffizi . . ."

"The director of the Uffizi?"

"I'm sure he'll know him. You need to get the painting back to Italy, where it belongs."

"You think the gallery would like to have her?"

"Not only that, you'll be the pride of the nation. But don't hesitate, you need to write to him soon. Write him a letter."

"I will not use my real name."

"Exactly. Very smart. Use something invented. A name you like."

Vincenzo is silent, considering. Mathilde waits patiently.

"I like Leonardo. A tribute to Leonardo da Vinci."

"That's good."

"Vincenzo Leonardo."

"It has a nice ring to it. Write to him in Florence."

"What shall I write?"

"The stolen work of Leonardo da Vinci is in my possession. It belongs to Italy since its painter was an Italian," says Mathilde, considering her cigarette and smiling. "Something like that."

CHAPTER THIRTY-EIGHT

Florence, 1913

Vincenzo hauls a suitcase and his large white trunk onto the train, third-class rail. He travels from Paris, switches tracks at Milan, and is in Florence before sundown. He remembers nothing about the landscape except as a blur of hills becoming mountains becoming hills again. He stays in a modest hotel called the Albergo close to the duomo. Room 20. He sits on the bed, paces the room, smokes cigarettes, looks out the window. The little hotel is iced over by a December frost even though the sky is summer blue above the terracotta rooftops. He wants to go out to walk the city, move his legs, see the sights. But, too risky; he stays inside to play his mandolin and wait. At the appointed time, after nightfall, there is a knock on the door and a fat, distinguished-looking Italian stands before him, a thick gold chain hanging across his dark blue vest. His jowls fold over his high white collar and his eyes bulge with curiosity and wonder. The man greets Vincenzo with a nod, shakes his hand. "Alfredo Geri, *piacere*."

Vincenzo responds with stiff formality: "Signore Vincenzo Leonardo. *Piacere*." He bows and welcomes the antiques dealer into the faded room with the sweep of an arm, as if it were a Medici banquet hall. The large man stands awkwardly, sandwiched between the armoire and the bed. "Thank you for your letter. I was delighted to receive it."

Vincenzo nods and keeps quiet. Mathilde had found this man, had assured him this was safe.

Geri asks to see the painting. Vincenzo goes quickly, too quickly, to the pine trunk that is wedged next to the wall and the single bed. He opens the large pine box, removes his packed clothing, and takes a pocketknife from his vest. He uses the blade to pry open the fake bottom and lifts the painting from its thin red shroud. He can hear the dealer exhale slowly as he bends to see the painting. He takes it to the window for closer inspection. Finally, he turns to Vincenzo and hands it back to him. "I will need to confirm its authenticity"

"I want five hundred thousand soldi for it."

"You are selling her?"

"Yes, I am selling her. To you, to Italy. This is where she belongs. She must never be returned to France." Saying this, Vincenzo touches the tips of his fingers together and extends his arm toward Geri, making a slight kissing sound with his lips. "Of course, this is how it must be," he adds.

Alfredo Geri smiles a little and looks benevolently at Vincenzo. "Yes, I understand. How you must be feeling," he says, speaking slowly, a teacher to a child. "But I have a responsibility. I must show it to Giovanni Poggi for authentication. Would you agree to allow me to take her overnight?"

"Giovanni Poggi," repeats Vincenzo. "At your office." His face goes dark, his hands are shaking.

"Yes, Signore Poggi. That's right, the director of the Uffizi Gallery."

"But I would prefer that she stay with me in this room."

"Of course, Signore Leonardo, I understand your feelings. Everything must be properly conducted. I can have the painting back to you tomorrow."

Vincenzo sighs, goes to the window, lights a cigarette. He offers one to Alfedo Geri, who hesitates and then accepts. The men smoke together, the *Mona Lisa* lying on the bed between them. "Do you come to Florence often?" Alfredo Geri asks.

"Only once before. But I like it here. The golden light at sunset. I am an artist and this appeals to me."

"I hope you will enjoy your stay here. May I recommend the duomo first thing in the morning before all the tourists arrive? And the *David* by Michelangelo. The sculpture stands in front of the Palazzo Vecchio."

"The *David* fighting the big giant. Yes, I would like to visit it again."

"Well, then, Vincenzo Leonardo," says Alfredo Geri, checking his pocket watch. "I shall take my leave and see you tomorrow. May I?" He reaches for the painting. Vincenzo slides himself quickly to the edge of the bed and produces a battered leather satchel. He secures the red wrap around it and slips the painting into the bag. "For the protection of the painting," he says, shaking the man's hand, feeling the man's quality or virtue, as his mother used to call it.

"Until tomorrow."

The door is opened and closed. His *Mona Lisa* disappears with the fat man.

CHAPTER THIRTY-NINE

Florence, 1913

That night, his head throbbing with a headache, Vincenzo eats a bone-dry baguette bought that morning in Paris. His slab of cheese has gone greasy. He sits on the narrow hotel bed with its coarse blanket and stares out the tall window with the view of the duomo. The orange dome of the church is bigger than what he remembered. More like a bear coming down from the mountains to fling its massive body over the city. He hears the excited sound of the crowds moving through the cobblestone streets. Somewhere in the city, likely nearby, is the famous Uffizi Gallery, where great Italian masterpieces are proudly exhibited. He knows that the *Birth of Venus* by Botticelli hangs on one of its walls. Soon, the *Mona Lisa* will take pride of place in the Uffizi, and every one of his Italian brothers and sisters will fall to their knees, prayers lifted in thanks.

He is shy by nature, a hard worker, not given to making a scene with bombastic speeches, but he smiles a little thinking about being celebrated as a hero in his homeland. No longer seen as a dirty macaroni but as a patriot. He can hear the roar and thunderous applause of the crowds, lifting him up on their shoulders, grateful beyond words for the return—after four hundred years—of Leonardo da Vinci's great masterpiece. He does not want for anything, only that his parents and his siblings and their children be given a comfortable apartment in Florence where they can all live together as they used to and eat meat whenever they like, instead of beans stewed in olive oil. Let good Tuscan wine flow on that day and for years to come!

He falls asleep but wakes in the middle of the night, his head still throbbing. He feels nervous about what is about to happen on this very day after two long years of waiting. He paces the room, looking out into darkness, seeing the inky shape of the duomo weighing down on the city like judgment. In the morning, he takes extra time to smooth the wax onto his upturned moustache, his heart pounding beneath his starched white shirt. He is desperate for an espresso, for something to eat. Rushing out to the street to a café, he buys a tiny cup of coffee and two cornetti before running back to his hotel room, taking the stairs two at a time. He digs the key into the lock of Room 20. Out of breath, panicking, he throws himself onto the creaky bed and lifts the lid of the trunk. Empty. Of course it is. He should never have allowed the gentleman to take the portrait yesterday. He is sure that the ghost of this Tuscan woman, this *Mona Lisa*, would prefer to continue living with him in his Paris garret. Maybe selling her to an Italian museum with hundreds of strangers staring out from the walls is no better than living in a French museum with paintings stolen from Italy.

Finally, everything changes. There is a loud, urgent knock on his door and Vincenzo leaps to his feet, ecstatic that, at last, his fellow Italians can enjoy the "fruits of his labours." His courage. His daring heist! He remembers his father impressing that biblical teaching upon him before sending him off to work in Milan as a child. A lifetime of sacrifices, all of it has been worth it. He extends his hand gallantly to welcome the art brokers, but an Italian policeman knocks him to the floor, another puts him into handcuffs. He is too stunned to protest. There must be a terrible mistake. He wants to stand and shake the hand of the art dealer, the man of virtue, who surely will want to assure him that the painting is authentic and he is ready to pay for it. Out on the street, the duomo looming above him, Vincenzo shouts in Italian for them to stop, they are mistaken, he is not a criminal but a hero! The antiques dealer, the man who was kind to him, has betrayed him. People in the streets turn to gawk at him, curious to see a criminal, while shouting their questions at the police:

"What crime did this man commit?"

"Did he murder somebody?"

"If he killed somebody, let justice be done."

The people in the streets do not want a criminal to taint their happy experience of the beautiful duomo. Vincenzo sees their looks of disgust, their disappointment that he is wrecking the image of their golden city. He twists and shouts but cannot escape the hands of the two policemen. They lower his head and push him hard into a wooden box on wheels. He no longer hears the jeering crowds in the streets. Only the clop-clop of the horses' hooves on the cobblestone. There are no windows in the jailhouse wagon; the sunlight is snuffed out. The city disappears.

CHAPTER FORTY

Loc-Dieu Abbey, 1940

The doctor, a bully with an air of superiority, gives Mathilde a shot of morphine in her buttocks and tells her to bite down on a wooden stick that he pulls from his medical satchel. Two workers from the abbey move to her good side to hold her down. The doctor wraps both hands around the wrist of her limp arm and she watches his face, the distress clouding his eyes, the bloating of his cheeks as he inhales sharply before pulling her arm with all of his strength. She groans like an animal and cries and begs him to stop through her clenched teeth, and the nurses soothe her and press a cool cloth to her forehead. The doctor removes the stick from her mouth and nods at her. It is over. The pain has stopped. Her arm, dislocated from falling over her handlebars into the ditch, has been inserted back into its socket.

Franz finds her in the abbey infirmary that night, lying with her arm in a sling and a bandaged hand across her body. She nods at the nurse to leave them. One of his hands reaches out spontaneously to hold her good hand, but he realizes too late that this is ill-advised. He sits back down on his chair. Looking out the window of the small room, Mathilde realizes she needs to hide her face or give away her feelings for the man in Nazi uniform. She wants his touch, even if she finds it repellent, and is mystified that he is here. He tells her that he needs to take *The Wedding Feast at Cana* back to Paris. There are some senior officials who greatly admire the work of Paolo Veronese. She turns back to him. "Say it. Just say the word," she says, anger rising through her body. "Say who the senior officials are, the ones you work for."

He hesitates, looks down at his knees. "Nazi," he says. "Is that what you need to hear? I can say the word and it is an ugly word. But saying it, Mathilde, does not mean I am complicit."

She feels a tear at the edge of her eye, blinks it back, thinks, *So, this is how it will go*. She has heard from her friend Rose Valland, who still works valiantly behind the scenes at the Jeu de Paume gallery in Paris. She has told Mathilde that the most senior Nazis have been taking whatever masterworks please them from the gallery. She has told Mathilde that sometimes the abstract paintings with sharp, uncompromising lines are burned in the courtyard because the Nazis consider them degenerate.

"The Veronese will not go to the Jeu de Paume or leave the country," Franz assures her, his blue eyes serious. "The painting will only be exhibited at the Louvre. You have my word."

Maybe he believes this, but Mathilde does not. She does not have the strength to say more, but she is resigned to *The Wedding Feast at Cana* being whisked away to a château in Germany. Maybe Hermann Göring's. Maybe Hitler's.

"I want you to come with me. You should oversee its transport." He lets his fingers press lightly on her good arm.

"That French farmer wanted to shoot you dead."

"I don't blame him. He saw me as the enemy. That is what war does. You are this or you are that. There is no room for subtlety."

"You might have died on the road."

"Yes," he says.

"You say this and yet you believe you can be somewhere in between and survive this war?"

He does not answer but his eyes float to the gold chain around her neck.

"I see you are still wearing it."

What is happening to them seems impossible. Unreal. Her mind fills with the sound of cabaret singers crooning about life in the wine-soaked taverns of Montmartre. Her nights with Picasso and his crew of artists only a year after Franz had left her to go back to Germany. How they had lingered on the platform of the train station in Haguenau, unable to release each other and say goodbye. He had slipped the necklace from his shirt pocket and fixed it around her neck before turning to climb aboard. In his pocket, a one-way ticket back to Germany. His future awaited him, marriage and a noble career, his parents would have it no other way.

"You have to trust me. We will travel by train tomorrow. You and I, we can work together to protect the art."

"Please don't. Please don't take that painting."

She remembers the time standing in front of the monumental *Wedding Feast at Cana* with Vincenzo, the two of them, young, crazy with desire for each other, gazing at the spectacular, raucous banquet, at which Jesus miraculously converts water into red wine.

"I am trying to help."

"I cannot."

"Only for a few days. I've arranged an entire train car for the oil painting to be secure. You can travel safely to Paris with me and my men. You can see your son. And then be back to move the works farther south."

"I will not travel with Nazis."

"Mathilde." He stops speaking and looks directly, fully, into her eyes. "You don't understand. I have been given my orders to have you travel with us. I need you to come with me. It's required."

He hesitates, looks up at the ceiling and back to her face. "We need to carry on as occupier and occupied, if you catch my meaning."

She watches him closely, his face, the outline of his mouth, his eyes. They are filled with longing and something else, a warmth, the colour of jade stone and devotion. She thinks he might cry. His face reminds her of his younger face. When he caught up to her running down the hill after the eclipse in Alsace. "Mathilde, stop, don't be like this, why are you running?"

She remembers how she shouted at him then. "What do you want from life, Franz? Tell me that. What is your dream? Your own dream, not your parents', wherever they live in some fancy château across the border."

He had stepped back as if his legs might give out. Overhead, purple clouds raced along the horizon. "Mathilde, I want to live free. And I want to love you."

She remembers how his answer had demolished all the anger she'd felt for him moments earlier. "Mathilde, I love you," he said.

"I love you too."

How he lifted her up and she wrapped her legs around him and they turned around and around until they stopped to cling desperately to each other.

In the infirmary, she feels weary. She wants the war to be over. A fog seems to have settled over her mind. The strength that she has displayed to her colleagues, the take-charge attitude she has honed and polished since the onset of the war, she feels it slipping away like blood running out of her veins. Her mind is playing tricks on her, of that she has no doubt. She knows that she is required to think of Franz as a Nazi. But she wants to believe him to be something human, not good but not evil.

CHAPTER FORTY-ONE

Paris, 1940

Picasso thought the future belonged to the strange, bulbous eyes of the African and Iberian sculptures. Georges Braque thought the future came in the shape of a hairbrush. But the train is the true vessel of modernity. Fast and furious, streamlined for speed, the promise of the future that Vincenzo and his Italian Futurist buddies used to obsess over. Mathilde feels herself travelling past all that is familiar and comforting into a hard, selfish place. She is living it now, the present, still wearing a blue shirt, canvas pants, and a gold necklace.

From her private cabin, she can see the trees blurring together as ghostly brigades and, along the road, a human convoy moving south in the opposite direction of her train. She sees lorries with families travelling in the back, baskets and chairs heaped onto their laps. People on bicycles, in two-wheeled carts powered by engines or horses, the lucky ones in cars, many children walking hand in hand, all of them refugees of the war whose faces and backs are breaking with sorrow.

The train gallops toward Paris, belching smoke, *The Wedding Feast at Cana* rolled meticulously inside a long wooden box and lying along the length of the corridor. Outside, the hills rise and fall, the forests billow and recede. She thinks about her son, about *Mona*

Lisa under her bed in the abbey, she thinks about Franz. She slips her dark beret off her hair, arranges her bangs, unbuttons her navy-blue wool coat. The future has already arrived. What is known about cruelty and kindness is being rewritten faster than the speed of the train.

There is a knock at her door, a polite tap, indulgent. She rises and flips up the metal latch and a young German soldier extends a tray to her, his eyes beseeching, "*S'il vous plaît.*" He picks up her lunch tray, untouched, from the banquette seat, and replaces it with the offering of dinner. The aroma of coq au vin and roast potatoes fills her compartment. She looks at the small bottle of Bordeaux and the demi-baguette, and wonders where the butter has come from; it had recently disappeared from the market stalls in Loc-Dieu. She places her scarf against her nose and leans her face against the window, gazes at the road clogged with human traffic. She will not eat or drink. A small sacrifice, though she knows it is useless. *Where will they go, all these people?*

She called Philippe to let him know that she is arriving tonight. He sounded desperate, his voice cracking, but the line garbled his words. He is studying at the law school and yet it sounded like he was crying? She has become negligent, forgotten to pay attention to the ruin of her nation or her son. It has been three months since they have seen each other.

The train slows suddenly and she looks out to see a mess of electric cables overhead and Nazi soldiers knotted on the platform. Black clouds of steam engulf the train. It's impossible to see outside. She listens to the sound of running on the platform, heavy boots entering the train car. Loud voices, an argument. She stands up, her heart pounds; if they step into the narrow hall, they are sure to crush *The Wedding Feast at Cana*. She wrenches open her doors, looks out, and sees Nazi soldiers at the far end of the train car. One of them is pointing at her and the painting rolled up on the ground. It could be bags of flour for all they know. The sooty steam clears. Not Paris, not yet. She steps over the roll, lights a cigarette, unlocks one of the upper windows.

Another voice booms from the other end of the train car, ordering the soldiers to step back, clear the carriage. Franz walks toward her, careful to not trample the boxed canvas, brushing past her, his fingers gently on her back, breathing her name, "Mathilde," as he goes to meet with the soldier's captain. Within minutes, the soldiers exit and return to the platform. The train jolts and slowly its wheels turn, moving again toward Paris. The sound of its locomotion is deafening. She does not mind the screaming noise, as she always loved the stampeding of wild boars and deer during the spring rutting season. She watches the sky being subdued, the golden fleece of the clouds, the reluctance of day becoming night.

The train is a beast. Belching sooty billows. Obscuring her vision again.

It is late when he knocks on the door of her *wagon-lit*. She has turned on a small lamp on her side table. Her dinner tray, untouched, has been removed and she has swung her legs onto the couchette in an attempt to find sleep and rest. She arises reluctantly to open up.

He does not stay in the hallway but comes in and slides the door shut behind him.

"Not long now. Another hour."

She does not speak to him. She crosses her legs away from him and looks out the window.

"We will pull into the Gare d'Austerlitz. The artwork will be transported by truck directly to the Louvre."

He takes off his military cap and sits across from her. His blue eyes look over at her sadly, as if they have seen all the wrongs in the world.

"Don't look at me like that. I can't bear it."

He turns to stare out the window of the train. "I would like you to supervise the hanging of the artwork," he says, at last.

"I can't do that."

"Jacques Jaujard is aware of our arrival."

"With *The Wedding Feast at Cana*? He knows this?"

"Not exactly."

"Lies."

"Strategy."

"Meaning?"

"I did not want him to ignite panic at the Louvre. That might only bring stiffer rules from my superiors."

"You mean the Nazis."

He nods. "I want everybody to play nice for now. It helps to buy time."

"Play nice, even though we are all acting?"

"Mathilde, you have no idea. I feel we are all trapped inside a nightmare."

She scoffs, uncrosses her legs, crosses them again.

The train pounds forward and a long, wolfish howl cuts through the night air. She feels detached from the terrible reality of the war. Is it possible that the speed of the train blurs the demarcation lines that should exist between them? The carriage is cast in darkness as it pierces a long tunnel, but she can see his eyes, the way they stay on her. "I've never stopped thinking about you," he says, at last, leaning forward. "Apologies if I sound like a hopeless romantic but the truth is—" He hesitates and looks fully at her before taking a breath. "I never loved anybody else the same as you, if you can believe that."

Hearing this, she is flooded with joy and shame. She wants to climb onto his lap, put her hands all over him, this man from her past who is now her enemy. All these years, she thought he had forgotten her. She sits on the edge of her seat, her fingers on her gold necklace, looking softly at him. She can hear his breathing catch, a slight groan as he looks away, shakes his head, and sets his eyes back on her. Her mind races with images of tragedy, the collapsed homes of millions of wartime refugees, borders disrespected, war campaigns exposed and honed. The time and distance between them seem to fade away. Surely this is why human beings exist. To try to find the ones they love even if they have been lost for a long time. "You're killing me, Mathilde," he says, pushing off his seat, gripping her thighs with his hands. He angles his head and lets his mouth hover next to hers. Just for this moment, she wants to chuck her scruples and give in to this man. She feels dirty, she feels intoxicated, she feels loved and desired, she feels all of it, such is her need to be with him. Until she sets her hand to his chest and gently pushes him away.

CHAPTER FORTY-TWO

Paris, 1940

She steps quickly into the anonymous crowd, away from the Nazi train, away from Franz.

She is trembling, needs a drink, takes a cab to La Coupole in Montparnasse. Inside, she curves her body into a leather banquette in a corner of the restaurant. The elegant dining room is packed with Parisians. Men remove their overcoats and fedoras, handing them off to waiters. Women with short sultry nets across their eyes sashay through the restaurant to meet their companions. She orders a Kir Royale but the waiter informs her that the champagne has run out. "Unless you're a high-command Kraut, of course," he says, looking angrily out to the street. One table over, a couple of women wearing long pearl necklaces doubled around their necks sip their drinks. They are whispering through red lacquered lips.

"Do you have any Jews in your family? In your extended family?" says one to the other.

They are both wearing classic dresses, simply cut, expensive. Mathilde marvels at their beautifully coiffed hair rolled away from their patrician foreheads. Next to them, she feels unkempt, a cat that's been dirtying its paws in the back alley.

"*Chérie*." The friend laughs. "We have been French and Catholic since Louis XIV!"

"I pity anybody who is not," says the other, adjusting the large gold bow on her head, drinking her pink cocktail. "You'd be banned from this place."

"Oh, don't lay an egg, the Jews know how to make pennies fall from heaven. I wouldn't worry about them. Besides, look at the bright side, more gin for us!"

Rising above the din of the conversation is the shrill ringing of bells. Mathilde looks over at an approaching busboy, green-eyed, wearing a round cap with a chin strap and a jacket garish with brass buttons. He is carrying a blackboard with somebody's name written on it. He walks closer, ringing the bells loudly, filling her ears. She is gripped by a sudden fear that her name is written out: *Mathilde Payer, Collaborator*. The ringing bells threaten to deafen her and she stands up, ready to run to save her life, but she notices somebody raising their hand nearby. The customer rises and pays the busboy a tip, apparently happy to receive a phone call in the restaurant's office. She sits down quickly, lights another cigarette, knocks back her gin cocktail.

She pays, leaves the restaurant, and walks down Boulevard Raspail to her apartment on Rue de la Seine. Some of the restaurants and shops are boarded up, and there is a subtle but noticeable state of disrepair in the city: chipped paint on windowsills, litter clogging the gutters of the sidewalks. Otherwise Paris looks fine to her. Peaceful. No risk of being shot dead in the road. Her corner grocery, the one she always frequented as much for its fresh flowers as for the charcuterie, has closed. She turns instead into the other, shabbier option and buys some dinner.

She climbs the winding stairs to her apartment, running her hand lovingly along the wooden banister carved with acorns and rosettes.

It is so good to be home, her sanctuary with Philippe. She turns the key in her apartment door and switches on the entrance lights. She washes at the kitchen sink, annoyed that the water is running cold here in her Paris apartment, as it always does in the old châteaux. She refuses to focus on the pile of dirty dishes cluttering the counter. Instead, she looks through an old wooden cabinet and finds the gin and vodka bottles to be empty, but there is a bottle of Bourgogne still corked. She pours herself a glass and tours the living room as if for the first time. On the wall behind the green couch is the floral wallpaper that Philippe helped her to hang nearly ten years ago and the gilded mirror over the modest brick fireplace. The apartment is small with only a Juliette balcony overlooking the street. But she is overwhelmed with gratitude for her home.

She arranges their dinner on two plates: cooked slices of ham, an endive salad, and a baguette. Looking around, wondering what to do next, she goes into her bedroom to unpack. Her bed is exactly as she left it months before, the chenille cover pulled tightly around the mattress, two pillows with lace edges bought at the Clignancourt flea market. She peers at the black-and-white photographs of her and Philippe in oval gold frames. Another shows her grandparents posing stiffly in an Alsace photo studio.

She wonders where he might be. Philippe is never late. She throws her clothes into drawers and, famished, eats while standing up. Exhausted, she cannot bring herself to do the dishes. She wonders what is keeping Philippe. Something must have come up. A study session, or too many drinks at a *bals-musette*, but her mind is tricking her into such naive thoughts. The city is walking on a knife's edge. Anything could have happened to her son. She sits rigidly on the couch, hugging a pillow to her stomach.

He does not wake her gently but by shaking her shoulders and shouting her name, "Maman, Maman!" She lurches awake and sits up.

"There you are." She reaches up her arms to embrace him, but he grabs her hands.

"Listen to me, they have raided Rachel's apartment."

She nods, trying to grasp what he is telling her. "When?" she asks.

"Today. All day. Taking their stuff, their belongings."

"Who? Who did this?" Her mind races to catch up. She thinks of Franz's lips hovering near hers and drags her shirtsleeve across her mouth, purifying herself.

"The Nazis. The Nazis, of course! Don't you realize what's happening? They took the family jewellery, the paintings off the wall, they took the necklace and earrings that Rachel was wearing, and when she begged them and told them that her grandmother had given her the jewellery, they laughed and pointed guns at her."

"But they have no right. To enter people's private homes and take their things."

"Maman, you're joking, right?" He lets go of her hands with disgust and paces the room. "The Nazis are targeting the Jews. How do you not know this? There's talk of forcing them to wear yellow stars, moving them out of the city by train."

"But Paris looks the same," she says weakly, recognizing her stupidity the moment she speaks. The back of her neck hurts. "Where is she now, Rachel?"

"Over in the 16th at her cousin's apartment. Her entire family is hiding there."

She thinks of how she stepped over *The Wedding Feast at Cana* on the train, blowing smoke nonchalantly out the window. She can still feel the rocking of the train, how she almost allowed Franz to kiss her.

"Yes, good, that's good. Thank God she's safe."

"It's only good until it goes bad. Tomorrow, there's a big protest. November 11. The Nazis cancelled our Day of Remembrance. Obviously to provoke the French. All the university and high school students are going."

"Philippe, please, no, please don't. Protesting is against the law. Don't."

She hears the busboy's bells ringing loudly in her ears. She tries to silence them, wills them into oblivion, or back to the restaurant where they belong. But they ring on with a lusty, relentless energy. Somebody is sure to find her out. It's only a matter of time.

"Against the law? Do you hear yourself? The Nazi occupation is against the law. Maman, I'm going. Obviously. We're at war." He storms away from her, leaving her with a new scent—an odour of rage and desperation—the first time she has smelled that on her son.

CHAPTER FORTY-THREE

Paris, 1940

She wants to open her eyes wide because she is having trouble believing Philippe, and this cannot stand because they need to trust each other. She has taken a long time, decades, in fact, to understand that to love is to trust absolutely. These should be the ground rules for any relationship: mother and child; sibling to sibling; lover to lover. This is what she is thinking as she walks from the Louvre into the Tuileries Garden, resplendent as always with its circular fountains and little children floating wooden boats in the pools. She walks along the long allées of plane trees, their grey sylvan branches as elegant as the fine silver gravel. French police in black capes strut, as always, through the garden. A couple of Nazi soldiers appear every once in a while, in the park and on the streets. Mathilde realizes that the French are ignoring them, as if they were stray cats or dogs. Undesirable. Odoriferous.

When she reaches the Jeu de Paume at the end of the park, she lowers her beret, pulls up her coat collar, and steps to a stone wall overlooking the street. She can see the Nazi banners unfurled on the Hôtel de Crillon and on all of the major buildings along the Rue de Rivoli, even the fancy Meurice restaurant. The swastikas sway in the wind.

She registers the calm of the city, the lack of car travel; mostly people are using bicycles.

"Mathilde?"

She turns to see Rose Valland standing nearby at their prearranged meeting spot. They have been sending occasional telegrams to each other, but she sees fatigue in Rose's face that a telegram does not communicate. "It's good to see you. I noticed how peaceful the city seems. The air seems cleaner."

"Four million people have fled Paris. Most of them in cars."

"Can you talk? Is it safe?

"For a few minutes. We're expecting German high officials tomorrow, not today." Rose Valland has refused to leave her work as a curator at the Jeu de Paume. She is a secretive person by nature, plain and unremarkable, meticulous at keeping records. Mathilde suspects she will do an excellent job keeping track of the Nazis.

"*The Wedding Feast at Cana* is back up on the walls at the Louvre," says Mathilde, lighting a cigarette for Rose, another for herself.

"The Nazis might be visiting tomorrow after they make their rounds here. Hermann Göring is shopping," Rose says.

"How many French artworks have been stolen so far from your museum?"

"A few dozen. The Germans have established a complex bureaucracy with many steps of approval before an artwork can leave this country. Franz Metternich is making sure of that." At the mention of Franz, Mathilde feels her breath catch in her throat. She saw him briefly in the morning while she inspected and approved the hanging of the returned painting. "Respecting Hague Conventions and so forth," says Rose, exhaling the smoke, speaking quickly. "But the top officials have ways of getting past him. You've been in the south protecting thousands of works and I admire your courage,

Mathilde. I'm here witnessing the seizure of artworks owned by the Jews. It's like living through a very bad dream. A couple months ago, the Führer decreed the seizure of art. It's called ownerless. The Paris palaces where the Rothschilds used to live have all been looted. I've seen jewellery from the Renaissance come through our museum, exhibited and then packed up for freight trains heading to Germany." She draws on her cigarette, looks all around her, leans closer to Mathilde. "Last month a group of Nazi officials moved into the Jeu de Paume. They call themselves the Special Staff for Pictorial Art. Very efficient at moving artworks from Paris to Germany. I keep track of the freight trains the Nazis are using. The numbers, the dates, the works of art."

Mathilde suspects that Rose is working with the French Resistance. But she will never ask.

"We recovered a crate on the road to Loc-Dieu," she says, looking around, ensuring their privacy. Suddenly even the public space of Paris seems corrupted. "Filled with masterworks, of course."

"I'm not surprised. The French police are collaborating with the Nazis, they source the Jewish records with all the details of where the art is kept, in their mansions or warehouses in Paris or Bordeaux."

"Seeing that crate on the side of the road. It was awful."

"I've seen signed works by Rembrandt, Vermeer, Velázquez, Goya. All of it looted by the Nazis."

"I've heard that Hitler's vision is to create a new art museum in Germany with the best of European collections," says Mathilde. She feels her body shake with anxiety about the thousands of artworks under her care at the damp Loc-Dieu Abbey. She wants to share with Rose the farcical conditions there, the black mildew crawling over some of the Renaissance paintings, but saves it. Rose has her own battles to fight.

"The hardest is watching the Nazis burn the paintings they call degenerate outside in the museum courtyard."

"It's appalling," says Mathilde, stubbing out her cigarette with the heel of her boot. She wishes she had worn a scarf, the red one from Picasso she saw hanging yesterday on a hook in Philippe's bedroom. "Bright red, the colour of fierce new ideas," he always told her. "Surely the French police or the army can stop them?" she adds. "It's against the law to destroy cultural property. But nobody, except for us, seems to care."

Even in the fading light, Mathilde can tell Rose is sizing her up. "The French police have long ago capitulated to assist the new regime. Once that was unthinkable, but now it's become normal."

"Their normal is disgusting."

"They confirm Jewish identity, opening their books at police headquarters so they can hunt down all of their property." She takes a deep drag on her cigarette. "A Cubist work by Picasso the other night. There," she says, lifting her chin in the direction of the museum. "You can still see the pile of cinders."

Mathilde feels a hot rage running through her. She remembers standing next to Picasso as he originated his Cubist works at the Bateau-Lavoir. She wonders what he would have to say about this. She hasn't seen him for decades, although their apartments are just blocks apart from each other. He has apparently refused to leave Paris.

"If there's anything I can do, or the Louvre . . ." says Mathilde, but she knows her words fall flat. Rose lifts her chin to the grand Champs-Élysées. "Best to go home. There's a demonstration and it'll likely get nasty."

"Good advice. Thank you." The women do *la bise* and Mathilde turns as if to walk home in the direction of the Louvre. "Rose, please, take care," she adds. The women grip each other's arms.

"You too," Rose answers.

Mathilde scrutinizes the park in the gloaming; how sinister it looks at night compared to the landscape of symmetry that calms the mind in daytime. Thinking of everything that Rose has told her, she circles the museum and heads down the steps to the Place de la Concorde. She wants to observe how the Nazis treat the students, and applaud Philippe and his friends for their young, valiant defence of their nation. They can go for dinner and drinks afterward. She lifts her skirts and walks briskly along the boulevard, buttoning her coat collar around her neck, watching hundreds of cyclists pedalling in the same direction up the Champs-Élysées. The plane trees arch their muscular branches above her path. A hundred years ago, Napoleon ordered the planting of the trees to provide shade for French soldiers. Now, she muses bitterly, they're providing shade for the occupiers.

Up ahead, running the length of the Champs-Élysées, she can see that the tricolour French flag has been replaced by Nazi swastikas. Does Franz know about this provocation? It's hideous to her, to anybody in their right mind. She surveys the scene, innocent students on the streets gathered to exercise their French right to protest in public, a collective act honed through generations. At the edge of the boulevard, a group has gathered. Some of them are sitting at café tables below the striped awning. She sees that most of them are boys no more than seventeen years old, dressed in classic navy-blue sweaters and pants, polished leather shoes, rumpled hair, cheeks blossoming red from the cold. From a newspaper kiosk, she looks among many prominently displayed German magazines for a Paris newspaper, finally pulling *Le Matin* from the stacks. She walks inside an elegant brasserie and sits at a table with an oblique view to the street. Outside, the crowd of students is growing past the sidewalk to spill onto the street. Older, taller students are arriving on bicycles and on foot.

She can watch but not be seen. Philippe is not in the crowd. Maybe he decided against joining the protest. Flipping open the newspaper, she regrets seeing its censored pages, all the upbeat articles about the Nazi occupation, the allure of German hairstyles, even the power of German artists to uplift a nation's spirits.

The waiter sets her glass of Bordeaux down on the table and stands back. "They're stupid and they're brave. I admire them," he says, adjusting his bow tie.

"They're young," says Mathilde, trying her best to be lighthearted. "I think they should get home and start studying for tomorrow's lessons."

"Maybe," he says, turning away from her. "But the Nazis had no right to cancel our Day of Remembrance. The First World War was not that long ago." He steps closer to the door and looks out on the gathering crowds. "Something's in the air. I feel it."

She watches through the glass as one of the bigger, older students stands up on a café chair and starts singing "La Marseillaise." The waiter is right. November 11 has long been a sacred day of remembrance. A rowdy cheer goes up and everybody raises their fingers in a V for victory. Mathilde knows that the French national anthem has been banned, and she looks around anxiously for the arrival of police. But war seems to have thoughtfully skipped over the boulevard.

Sipping her wine, she goes back to her magazine and flips through its pages. It's regrettable that the Nazis have stolen from Rachel's family, but maybe there is a reason, some criminal business activities they were involved in? Some outstanding taxes that need to be covered?

Looking up, setting her magazine aside, she is surprised to see that the street has become clogged with protestors. Too many to count. The leader is pointing toward the Arc de Triomphe. Banners with the tricolours of the French flag appear out of nowhere and are unfurled.

Students raise placards painted with the V sign. People walking by stop in their tracks to join the protest. Students paint the *V* symbol on their faces. More fists punch into the sky. There is laughter but there is also a feral energy. The crowd heaves forward, chanting the name of a popular French general in exile in London: "De Gaulle. De Gaulle."

"Messieurs, dames, we're closing for the night," shouts the waiter, a panicked edge to his voice. In the distance, somewhere outside, the sound of collapsing, shattered glass. Mathilde pays for her drink and half walks, half runs, the mob carrying her up the boulevard. She cranes her neck to try to find Philippe in the crowd. But no chance. There are too many people, hundreds, likely thousands. Her ears fill with collective rage, the vocal cords of the young students suddenly thickening, dropping low to become fearless and flint-axed.

Her mind flashes to a painting at the Louvre. Bringing home the bodies of the sons. Its official title was something like *Bringing to Brutus the Bodies of His Sons*, but Mathilde was mesmerized not by the political motivations of Brutus but by what was happening on the other half of the painting: the raw emotion of a grieving mother reaching an arm to the stretchers where her murdered sons lay. Jacques-Louis David was a master at exposing the terrible truths of life. He painted a mother yearning for her sons, desperate to press her cheek against the final beating of their hearts. But she cannot move because her daughters are collapsing against her. She needs to hold them up and guide them through what is unimaginable: that their father arranged the murder of their brothers for apparent acts of treason.

Night falls. The globes of the Champs-Élysées scatter golden crystals of light, the Arc de Triomphe rises, solid and muscular, in the near distance. Mathilde is beginning to understand the gravity of the situation. The students are marching en masse to the symbol of the French nation. She runs again to try to keep up with the pace of the protestors.

Her feet hurt from her shoes; she considers taking them off, but no time. She sees French police being knocked to the ground, their black caps rolling along the sidewalk. She sees some of them hiding in cafés. She sees a Nazi soldier being beaten by the mob with sticks. "Boche, Boche," the crowd jeers, before moving past his trampled body.

More glass shattering. Waiters and barmen in tuxedos are rushing to pull down metal shutters to protect the elegant shops and bistros. She runs along the sidewalk, staying close to the buildings, and watches the protestors march forward. Without warning, they stop, and the skies unleash torrents of rain. For one moment, the shouting and whistling goes quiet. She tucks herself into the entry alcove of a pastry shop and is shocked to see why the protestors are standing still. Ahead of her, marching from the side streets, are battalions of Nazi soldiers wearing heavy riot gear. They are pointing at the crowd with rifles, their bayonets are fixed. The teenage protestors do not turn and run. Their eyes go large and round and they look quizzically at the approaching troops. Up goes their cry: "*Vive de Gaulle*." They throw stones at the soldiers and at the German trucks that have appeared, attempting to force them away from the sidewalks. But the students are young and naive, full of bravado, not the smarts that come from long, hard-fought battles. Mathilde watches in horror as one of the students is crushed below the wheels of a truck. She sees students fall like puppets in a rain of bullets. She sees their bodies ooze with blood. She wants to run into the crowd but a Nazi truck is ploughing down the sidewalk, clearing the protestors. In the distance, she spots Philippe as he raises his fists in the air, the red scarf tied around his neck. She jumps onto a bistro chair and screams his name. She is terrified, not for herself, but for her son, for his innocence that is about to be destroyed. Her eyes are fixed on him; she believes he can see her, that he is staring in wonder at her, his eyes shining the way they always did when he spotted her seated in the audience for one of his school plays.

Mathilde is convinced she can save Philippe, protect him from his outrage and naivete. She pushes through the crowd, loses a shoe, pummels her way forward. Students are scattering, trying to escape, holding their hands to bloodied faces, clutching their stomachs. She steps over broken, dead bodies. Somebody unseen punches Mathilde in the stomach and she gasps from the force of the assault. Still she lunges forward, powered by a feral energy. A teenager is screaming on the ground and she stops to help lift him into the arms of his classmates. Looking up, wild with desperation, knowing she must reach her son to save him from this nightmare. Her screams pierce the roar of the crowd. She watches Philippe being kicked and beaten by three Nazi soldiers. She begs them to stop. His beautiful face is cracked open, covered in blood. Her arm reaches forward, she lunges at the Nazis, offers to give her life to save her son. He is innocent, he is a student of French law. But there is no law. There is only brutality and humiliation. A soldier pushes her to the ground, and she stays low, pounded by the rain until a hole opens in the crowd and she raises her head to see soldiers dragging Philippe to a truck. She stands up, sees his scarf on the ground, the doors opening. His legs do not seem to be working. They throw him inside. She screams, lifts her fist, but there is nothing to punch but the air in a city that stinks of gunpowder and bloodshed.

CHAPTER FORTY-FOUR

Paris, 1940

Shoeless, sobbing, half blind, she stumbles away from the Champs-Élysées in the rain. When the black police cars approach on the roadway, she hides against the tree trunks. She doesn't feel the cold or the wet, only a seething rage at the Nazis. The beating of her son, the shooting of young intellectuals, killing their ideas because they run contrary to the new immorality. The demonization of Jews, the declaration that they are stateless. Her City of Light has been stolen from her, its beauty defiled. She curls her fingers with hatred for the invaders, feels reckless, would kill them if she could.

She stops on the bridge next to the Louvre to look down into the cold, rippling waters of the Seine. She knows that they are there, the glassy-eyed carp and whiskered catfish. All that used to be unseen in the city, that she once ignored has become crystal clear. Her refusal to see the truth made her son especially vulnerable. How to make sense of it? Was her brain dulled by opium smoked decades ago? The rain lashes at her, drives her into the alcove of a fancy milliner's shop, colourful felt hats atop dead-faced mannequins. She cannot face going home to her empty apartment, where she and Philippe last saw each other, where they argued about the grim reality of the Nazis. Panic courses through her veins. She has no idea where they have taken him. In ordinary times, if he had broken a law, she would have a right to know what jail he would be sent to, how to post bail, how to present at a trial. But no longer. The enemy keeps secrets. This is their new law. Secrets about where they send people they do not like, secrets about what they do to people who have disobeyed their newly invented codes.

Through the puddles, shoeless, she runs past her Paris apartment and cuts onto Rue de Buci to turn onto Rue des Grands-Augustins. In a daze, she finds herself banging on Picasso's door without any idea of how she got there. She knows his address, it is a three-minute walk from her home; she has always been aware of his movements, as most artists have, from Montmartre to Montparnasse to 7 Rue des Grands-Augustins. A new address, a new love. She bangs again on the door. A woman with dark hair framing her face opens it, alarmed, clutching a silk robe around her body. She examines Mathilde, a woman without shoes, soaked, her hair ragged around her face, presenting herself at midnight.

"I need to speak to Pablo," says Mathilde, sobbing. "They took his scarf, his red scarf. . . . They took my son. I couldn't find the scarf."

The woman listens to the garbled words of this woman she does not know. Finally, lifting her chin, showing her handsome face, she says, "The Nazis?"

"I hate them," says Mathilde, her voice low and haunted.

"Please, come in and get warm," she says quietly, extending both her hands, drawing Mathilde inside. "I will call Pablo."

An Afghan dog with thick, silky fur circles Mathilde, excited by the arrival of a late-night visitor. The woman pushes the dog away—"Shhh, Kasbek, not now"—and eases Mathilde onto a blue velvet couch in the living room. Picasso's busts of women with jagged, distorted faces stare out into space from marble side tables. The room is high-ceilinged, elegant, seething with creative output. A large painting of muscular, laughing women running hand in hand on a beach hangs over a baroque fireplace. Picasso rushes in, carrying a paintbrush. He hesitates when he sees Mathilde, her body crumpled in grief, her short brown hair where once he used to caress a long blonde ponytail. It has been thirty years. Recognizing her at last, he falls to the couch and wraps his arms around her, holding her wet, limp body to his.

"Mathilde? Mathi, what's happened?"

"Pablo, help me." Her voice is barely a whisper. "They took him."

"Your son," he says quietly, with a tone that says he understands everything.

She nods, demolished, does not look up.

"Where is he?"

"I don't know," she says, weeping.

"From the student protest? The Champs-Élysées tonight?"

"They were shooting teenagers, the Nazis beat him, broke his bones, his beautiful face." She collapses against him. "I don't know if he is alive."

Picasso's face twists bitterly. "Bastards, they have no right."

The rain pours down. Midnight, the sound of clock bells tolling long and mournful. "Dora, could you bring some whiskey?" says Picasso. He wraps a white blanket around her shoulders.

Dora pads barefoot across the carpeted floor and returns with a tray of tea, biscuits, and whiskey glasses. She uncorks a bottle, pours a glass, drops a teaspoon of honey into the amber liquid, and brings it to Mathilde, urging her to sip. Picasso leaves the women on the couch and crosses the room to a round marble table. He pulls a telephone forward and dials a number. There is a short conversation. He asks questions softly and waits for the answers. "How many? Where?

Visitors? Conditions for release?" He cups the handset and turns to Mathilde. "Mathi, what is his name, the name of your son?"

She looks up wearily. "Philippe. Philippe Payer."

"Philippe Payer," he says into the phone.

Finally, he replaces the receiver on the cradle and turns to Mathilde.

"Have another sip," he says quietly, kneeling by her side. He looks at Dora, who nods at him. "My contact in the French police prefecture is looking for your son."

Mathilde wipes her eyes with the back of her hand and sits up. "Maybe there is hope."

"Mathi, you are a dear friend. I thought I would never see you again. But here you are." He grips her hands. "It is strange but not surprising that we have found each other again, this time in occupied Paris." He exhales and rubs a hand over his forehead. "Where dark times just got darker."

"I feel empty," says Mathilde, her face twisted in anguish. She shakes her head in disbelief. "I should have protected him. Never let him go to the protest. This is all my fault."

"Not your fault. The Nazis are to blame."

He hugs Dora to his side.

"Dora Maar and I, we'll do everything we can to help you."

"You can sleep here, Mathilde," says the woman, her eyes brimming with tears. "Until it's safe to go home."

CHAPTER FORTY-FIVE

Paris, 1940

That night, the rain pounds down on the zinc roofs of Paris, sending birds deep into their feathered nests. Mathilde stands at the bedroom window of Picasso's apartment, replaying the horror in her mind, her son being beaten and thrown into a Nazi truck. Her hand is pressed on the windowpane, and she looks down on the street where black police cars are slowly cruising. It is a moonless night. Cursed. She looks over at an ancient wooden Christ hanging on the wall of the bedroom. She gets down on her knees and does something she has not done since a child in Alsace: She prays. Hands clenched together, she prays that her son is still alive.

Mathilde wakes to the sound of Picasso calling her name gently, "Mathi," as he touches her arm with one hand. She fell asleep on the floor with the white blanket pulled roughly over her. Picasso rises and looks outside, checks the weather, and sees that the rain has stopped. It is dawn. Her thoughts are clouded and confused. "Why are you here?"

"When you are ready, we will go together," he says softly.

"Where are we going?" Getting heavily to her feet, she feels the trauma rush back at her. She is sure he can see all the world's bitter sorrows written all over her face.

"I'm sorry, Mathi, but we should go as soon as possible."

"Yes, we need to, it's the right thing. We must," she says, as if echoing words from Philippe that she had just remembered or dreamed. She rubs her eyes, trying to understand where she is. In a bedroom, with a carved antique couch and gilded chairs, with a plaster sculpture of a man holding a sheep in his arms. She remembers now. Picasso's apartment. He usually wears a blue-and-white striped sailor's jersey. But today he is wearing an expensive wool suit, a shirt and tie. She looks up at him intensely as if seeing him for the first time. She notices dully that he combs his grey hair over his skull from the side. The skin around his neck hangs loose. The light in his eyes has dimmed with age and softened with kindness. Last night's horror: she feels her wound gape open, fresh and raw.

What matters is that she is in the care of her old friend.

"Philippe. Where is he? Do you know?"

"When you are ready, we go out. We need to go to the prison where they're holding the students."

"The prison?"

"Cherche-Midi. Not far from here. We can walk. We will go together."

She and Picasso cross the courtyard together and step into the street. He links his arm through Mathilde's, and they walk like an old bourgeois couple toward the Boulevard Raspail. They stop at a café, and he insists that Mathilde have an espresso and a croissant before pressing on. She notices for the first time a sign posted in the window to ward off Jews: *Interdit aux Juifs*. She drinks the coffee, ignores the croissant. Eating is not a possibility while her stomach twists in despair. The streets are busy with passersby and no sign of soldiers. But she will not rest until she finds Philippe. She does not speak to Picasso as they walk, and he does not seem to mind. His gaze is firmly ahead, his arm hooked through Mathilde's; she leans against him, feels she might be sick to her stomach. She knows the Cherche-Midi by reputation as a French military prison with hundreds of cells for solitary confinement. With all the laws that the Nazis have broken since the war started, this old prison would be a fine place to contain the occupation forces. Innocent French citizens have no place there. "Insanity has replaced sanity, am I right, Pablo?"

He looks at her and his black eyes flash with anger. "That's how it happens. Justice and morality are replaced overnight. Here and in many places. In Spain, the people suffer under the fascist pigs."

"Isn't it always true? The young, the innocent are the first to be sacrificed," she says, depleted, her voice barely a whisper. She says a silent prayer to whichever god might be listening. She asks that her son be alive. She asks to see him and wrap her arms around him.

"Not much farther, Mathi," Picasso says, squeezing her hand, holding her up.

Up ahead, a tall brick wall wraps around the military prison. She looks up to the small square windows dotting the facade. Could Philippe be looking back at her? She strains her eyes trying to see a face. But Picasso is slowing his step and exhaling loudly. "There's a lineup. Let's see what we can find out." She sees hundreds of people pressed against the prison wall, waiting quietly, their faces twisted with anguish. They wait. Picasso wanders short distances away from Mathilde to try to gather information but everybody seems to be at a loss. There is nothing to do but be there. She stands resolute, straight-backed, trying to get her bearings. She sees a crowd of mothers and fathers, sisters and brothers, young students and possibly some of their professors. In the old France, before the war, this waiting without any information or explanation would have been met with cries of outrage. People would have stomped their feet and banged their fists on the prison entrance. But the occupation has made the French cower. They look down rather than up, they lower their voices to obedient whispers.

"Overnight our democracy has crumbled, and our power," she whispers to Picasso. "I thought there were rules preventing an unprovoked invasion."

"It's a sick version of *Alice in Wonderland*. She goes through the hole and discovers a hideous new world," says Picasso. His face is grim.

They stand. They smoke cigarettes. They barely speak. Finally, she leans her back against the brick wall of the prison. It doesn't matter that Picasso is a famous artist, that he is wearing a bespoke suit from Savile Row. They wait for three hours. They smoke, they eat some chocolate that Picasso pulls from his pocket. Most of the women sit on the sidewalk, their heads bowed on baskets of food and blankets that they have brought to nurture their sons and daughters. The clouds gather overhead, it threatens to rain again. Then, without warning, the double reinforced doors of the prison creak open and several Nazi soldiers step onto the sidewalk, rifles lifted. Nobody speaks. Everybody looks to the ground. The hope is that utter submission will allow their missing children to walk free. Mathilde can hear orders being shouted and another series of metal doors clanging open. Students begin to walk out onto the sidewalks. Some of them are limping. Others are holding their bloodied faces, their arms across their chests at strange angles. Their mothers rush to their child first, and cries of relief that cannot be repressed go up into the air like answered prayers. Mathilde and Picasso press forward in the crowd. They are nearly at the gate. She counts fifty, seventy, then one hundred students. They stream out of the prison and into the arms of their loved ones. She records all of their faces twisted and dazed with grief, their innocence stamped out, the tears streaming down their cheeks. The crowd diminishes, and only a dozen parents, hands wrapped around the bars of the iron gates, stay at the prison entrance, this horrible place that had been invisible to Mathilde before the war. She does not see Philippe. He is not walking out and into her arms. She begins to panic, stands on her tiptoes, shouts his name. Picasso presses her against him and begs her to stop. "We must wait," he says. She calls out, beseeching him to appear. She screams his name. The guards jerk their rifles toward her, looking annoyed by this hysterical woman. Picasso turns and rushes her down the street, out of sight. Finally, the guards retreat from the sidewalk, stepping back into the secret, shrouded world of the prison. The gate closes with a heavy thud. *What does it mean*, thinks Mathilde darkly, clinging to Picasso, *when people pass through the gates but never come out again?*

CHAPTER FORTY-SIX

Paris, 1940

Picasso calls his contact in the French prefecture of police again. He learns that about 150 students were arrested, many of them beaten, forced to stand outside all night in the prison courtyard. At dawn, the mock executions began. The students were lined up in groups of ten and shot at with blanks. Most of them collapsed on the ground, believing their lives had ended. They were ushered into the prison, fingerprinted, and warned to never protest again. About twenty students were still being held inside the prison for mysterious reasons.

Picasso does not relay any of these gruesome details to Mathilde. He finds her lying on the carpet in the guest bedroom staring at his sculpture of the man with the lamb.

"The lamb looks frightened," she says dully, not bothering to look at Picasso. "Twisting to escape."

"I was thinking about my country when I sculpted that. How the Spanish people are struggling under Franco. And now the French are condemned to an unholy occupation."

"A sacrificial lamb. We've become that animal."

"A lamb desperate to escape."

"Pablo, I will do anything. I need to see Philippe. Why are they keeping him? He has done nothing wrong." Her hands are curled into fists.

"Mathi," says Picasso quietly, sitting on the floor beside her. "Now that the Nazis have occupied France . . ." He hesitates, looks to the window and back to her, his eyes filling with tears. "*Biens*, what is now true is that there is no longer right and wrong. What we used to know. There is only them and us. The occupiers and the occupied." He holds her hand in his own and grips it to make sure she is listening. "I have many friends with contacts on the inside. Good people, some working for the Resistance. But this is a difficult situation."

All of this, Mathilde's meeting with Picasso at his posh apartment, Dora Maar's wrapping her in a woollen blanket, serving her coffee this morning, is overwhelming to her. Mathilde knows her by reputation, that she is an exceptional photographer, one of the brightest members of the Surrealists, her dreamlike photo collages a revelation. Mathilde wonders idly whether her reputation will withstand the narcissism of Picasso. Nearly three decades ago, Picasso dumped Mathilde to shine his light on a new muse. She remembers the emptiness that accompanied his steely rejection. The way her knocks on his door went unanswered. No letter to explain. No phone call. Finally, standing on the Pont Neuf looking out over the Seine, the feeling of her body poisoned by the rejection, she came to grips with the breakup. Mathilde realized that Picasso clipped the wings of women so he could fly higher. And yet she has come to him now in this time of desperation. Without hesitating, he has thrown himself into helping her.

"Can they do something?" she asks Picasso, her voice hoarse. "Release Philippe?"

"I'm afraid the Nazis control Cherche-Midi prison," he says more quietly.

She nods listlessly and looks back at the sculpture.

"I'm on a list of degenerate artists. I must be careful," says Picasso.

"Yes."

"The German soldiers come to visit me often."

He has changed out of his suit and is wearing a striped jersey and paint-smeared pants. Mathilde looks at the lamb, writhing to escape the arms of a tall, strong man. She thinks about how the enemy wants her to lie down and be defeated. To not stand up is to succumb to the wishes of the occupiers. To not try is to be complicit with the humiliation. She must act or let the Nazis win with their evil new code of morality. Picasso gets to his feet and helps her stand up.

"Mathilde, I need to apologize to you. These dark times have humbled me, it seems, and I need to be honest with you at last about why I abandoned you, what we had, back then."

"Pablo, I don't know what . . ."

But she wants to hear his story, after all these years cleaved apart.

"You were very young, and I was selfish with you, and many others," he says, his dark eyes boring into hers. "A very good friend of mine died of opium at that time, by suicide, or overdose, we will never know. And there was the trial about the stolen sculptures from the Louvre. It was all wrong and I felt broken by all of it. I couldn't see you any longer. It was too painful."

"I see," says Mathilde, stunned by his confession.

"I'm so sorry."

"It's all right. I understand now, it was a long time ago." Saying this, she realizes all over again that her provocation of the theft had exposed Picasso and Apollinaire to public scrutiny, and she regrets that now.

"You disappeared, though. After your boyfriend was found with the *Mona Lisa*, his face printed on the front pages of all the newspapers in Italy and France, I mean, unbelievable."

"Vincenzo. I—" Her voice cracks and she starts to cough.

"Vincenzo, yes. He turned out to be fearless. Or insane."

"A bit of both, I guess." She feels faint, desperate for a glass of water.

They look at each other for a long time without speaking.

"*Biens, biens,*" he says, sighing, rubbing his tired eyes with his hands. "That was a long time ago. Now we are at war. More absurdity, more violence, despots never get tired of their excesses. I am glad you came to me, Mathilde. What else can I do?"

She shakes her head. "Can I use your telephone?" she asks.

She calls her ex-husband in London. Their communication is rare, but he is, after all, the father of Philippe and deserves to know. The line rings but he does not pick up. She tries again. No answer. She will try later but there is no time now. She must act immediately. Picking up clothes lent to her by Dora, she goes to the washroom and showers. The water is hot and the pressure is luxurious but she hurries rather than lingering. She dries herself, gets dressed in the navy-blue tunic dress, arranges her hair, and pulls on her black beret. She hesitates in front of the ornate golden mirror. She looks at herself, knows what she is capable of. She presses her cheeks with pink powder and stains her lips red. She picks up her purse, puts on pumps, and walks to the Louvre by the fading daylight. Bicycles criss-cross the public square in front of the museum. Police cars race along the river. The invaders are posted at regular intervals along the main streets. She stops on the Pont Alexandre and looks out onto the Seine. The orb of the sun hangs low, glistening like pale honey.

She walks unsteadily across the courtyard of the Louvre, feeling vulnerable and off balance, like an aged woman in need of a cane.

The helmeted guards flip through her identification and, wordlessly, gesture for her to pass into the museum. She trips along the ground floor, her heels echoing in the stone hall like the loud ticking of a grandfather clock. She slows her pace and stops in front of the *Great Sphinx of Tanis*. Mathilde has walked by the monumental creature hundreds of times during her years working at the Louvre, but today she stops to press her hands against its giant paws of rose granite. She considers all the wars and occupations the stone beast has witnessed throughout time. How oppressors destroy until they themselves are destroyed. More than four thousand years old, she thinks, this creature, all-seeing, all-knowing. Too heavy to be transported away from the Nazi occupation. If it were winged, surely it would have flown from earth long ago. She reaches her arms around the sphinx's huge, noble head, touches her fingers to its eyes, its mouth, then its ears. "Help me," she whispers. "Give me back my son."

CHAPTER FORTY-SEVEN

Paris, 1940

She is terrified for Philippe. For Paris. For her entire country. But something happened when she wrapped her arms around the neck of the sphinx. Her body filled with courage, deep and unshakeable like the granite rock from which the beast was carved.

Head lifted, she walks through the grainy shadows of the hallways, dusk descending, the lights switched off to darken the museum, attempting to save it from expected air raids. This is how Franz finds her, pacing the hallways.

"Mathilde?"

She stops and turns to him, finding his eyes.

"Madame Payer, it's good of you to come," he says in a loud, officious voice. "I think you'll be pleased with the exhibition of *The Wedding Feast at Cana*. This way, please," he adds, boots clicking on the parquet floors as he walks briskly forward, all business. He does not leave space for her to question his direction, and suddenly they are breezing down the corridor, past other German officers and soldiers of common rank, together but apart, careful to not come close to grazing shoulders. Now he is gesturing to the left until they enter the Salle des États. The gallery is empty, save for the monumental masterpiece. She tries to manage her emotions, the animal rage she feels toward the Nazis for what they have done to her son. "I think you will agree that the canvas is still in good condition," he says, stepping away from her, speaking into the air, and turning a circle in the gallery. "We are most pleased about having *The Wedding Feast at Cana* exhibited here," he says, stepping back, looking intensely at her, "placing it back to its rightful place." He stops speaking as he examines her face. Lowering his voice to a whisper, he says, "Mathilde, what is it? You've been crying."

Now it is her turn to step away from the painting. She cuts a wide path to the gallery entrance and back again, gathering herself, finally responding loudly, "I think Paolo Veronese would be pleased to see his work back at the Louvre." She does not look at him. "Monsieur Metternich," she adds. She looks at Franz from across the gallery and nods once. "I hope it will enjoy a long stay in the safety of the museum."

"We only need to sign the papers then, per German regulations now standardized within the French bureaucracy. If you will follow me to my office."

They leave the gallery and walk through the dimly lit corridor, maintaining a safe distance apart. Her shoes click on the parquet floors, his boots echo heavily. A helmeted soldier stands at the entrance to a gallery. With his eyes on the high-rank eagle embroidered on Franz's collar, he salutes with his right arm hoisted powerfully into the air and shouts, "Heil Hitler."

Franz nods blithely and continues walking with Mathilde. "Tell me. Something has happened. Something has upset you," he says, whispering, turning his head slightly toward her.

She tilts her head to look up to a gold-coffered ceiling decorated with merciful gods and goddesses. It helps to distract her. She wonders where all the mercy in the world has gone and whether it will ever return. He unlocks a door and shows her into his spacious office. The arched window overlooks the Seine. She wants to hold it together, show nothing to this man, for he is the enemy. She must remember that, and the enemy has brutalized her son and the other brave students. "Mathilde, tell me, please, if you can?" He removes his grey military jacket and tosses it on a chair. She wants to hate him but she cannot. She faces the door away from him and weeps silently.

"Are you upset about the painting? Moving it back to the Louvre. I promise it will stay here where I can watch over it."

She does not respond but her entire body is trembling with sorrow. She knows that in her past, she has been bitter and manipulative. She knows what she has done, has reviewed her life as if a book, cover to cover, forward and backward, left to right, right to left. Fine. Her sorrow tonight comes from feeling small and powerless against a mighty regime that cares not at all about her pain. They care not at all about the lives they will destroy. And so she waits in limbo, not knowing whether her son is alive or dead. One thing is certain: The laws that would have protected him have been ripped up by the occupiers.

Then she feels his hands on her hips and he is turning her toward him. His arms wrap around her, and rather than resisting, she presses her entire body against him. For a moment, she welcomes his comfort, wants to believe he can help. One of his hands is stroking her back, the other holds her firmly against him.

She takes the white handkerchief that he offers and wipes her face. At last, she looks at him. "How can I know? How can I know you are still the same man?" Nothing he can say at this moment can change her mind about how much she hates the Nazis, including Franz. She will stay soft for a while more, dab at her eyes a touch, until she does what needs to be done. She is prepared to get down on her knees and beg, if only to save her son.

He nods a little. "I wish this war had never started, that the occupation had never been allowed, that the armistice had never been granted between the Nazis and your French government. I'm grateful to see you again, though the circumstances are insupportable. But please know, if you need me, I will do what I can to help you." She nods and presses her hands gently against his chest.

"The Nazis . . ." She tries to find the words for the way her world has been turned upside down. "I don't think any of us were prepared for how cruel they can be."

Nodding again, lowering his voice, he says, "Hitler is obsessed with power. But, Mathilde, this is me. An older version of the man you knew in Alsace." He presses one of her hands against his chest. Through his grey shirt, she feels the warmth of his skin, the beating of his heart. "Can you feel that? Please, trust me with whatever it is that is upsetting you."

She does not say anything for a long time. Finally, she removes her hand and looks up at him. "My son was part of the student protest yesterday."

"On the Champs-Élysées?"

"Yes." She swallows before going on. "They beat him. I was watching. His face . . ." She trails off, will not speak of it. "His legs looked broken." Franz exhales loudly and wraps his arms around her once more. She wants to sink again into his comfort, which seems about the only human right left to her at this point, but instead, frantic, she pushes away to look directly at him. "We went to Cherche-Midi prison this morning. They released many students. But not Philippe. I don't know why. He did nothing. I don't know if he is alive."

"This is very tragic, I'm so sorry. The plan is going to extremes." He takes her hands in his and grips them tightly. Tears form at the corners of his eyes. For a long moment, neither of them speaks. Finally, he says, "I fear the Nazis might be more hardline than I had ever imagined."

"They will not succeed," she says. "They will never win this war."

"Perhaps. But they are a large machine and the machine likes to punish. They will try to silence dissent." He shakes his head as if trying to clear his mind. "I cannot change that. But let me try to bring your son home."

She stands apart from him. "I am full of hate for what they have done. They have taken my son. They have destroyed people's lives. It is evil, unthinkable evil. When will it end?"

"I know. I wish it would all be over," he says, pressing his forehead against hers. "Please let me see if I can help." They stand for a long time without saying anything further. Boots approaching from the corridor interrupt them. He turns to put on his military tunic and sits at his desk. "As you were saying, madame, about the collection?"

"His name is Philippe Payer," she whispers before opening the door to leave. "My son." He writes down the name and puts the slip of paper in the pocket of his uniform. She hesitates and then asks, "Do you have children?" He nods and half smiles. "Two sons. One daughter."

"Are they safe?"

"I pray they are, but I don't know for sure."

Mathilde feels suddenly frightened for these children she has never met. They must all be kept safe from collapsing buildings and aerial bombings. "They did not choose war," she says to Franz.

"No, they did not. They did not choose war."

She turns to walk down the long corridor, past the towering galleries with coffered ceilings and monumental skylights, emotionally exhausted but buoyed by Franz's promise to help her. She stands up on her tiptoes to touch the nails where great paintings used to hang, gazes dumbfounded at the countless ornate frames lying down on the floor, emptied of their canvases. She knows, of course, that the canvases were removed from their frames in order to make for efficient transport to Chambord and other storage depots. But, seeing the museum empty of its staff, the frames look like wooden corpses. She kicks angrily at dust balls floating in her path. Before the stairs leading to the exit, she passes the door to the storage closet where she and Vincenzo used to have desperate, passionate sex, when Paris was vibrating with new music and art, when world wars had not been unleashed, when she was an innocent with a long ponytail wearing her grandmother's embroidered blouse.

She is about to descend the stairs, but a man's voice interrupts her. "Madame Payer, *bonsoir*." Jacques Jaujard, the director of the Louvre, appears from his office. He steps out of the evening shadows, his face drawn, his eyes hooded. "I'm glad to see you," he says somberly, "although I was not informed of your visit."

Mathilde is astonished by the way her boss has aged in less than one year.

She rushes forward and seizes both of his hands. "Monsieur Jaujard, *c'est toujours un grand plaisir de vous voir*." She is no longer under his direct command but under the thumb of the German bosses, but, to Mathilde, Jacques Jaujard will always be her leader. "I'm only here to inspect the hanging of *The Wedding Feast at Cana*."

"Yes, I inspected it myself yesterday," he says. "It looks fine, all things considered."

"Tell me, how is everything with you? You come to work every day even with all these"—lowering her voice—"these occupiers everywhere?"

"I show up every day, and I will continue to do so. Let them try to stop me."

"They will take everything if we let them," she says.

"Of course they will. They want to break us, take everything we cherish. Our democracy, our justice, our homes. But, Madame Payer, I am most concerned about the health of the artworks I entrusted to you." He walks next to her and whispers "*La Joconde*" into her ear. He steps back, and she notices his fine black suit is rumpled and worn. The truth is that she must also look a shadow of her previous self, wearing Dora Maar's oversized clothes.

"You must return immediately to move the artworks out of Loc-Dieu," he says, a hand placed gently on her shoulder. "The black mildew, it's too great a risk. And the Nazis are on the move. The free zone is being squeezed again. We have to do everything in our control to protect the art."

She wants to explain that her son has been imprisoned, that his condition is unknown, that she is paralyzed with grief. But, of course, she cannot. Any revelations about him would only reveal her plan—her collaboration with a Nazi—for having him released.

"Yes, of course, I am planning to . . ."

"You must take the first train in the morning. Your assignment is to lead the convoy to Montauban. It's all arranged. The Musée Ingres can accommodate the crates and the village can billet the staff."

"The Musée Ingres?" She knows the museum by reputation, a handsome medieval abbey built on dry land somewhere between Toulouse and Bordeaux. She often scrutinized one of Ingres's paintings at the Louvre. A naked, beautiful woman in a turban lounging on a sumptuous couch, framed by blue silk curtains. *La Grande Odalisque*, it was titled, meaning a chambermaid or slave belonging to the Turkish empire. In other words, a woman that a man could have his way with for free. Mathilde was impressed by the painting's perfect coloration, but always wondered why so many women were painted naked and most of the men in museums were clothed.

"I was hoping to spend a few more days here." She feels panicked, unable to breathe. Leaving Paris tomorrow is impossible. Without Philippe? She must tell him, let him know how she is suffering.

But Jaujard is in no mood for indulging Mathilde. "May I remind you that I expressly put you in charge of protecting the greatest treasure of our nation," he says, removing his hand from her shoulder. "This is the icon of Europe, indeed of the world. Your utmost dedication is required."

She cannot speak.

"Mathilde?"

She looks at him, hesitating.

"This war requires all of us to sacrifice. All of us. Except for *La Joconde*. She will not be sacrificed under any circumstances. Am I clear?"

"*Oui*, monsieur," she says, her eyes turning icy blue. "I understand. Your plan is good. It is a good plan."

She bows slightly and shakes his hand. He nods and she turns away, moving woodenly.

Finally, she reaches the main floor. She stops to lean her body against the sphinx's granite shoulder. She looks at the noble face of the beast. "Are you not a messenger from the sun goddess?" She knows that she sounds foolish. Philippe would tease her if he could hear her now. But she has nothing else. "Give me back my son. I beg you. I will give you anything."

CHAPTER FORTY-EIGHT

Loc-Dieu Abbey, 1940

Travelling south from Paris to Loc-Dieu is long and arduous. Certain train lines have been blocked. Stone-eyed Nazis conduct passport inspections on the platforms. Finally, Mathilde arrives at the abbey, exhausted and unsteady, in a small truck from the train station, unnoticed, except by Suzanne, who appears suddenly, her white curator's smock streaked with dirt. "You've been missed."

A group of men with crates balanced on dollies walk by. "Madame, which trucks?" they ask loudly.

"Straight ahead to the one painted yellow," shouts back Suzanne. "We're about halfway loaded," she says to Mathilde. "Where do you want the Italian Renaissance collection? Front or back of the convoy?"

"In the middle. Less visibility." Mathilde feels her life force has gone out of her. She thinks she's shouting but her voice is barely a whisper.

"The Greek and Roman urns?"

"At the back. You can ride in that truck."

"That puts you in the front, Mathilde. With your wooden case." Suzanne hesitates, scanning Mathilde's ashen face, her eyes, cloudy and distant. "My God, what happened?" She wraps an arm around her friend and draws her into an alcove. "Something happened in Paris. Tell me. Can you tell me?"

Mathilde thinks, *Is love worth the pain?* She is too exhausted and torn apart to know. Her mind casts back to Philippe in the first cloudy moments after his birth. A film of silky vernix still covering his little bony shoulders, a hint of black hair, his eyes dark and penetrating. His tongue poked out of his mouth. The truth is she hadn't really wanted him, this tiny, withered turtle. Not at first. Her ambivalence about motherhood was acute, never having been mothered herself. Nobody had warned her of the torture of being a new mother, the unthinkable pain of a forceps birth and the sharp sting of breastfeeding that made her howl every time he latched on. It was all humiliating and undesired. Her husband brought her tea and cake and disappeared at night. She enlisted a wet nurse, then fired her, and finally, she settled into breastfeeding her son. On day six, he smiled at her. The midwife dismissed it as a newborn merely passing gas. But Mathilde trusted Philippe. And he bonded deeply with his mother. Nobody else could hold him for the first two years of his life.

"They took Philippe," she says to Suzanne, wide-eyed, finally weeping, her shoulders convulsing. "The Nazis beat him and then took him."

Suzanne grips Mathilde harder in her arms. A low growl vibrates so powerfully from Suzanne that Mathilde can feel it inside her own rib cage. "No," Suzanne says, finally. "They can't do that. They can't. He's coming back. Trust me. Your boy is coming back to you. Damn it. He's coming back."

They cling to each other for another long moment.

"Let's leave tomorrow at sunrise," says Mathilde, wiping her tears harshly with the back of her hands.

"There's a bottle waiting for us in the cellar."

"Only one?" she says listlessly. She craves something stronger, opium, to leave her life for a night. She touches her golden necklace and desperately wants Philippe's red scarf around her neck, something comfortable to hold on to like freedom. "Paris is in a war zone. I wasn't prepared."

Leaving her friend, holding tight to the banister, she climbs the stairs and unlocks her bedroom door. Dropping to her knees, she reaches an arm below her bed and slides the wooden case toward her. She hesitates, gets to her feet, and locks the door. Then, breathing deeply, she uses both hands to push away the wooden lid and lift out the bespoke case inside. She unclips the metal fasteners. With tenderness, she lifts away the layers of protective paper before revealing the *Mona Lisa*. "There you are," she says. The woman in the portrait gazes directly at her without judgment or expectation. "I see it now," says Mathilde to *Mona Lisa*. "Your empathy."

She wraps up the painting and slides it back under the bed to lie next to the other special package there: Leonardo's drawing of Isabella d'Este. In the distance, she can see dozens of wooden crates being loaded into the old, battered trucks. She pulls on her canvas pants and a thick black turtleneck. Maybe news will come later tonight, or tomorrow. She has to believe that Philippe will be saved. But now she turns to the work at hand. At her desk, she takes out a pen and paper to scribble a telegram to the man she desperately wants to trust, who holds the fate of her son in his hands. *Bats will be out soon. I must be getting on. Odalisque creator. Hometown.*

CHAPTER FORTY-NINE

Musée Ingres, 1940

At dawn, many of the custodians and guards beg off, preferring to risk all to return to their families in the occupied zone. Mathilde shakes their hands and nods at them to go home. To be with kin is what matters most, even if she herself is prevented from doing so. The remaining convoy travels to the southwestern pocket of France, to Montauban. The road is flat and forgiving. They rumble past houses built from stone that look bleached white, past vast agricultural lands, squashed melons in fields, sunflowers gone brown and limp in the cold. Their destination, the Musée Ingres, is located at the bottom of a hill so steep that the lead truck comes to a sudden halt at the top. From inside the cab, it's impossible to see what lies beyond the crest. The driver steps out of his lorry, looks down, and immediately signals to the truck drivers behind him to reverse. Rumbling loudly, grudgingly, the trucks roll backward until finally they come upon a road that cuts across the slope, allowing for a less perilous arrival into the museum courtyard without having to sacrifice their precious, threadbare brakes.

The museum is a refuge of charming beauty. The paintings by Ingres pay homage to the elegant Greek fashion of the 1800s, and there are many erotic depictions of golden-skinned lovelies, male and female. In other rooms, his landscapes of rivers cutting through valleys with skies blossoming peach offer views past the horizon line into something sublime, like infinity. But Mathilde notices that most of the windows face north, allowing only a mean grey light into the interior. The men are grim-faced as they unload the crates in the cold. Steam pumps out of their mouths as they lug objects inside the dark, musty rooms. Mathilde walks the galleries, inhaling deeply. But she does not detect the damp smell of mildew. Wearing her white curator's smock, she speaks listlessly, pointing the collections into certain vast halls, directing smaller crates into windowless galleries papered in velvet brocade. For accommodation she is given a small compartment with gilded furniture on rickety legs and a canopied bed with a horsehair mattress. Her bedside light flickers, brightens, and then dies. She slumps on the bed, leaving her white coat on the floor, touching a hand to the side of her head to alleviate the throbbing. It's as if somebody is pressing a boot against her neck.

Earlier, in the sweltering summer of the Château de Chambord, she lay naked on her narrow bed and thought of herself as a musical instrument. Imagined a life that played all the movements of a symphonic work at every speed, from slow and meditative to lively and fierce, *lento, adagio, vivace*. In Alsace, she was a flute, flitting across fields, sniffing for wonder, quivering in space. Franz taught her how to trust herself enough to play trumpet, when she found confidence enough to slap down ragged rhythms and laugh at people with her horn. With Picasso, she was a violin capable of making ear-piercing sounds, and in those early years in Paris, she liked to drag the bow along the frets to birth animal sounds. With Vincenzo, she created low string notes, foreshadowing. But now, during the war, she rarely plays. She no longer laughs. Except when she becomes a cellist so she can lean into the torment of her life. When she stops, it is because she cannot find notes that are magnificent and sweet. She reaches a hand to turn the pages but the music is no longer being written.

She tries to think of nothing, pressing thoughts of her son away in order to survive the day. Instead, she thinks of Lisa. When she was told that she would be personally responsible for protecting *La Joconde* during the occupation, she went to the Bibliothèque Sainte-Geneviève, a library near the Panthéon in Paris. She asked whether she was a real woman. The librarian, hair swept back in an elegant bun, angled her head and nodded. "Interesting. Nobody has asked that before."

On a long oak table, the librarian switched on the reading light with its green glass shade. She piled up books and archival records beside Mathilde. Accounts about Leonardo da Vinci in Giorgio Vasari's *Lives of the Artists*. Tax records from the 1500s were readily available but they needed to be requested. Two weeks later, the tax records arrived, photocopied from the Florence State Archive and mailed to the Paris library. She helped her to find the correct pages. Together, they discovered that *Mona Lisa*'s real name was Lisa Gherardini, that she was married at fifteen to Francesco del Giocondo, a silk merchant. That she was raised poor on the wrong side of Florence in the Oltrarno neighbourhood. That her family was nobility from the Chianti region, land rich but cash poor. That Lisa had six children by the time she was twenty-four years old. That three of them would die early from illness, two as toddlers, another as a teenager. That she was buried not with her husband in the del Giocondo crypt but in a pauper's grave next to the Sant'Orsola convent, where one of her daughters had taken her vows.

All of these facts are discovered and shared, but do they get to the essence of the woman? That she is terra firma?

The days unwind at the end of a low, burning coil. Silence from Paris. After several attempts, she finally reaches her ex on the telephone, tells him about Philippe, the protest, his incarceration, and Picasso's attempts to help her. There is a long silence at the end of the line. She thinks he might be crying or simply rubbing his forehead with his long fingers. At last, her husband speaks. "You should have taken him out of Paris. He should have gotten out and saved his skin. You call me giving me this news two weeks after his imprisonment? What kind of mother are you? This is your fault. All of it."

She is accustomed to his accusations, assessing blame, revealing her many weaknesses. "Can you help? Speak to your colleagues? De Gaulle? Maybe he can do something?"

"Of course he can't help. He's trying to mastermind the return of a new French government when the time is right. The Nazis are blowing up our country, all our infrastructure, everything we've built. He can't bend his mind to our personal affairs. This is your mess. Not his."

She hangs up and stumbles outside for a cigarette. Two weeks and there has been no word from Philippe. Nothing from Picasso. No telegrams from Franz. She contemplates going back to Paris on the train but fears being found out by Jacques Jaujard. What was the word he kept repeating to her? *Sacrifice. Sacrifice. Sacrifice.*

CHAPTER FIFTY

Musée Ingres, 1940

Suzanne takes the lead on arranging the artworks, airing out the crates that had succumbed to black mildew at Loc-Dieu, covering the large Greek sculptures with white sheets to keep the dust off. Mathilde stays in her room, feigning the flu, and though she knows there is nothing physically wrong with her, her body pricks with a clammy sweat. She crawls into bed, leaving her canvas pants and sweater on, for it would require too much effort to remove them. Her mind meanders like oil in water: She thinks of Picasso eating bowls of spinach and feeding her rice pudding with a small silver spoon, his Afghan dog watching her with mournful eyes, its shaggy head on her bed at the Grands-Augustins apartment. Next she is lying in a ditch with Franz wrapping her in his Nazi tunic, his fingers gliding over her stomach. She recalls the early days of the war when she led the way into the Cosson River next to the Château de Chambord, fully clothed, holding a bottle of sparkling wine aloft; the other curators floated beside her, everybody laughing hysterically at the terrifying prospect of being devoured by catfish, when it felt that the invaders would never come. That past seems like a dream, but nothing is more abstract than reality. She wants to remember what it was like. Back then, when discovering the joy of life was everybody's right.

Her thoughts curl around her son, memories from his childhood, dancing together in their Paris apartment, the lamb that he insisted on saving in the mountains. About Franz, she has resigned herself to his Nazi status. His very presence in Paris makes him intolerable. None of their happy moments in Alsace—amounting to a year of classic teenage infatuation between two people lusting after each other—make him bearable. Franz is a Nazi, though he denies it. From her feverish state below the antique canopy of her four-poster bed at the Musée Ingres, she feels herself drowning in a pool of hopelessness. Darkness has become a faithful companion.

She is thirsty. She should get up to drink some water. But the energy required to lift herself up has gone. Her will has evaporated. She touches a hand to her necklace, seeking comfort. She thinks of Franz, her one love from long ago before her life became complicated, before, more accurately, she complicated her life. She thinks of Vincenzo. What he did for her. Adoring her, laughing with her in a Paris fountain, making love in the Louvre's storage closet. What else? Oh, yes, lying and stealing, to make himself more of a man in her eyes. Surely, he was the best of them, resolute in his conviction to steal back what had been taken from his home country. After he left France for Italy, she followed his story carefully in the newspapers. At his trial, he was interrogated about accomplices but never did he name Mathilde. He alone was jailed for being the Paris thief. The *Mona Lisa* was put on exhibit at the Uffizi. More than thirty thousand people pushed their way into the great portrait gallery to see her. Mathilde read in the newspapers that there were riots in the streets when thousands of others were unable to see her. The painting was exhibited in other cities in Italy. Vincenzo served six months in jail in Florence, during which time he was given special treatment. One Italian newspaper reported that the other inmates treated him as a special guest, arranging extra cigarettes and, on Easter Sunday, a chocolate panettone. Finally, on Sunday, January 4, 1914, the *Mona Lisa* was returned to the Salon Carré at the Louvre museum. But Mathilde did not attend. She had already travelled to the south of France to begin a quiet life in Chambéry.

Turning over in her bed, she thinks of Vincenzo. Did he die in the Great War not long after being imprisoned in Florence, or does he still live? Has he gone mad with lead poisoning? She hopes not. She hopes he is well. She thinks of his animal energy, of the rush he gave her, of his tongue sliding from her mouth down her neck when they lay next to the fountain at the Luxembourg Gardens. He was damned and he was charmed. She hopes he is living a life without regret, waking every day with a view of the duomo and an adoring wife and children stepping through the cobblestone streets next to him. Maybe he will always hate her. Maybe he wants to thank her for making him do something honourable with his life. Few people have the opportunity.

She pushes the blankets from her bed. The air in the bedroom is suffocating her. She decides she will find Vincenzo after the war and apologize to him. She will knock at his door, wherever he may be living, in France or Italy, and he will welcome her with his accented French and he will listen and look at her with his dark brown eyes, and maybe they will laugh about all that they risked in Paris. She will knock on his door at the first crack of dawn, and if he doesn't answer, she will knock again at dusk and again at night.

But that is not her knocking. That is somebody rapping hard on her bedroom door. "Madame, Madame Payer!" She is being called from the other side of her door.

Mathilde blinks but does not stir. She recognizes the voice of a woman gone hoarse from too many years of feather-dusting paintings. The manager of the museum. "*Oui?*" she asks from her bed.

The door opens. "Somebody to see you. Come quickly."

Mathilde rolls over slowly and drops her feet over the edge of the bed. She waits, breathing heavily, dread settling in her bones. Finally, she stands up, drags a reluctant hand through her hair, straightens her clothes.

"*Oui?*" she says again, but the woman has gone, leaving the door wide open.

She moves along the corridor, her hand on the wall to steady herself, gripping the wooden banister as she steps barefoot down the carpeted stairs. Her clothes hang loose on her frame, for she has barely eaten these past weeks. In the distance, a door bangs open and shut. She hears somebody shouting a command and a truck rumbling out of the museum courtyard. They have delivered his body is what she thinks. Her hands are trembling, they will not quiet. A brash light draws her attention to a narrow window. She had expected it to be night. She blinks at the unexpected sunshine, the sky a patch of brilliant ultramarine, as if lapis lazuli had been ground and thrown into the air. Perhaps it is no longer today but tomorrow.

Breathing through her panic, she descends the rest of the stairs. An eerie silence has fallen over the museum. She steps forward. Standing in the entrance hallway of the museum, below the grand arch, is a version of the son she last saw in Paris. His face is swollen with purple bruises. One leg is held rigid in a cast. When he smiles at her, she sees that he is missing a tooth. All her doubts and judgments about people and the state of the world evaporate. Everything feels drenched in goodness. She feels divinely blessed. For, just as the ocean inhales and exhales through the push and the pull of its tides, her son, her only child, breathes. He is whole. He is not dead, but in front of her. Alive. Philippe is alive.

She does not speak. She cannot. Her legs buckle, she drops to the ground.

"Maman," he says. "It's all right." Dropping his crutches, limping forward, he lifts her up and wraps his arms around her.

CHAPTER FIFTY-ONE

Musée Ingres, 1940

That night, the local women make a traditional cake, a Quercyan, peeling and slicing a bushel of apples picked from the orchards. Speaking in whispers, they exchange details about the arrival of Philippe and what he had suffered at the hands of the Nazis. The cooks in the kitchen press paring knives against their fingers until they go red from the effort, the apple skins piling high, spilling onto the floors. Jugs of rum are found within the cellars, and the slices of apple are set to marinade. In the morning, the sky blooms pink before succumbing to a silty blue. With the dawn, Philippe's story spreads across the village, to the women's husbands and children, to their grandmothers and neighbours. At the market, all of the villagers bend their ears to hear spoken fragments about the young man who survived the student protest on the Champs-Élysées in Paris, how he was beaten by the Nazis and incarcerated for two weeks in a solitary cell until finally, thankfully, he was seen by French doctors. A wave of unspoken love and respect for this young stranger ripples across the community like golden sunlight bathing a wheat field. The locals will gather at the museum to meet this hero. There will be enough cake to feed hundreds. At the back of Mathilde's mind, behind her tremendous bliss and thankfulness, she wonders who is responsible for the freeing of Philippe. His safe delivery out of prison was obviously orchestrated by somebody in a position of authority. Right now she need not know but she wonders who stepped up in the end. Picasso? Her ex-husband? Jacques Jaujard? Franz?

To prepare an ample feast, duck hunters arrive in muddied boots to slap ten birds, gutted and plucked, onto the kitchen counter. They stand quietly, shuffling next to the cooks, not wanting to wake the young man who sleeps in an adjoining gallery. But they whisper among themselves, learning Philippe's story from the chief cook, who has been speaking to the manager of the museum, and the truth emerges about the entourage from Paris who have taken refuge in their local museum. Among the crates of artworks and the dark tapestries and melancholic paintings by Ingres adorning the walls, Philippe's bright-white cast is a troubling, shining beacon, the wool blankets covering the rest of his body. Nobody talks about the depths of despair they feel learning how he had to endure two weeks of excruciating pain before the French doctors were allowed to set his leg. This young man, the son of Mathilde, the museum person from the Louvre in Paris, the guardian of thousands of artworks from the Louvre, embodies all the sacrifices of the nation. Their hate for the invaders deepens, as does their keening for the losses of their own kin gone to fight in the Resistance.

Later that day, when Philippe is awake and has been fed three bowls of porridge with honeyed preserves of melon, when Mathilde has arrived to sit anxiously by his side, one of the cooks wipes her hands on her apron and sits down at the piano to belt out a *bals-musette* dancing song. Mathilde looks up. She hasn't heard a piano being played for a long time. The sound resembles the nose-pinched pitch of a harpsichord. But the woman's fingers fly along the keys and people start to gather. A pair of women in linen aprons step down from ladders, where they are hanging garlands of dried lavender across the main archways. Custodians, swarthy-faced from a morning oiling their trucks, gather with arms folded across their chests. Some of the curators and conservators walk into the salon with arms full of local red wine, setting the bottles on a long table festooned in a variety of tablecloths in tones of purple and gold, the colours of the grasses and dogwood erupting on the land.

They gather to celebrate something good, and so a song is being played. It seems decadent, and also necessary if they are all going to avoid going mad. Mathilde joins the knot of people around the piano and she starts to sing, tentatively at first, but joined by Suzanne and other curators. No amount of coal or wood in the fireplaces can warm the museum as much as their voices.

Mathilde can see her son propping himself up on his elbows and looking over at her. She wonders if she should put an end to the singing. But Philippe would not want that, to impose his story on these people, for they have their own stories to tell, if not now, in the future. Instead, she goes to him and sits next to him at the edge of his bed. She watches his eyes darken with the telling of how Rachel and her family were forced out of hiding and onto trains heading to Germany. Of how the nightmares that he suffers are from the sounds of his classmates from law school being beaten, how they suffered more than he did, and how two of them died. She sits beside him and listens to his voice, twisted and hoarse from the telling. She knows he is saving her from the most terrible details. She knows she is helpless to take the pain away from him. The details of his release are set aside for another day. He slumps down in his bed, turns his back to her. But she sits close to him and waits until he falls into a fitful slumber.

It is mid-December and the museum has become bitterly cold. Her bones ache as she stands at last. Tentatively, she arranges the wool blanket over her son to keep him warm. It is all she can do. This is how they will greet Christmas, with hands, limp with exhaustion, raised in the name of human grace.

CHAPTER FIFTY-TWO

Musée Ingres, 1941

The invaders have come to occupy the southwestern land of France during the winter. Their trucks roar across the fallow winter fields, their boots pound on the cobblestones of the village squares. In Montauban, the soldiers take photographs of the rose-stoned village with the Pyrenees Mountains in the background, demanding to know from the cowering shopkeepers when the fields will turn golden with sunflowers and purple from lavender. The villagers seem quiet and submissive. Playing the part of "daft local yokels," as the Germans call them, is all part of the pain of the occupation. The Nazis sit back in their trucks, biding their time.

Inside the museum, the roughly paved kitchen is vast and polar cold. There are gaping openings for rats hungry for scraps to come and go as they please. The primitive mechanics of the museum are at dramatic odds with the beauty of the interior, its Persian carpets and Greek vases, statues of Beethoven by local sculptor Bourdelle standing next to Ingres's melancholic landscapes and perfect torsos of male models. All the water from their lodgings flows into an immense open-air sewer that freezes with a slick of lurid green during the hard months of the winter. The locals call the sewer the Mandoune, and they look kindly on it as just another stream feeding into the local River Tarn.

Every morning, teeth clenched, Mathilde breaks the ice in the bathroom sink with an iron pick and brings Philippe a glass of water to drink. She rolls away the canvas cot where she has arranged to bed down next to him in the gallery. His nightmares come in the way of dark murmurings or hoarse screams. Mathilde rises quickly and bends over him to tell him that he is safe, though she doubts the truth of her night counsel.

To help buoy the spirits of Philippe and all the staff in exile at the museum, Mathilde invents a game. She enlists Monsieur Thérizoles, a local carpenter who sings whenever his mouth is not full of nails. He builds four wooden easels in quick time and stands them up in a large main floor gallery. Mathilde gathers all the cooks, cleaners, and curators in front of them. Philippe leans on his crutches in the corner of the room, unamused, blithely eating an apple.

"Tell me, what would you like to see?" says Mathilde. She scans the faces of the two dozen people gathered in front of her. Their complexions have gone as grey as the brooding skies, their bodies thinner than they were a year ago. She notices their crossed legs, their shoes worn out, some of their leather heels replaced with cubes of wood.

For a long moment, there is silence. Nobody seems to be in the mood to play. She is not good at cheering people up. She barely knows how to smile. "I know it's cold, and I know we are all tired of eating potatoes and rutabaga. But I need a break from listening to the wartime reports coming from London." The crowd murmurs in agreement. "I need a break from the endless waiting, our lives put on hold without the promise of a future. I need a break from the terror of the war and the evil that the oppressors have brought to our country."

Some of the people start to clap and shout her name in agreement. "*C'est vrai*, Mathilde. *Oui*, Mathilde."

"This afternoon, let us pay homage to artists who never gave up on beauty." She looks around at the crowd. "Tell me, what would you like to see?"

Suzanne stands up and shouts, "A Manet!"

Mathilde smiles and opens up a black dossier held in her arms. The artworks have been organized with such extreme care that it is easy for her to flip through the pages of her master file to find the whereabouts of the Manet. She leans over to Thérizoles, his eyes twinkling, and points with her finger to the exact location. He runs off and in a flash returns carrying a large oil canvas in an ornate gold frame. The assembled crew applauds while he places the work on one of his easels. Their enthusiasm reminds her of a time when she would conduct tours in the Louvre for young schoolchildren, their eyes shining with delight at seeing Botticelli's frescoes, his dreamy, barefooted women in sumptuous, pastel gowns, and stepping into their parade, a little boy in a golden cloak!

"Cézanne!" shouts a local woman, an excellent baker, and within minutes, a marvel by Cézanne showing two men playing cards is placed on the next easel.

"Titian!"

"Poussin!"

"Veronese!"

There is wild clapping. With every request, Thérizoles disappears at a run only to reappear tenderly carrying the requested work of their dreams. The mood is altered, at least for the time being. Mathilde is grateful for the reprieve and allows herself the pleasure of a smile. She slides her hands inside her canvas pant pockets and starts to thank everybody for their dedication. "Because of you, these works of art, considered the most important in the Western world, have been protected from the occupiers. Every day, we fight against the risk of fire, flooding, or mildew—"

But she is interrupted.

"Da Vinci." A male voice unknown to them speaks from the corner of the room. "*Mona Lisa* by Leonardo da Vinci. I want to see her."

The Nazi official is flanked by five soldiers. He is tall and stocky, and he advances across the room to stand in front of Mathilde. "Bring her out for all of us to see."

Mathilde feels her face go ashen. They could not possibly know. "These works belong to the sovereign French nation," she says, avoiding the demand, her hands trembling in her pockets. Nobody has ever asked her directly about the whereabouts of the *Mona Lisa*. Neither Philippe nor her French colleagues. Yet, this occupier dares to ask the question in front of everybody. Is it possible he knows her secret? Lifting her chin, she speaks loudly, "By international cultural law, you have no right to any of the artworks. They are the property of the French government."

"The French government? Were you not advised? It buckled long ago." He sweeps a hand to his accompanying soldiers with their rifles pointed directly at the crowd. "Governments are decided by the regime that holds military power. It's that simple." He steps toward her.

"These works are protected by the Art Protection Unit," she says, holding her ground. A few voices from the crowd join with Mathilde in agreement. Some of them stand up.

The Nazi looks at her with disdain. Pushing his chest aggressively against hers, his mouth only a few inches from hers, he begins to speak.

"Don't touch her," shouts Thérizoles, leaping at the stranger. Without hesitating, the Nazi punches him hard in the face, dropping the carpenter to the ground. He puts a boot on the man's chest and turns back to Mathilde.

The crowd goes silent. "Never heard of it," he says, scowling.

"The Kunstschutz. Invented by you, the Nazis."

"You are wasting my time," says the uniformed man. "In twenty-four hours, we will be back to claim the best of our treasures." He releases his foot from Thérizoles and looks from Mathilde to the people gathered in the gallery. "Your country has surrendered to the Führer. The art belongs to us. Throughout history, this has always been the way." He marches out of the museum, his soldiers goose-stepping behind him. Thérizoles stands up and wipes the blood from his mouth.

CHAPTER FIFTY-THREE

Musée Ingres, 1941

Kunstschutz under attack. Mathilde writes the telegram to Franz quickly. She is desperate. Her mind warns her that he is not to be trusted but her gut tells her that he is her only hope. She hesitates, wondering if she should add another line to impress on him the urgency of what is at risk. That could be dangerous. Perhaps Franz ordered the Nazi to exert his authority at the Musée Ingres. Acting decisively, she seals the telegram and walks the short distance to the post office in Montauban to personally send it.

She returns to the museum and takes the back service stairs to access her bedroom. Locking the door, dropping to her knees, she reaches a hand below her bed and pulls the wooden case toward her. The lid sits lightly on top; Mathilde had released the nails at this museum the way she had previously done at Loc-Dieu and Chambord. In case of an approaching enemy, she could escape with the bespoke wooden case under her arm.

When Mathilde removes the white fire-retardant paper to look at the *Mona Lisa*, she is astonished by how old and tired the woman in the portrait looks. Her eyes seem to have gone dull with time, as if a sickly veneer has distorted the masterpiece. Even the landscape seems to be a faint shadow of its former monumentality. Mathilde's nose detects something noxious. There might be worms slithering inside the ancient poplar wood, too tiny to detect with the human eye. She leans down and inhales deeply. The smell is sickening. Possibly the walnut oil that da Vinci mixed with his pigments has gone rancid. His delicate layering of paint to achieve his smoky, mysterious technique of sfumato is rebelling at last. She blames herself. For exposing the masterpiece to unforgivable mildew at Loc-Dieu, for depriving the painting of oxygen for too long, hiding it like a crazed hoarder under her bed, the way she kept it for two years in a pine chest in her garret.

She should have shared her secret and told of the portrait's whereabouts during this long, excruciating exile. There were people who might have helped relieve the suffocation she is feeling now. Pierre Schommer at Chambord, or even the kindly, avuncular René here at the Musée Ingres. She feels herself plunging into a moment of truth. Her only desire now is to tell everybody from the top of the staircase that *La Joconde* is here, that they must do everything in their power to keep the enemy away. And more, she wants to confess to them all, rid herself of a burden she has carried for thirty years, that she was an accomplice to the theft of this masterpiece all those years ago. That she kept it hidden from the world and then sent her lovely, gullible Vincenzo directly into the hands of police in Florence when she decided that it was all enough. Picasso always said she was not a nice girl. The truth is that she was cruel to Vincenzo and cruel to this masterpiece.

To think that she is now in charge of protecting *La Joconde* from the enemy. What a joke! Because *look at me*, she wants to scream, *I'm the enemy that nobody thought to suspect.*

She feels herself drowning in panic, and her breathing accelerates, fear clawing at her throat. She crawls across the floor of her bedroom and looks out the window onto the picturesque village. Green tarped military trucks are travelling down the steep hill and parking outside the gates of the museum. The church bells toll six times. The stone roofs deepen in colour as night falls, inking her room with shadows. She lights her oil lamp and retreats from the window to bend over the *Mona Lisa*.

She feels the weight of her responsibility, the weight of her secret. Everything growing fetid under her watch. Nations destroying entire generations to rule over more land and seize one another's cultural prizes. Her son, broken and raging. With bitter hands, she wraps up the portrait, closes the case, and sets the latches in place. She slides the case into the hulking wooden box and pushes it into the darkest reaches below her bed. It feels all wrong. Like the occupation, the war, her descent into unwanted, unthinkable madness.

CHAPTER FIFTY-FOUR

Musée Ingres, 1941

A wind blows open her window, the wood frame banging loudly against the stone wall. It might be an ancestor filling her lungs. Somebody loving from her past, perhaps her mother, or her father, maybe the neighbour on the steps of the church. Slowly, as if learning to walk again, she steps out of her room and walks down the stairs, clutching the banister. She finds Philippe sitting with his eyes closed on his makeshift bed in the gallery. "It hurts," he says. She eases her body next to his and places a hand on his cast, as if she can massage away the pain of the break left to fester in the prison cell.

"I have something to tell you," she says.

Thérizoles interrupts them, arriving with a block of ice pressed over his nose.

"Is it broken?" she asks, lifting a hand to him.

"A new profile might improve my looks," he says.

"I'm very sorry about all of this." Her eyes sweep to the easels still holding the masterworks. "Will you stay for dinner?" This is her role as director of the evacuated collections. Stay optimistic, be the leader with an uplifted chin, and carry on as if nothing serious is going on, even now, when she is exhausted and her battle to defend beauty a broken dream.

"I'll spend the day at home with my wife and kids, if you don't mind, Madame Payer?"

"Of course. That sounds good." She nods and tries to rally. "That's a splendid idea."

He hesitates, steps away, and returns to face her. "We might go away for a time, if you get my meaning?"

She knows exactly what he means. That he fears being marked by the Nazis as somebody to track down and permanently quiet. The Resistance movement in the south has accelerated in the past month, and the Nazis are becoming brutal in their efforts to silence opposition. They go after individuals, and if the individuals refuse to talk, they bring in their families for questioning.

"Where will you go?" She asks the question thinking she would like to escape as well with Philippe.

"I can't say for sure," he says, looking to the floor.

This is to protect her, she knows, and the rest of the staff. To know specifics would only mean having details that the Nazis want to drag from people's mouths.

"Thank you. Be safe," she says, standing weakly, embracing the man warmly. Then, she returns to Philippe.

He looks down at her hand on his cast and shakes his head angrily. "Staying here, it's like we're all going to be hunted down."

"There are international laws . . ." But she stops herself, hearing how ridiculously naive she sounds. Philippe is proof that the occupiers are not being held to any moral or legal code.

"I want to go back to Paris," he says quietly. "I need to find out where Rachel has gone."

"Philippe, no, please don't. You're not safe in Paris. It's better here."

"Is it?"

Instead of answering, she looks at her son, his face still swollen, his tooth missing, leg in a cast. When he was a child, she could protect his innocence. She would avoid taking him to the pictures that might frighten him and make excuses when he wasn't invited to a schoolmate's birthday party. Later, she became an expert at hiding his father's affairs with men. The occupation has already wrecked Philippe's innocence. The scars from this war will be tattooed on his soul for years, and possibly on an entire generation, she thinks. He is damaged goods, they all are, and there is nothing she can do to stop the devastation.

The manager of the museum walks briskly into the gallery where Philippe and Mathilde are bent in conversation. "Madame Payer, *s'il vous plaît*, a telegram for you."

"Let's continue this later," she says to Philippe. Mathilde takes the telegram and crosses to the exit leading to an interior courtyard. Alone, she tears open the envelope and reads, *Taking the overnight train. Franz.*

CHAPTER FIFTY-FIVE

Musée Ingres, 1941

Waiting. She is waiting. For the Nazis to march into the museum and wrench the *Mona Lisa* from her arms. She expects the seizure of as many crates as they can haul and shove into their trucks with the swastikas covering the hoods and the doors. They will not know exactly what to take and they will compensate for their lack of expertise on the history of art by taking as much as possible. Eventually, she imagines, they will take the exquisite ink drawings by Ingres and some of his female nudes to amuse themselves. They will take some of Bourdelle's busts of Beethoven—every German schoolboy knows the musical genius was born in Bonn—but they will leave behind the coveted *Pietà de Villeneuve-lès-Avignon* from the fifteenth century, with the lean crucified figure of Jesus, his body curved into the lap of his stoic mother. The occupiers will overlook the Etruscan figures, even the Iberian heads of women with the large, staring eyes, one of which Picasso kept in his cupboard.

She slides her fingers along her gold necklace.

She anticipates the next sounds before they actually reach her ears. She hears Franz and a dozen soldiers marching down the hill. They must have walked from the train station about a mile away.

Philippe insists on walking across the courtyard with her, crutch-hopping, jaw set, sweat on his brow though it is cold outside. There are no windows facing out to the exterior courtyard but they can hear shouts of "*Heil* Hitler," a maniacal greeting from the Nazi—Philippe calls him the ape shit—who punched Monsieur Thérizoles, followed by a lower-pitched "*Sieg Heil*, Captain." She is certain this is Franz, assimilating the topography of the village, the status of the captain confronting him, the number of soldiers on the ground, the dozen Nazi trucks parked nearby.

She can only make out parts of the conversation in German:

"This . . . valuable artworks . . . no longer belong to the French state."

"Here to correct . . . your well-intentioned actions . . ."

"Our duty to seize . . ."

"Not at all . . . by international law."

"To fulfill the dream of the Führer . . ."

"Yes, his own grand museum . . ."

"Going in. Taking prisoners . . ."

"No . . . by order of . . . Kunstschutz . . ."

"You defy . . . authority?"

"You are outranked, and I place you under arrest." Mathilde can hear Franz shouting these last words. She hears a scuffle, the loading of guns, more shouts among men, protests, and indecipherable insults.

"Ape shit is getting his due," says Philippe grimly.

Finally, after several minutes, they hear trucks starting up and the revving of engines ascending the steep hill. They have yet to see anything for themselves, but Mathilde is certain that the Nazi from yesterday's altercation has been arrested, loaded onto a truck, and taken away. Silence descends on the courtyard. Birds begin to chirp high in the trees. Abruptly, there is a sharp rapping on the door. Philippe drops one of his crutches in alarm. Mathilde nods at him and opens the door. Franz is standing there, his helmeted men ranked behind him. He looks to Mathilde and then to her son. "Greetings from the Kunstschutz. The artwork you protect is honoured by the Art Protection Unit, as you know." His eyes sweep across the courtyard and back to Mathilde. "Apologies for yesterday's surprise encounter. That man was out of line and confused about his authority."

Now Franz moves from his official line of business to bow slightly. "Madame Payer," he says, acknowledging her, without giving away any emotion. Looking over at her son, he nods. "Hello, Philippe. It is good to see you again." He hesitates, looks grimly to the leg cast, and finally reaches into the leather case hanging from his shoulder. "I brought you this." He hands Philippe his red scarf and nods goodbye.

CHAPTER FIFTY-SIX

Musée Ingres, 1941

Living inside an occupation is like sitting inside the waiting room of a train station. Everybody is smoking. There is no way to unlock the door to escape to that previous life, the world on the other side of the glass that everybody wants but is unable to have. The fumes from the cigarettes grow thick until the toxins in the air block out all the daylight, making it impossible to breathe. Biking away together along the country lanes would be a dream. But, not a chance, thinks Mathilde. For Philippe and Mathilde, their only hope of survival is to stay quiet inside the waiting room.

The afternoon bleeds into the evening and still they wait. The museum sits quiet in the town as if everybody has retreated behind heavily shuttered rooms. The birds sing an anthem to the sunset, their calling across the museum courtyard offering a welcome distraction. Philippe hears the approach of footsteps first. Rising, hobbling on crutches, he opens the door of the courtyard and allows Franz inside the main lobby of the museum. The richly brocaded tapestries absorb the darkness of the night, converting the walls into black sucking holes. Mathilde arrives, glances at Franz, his swift removal of his military cap, and strikes matches to light candles, but her hands are shaking and she misses on the first several tries.

"May I?" offers Franz, taking the matchbox from her hands. The gesture is intimate, and she stiffens, not wanting to divulge anything to Philippe.

"Monsieur Metternich, we can meet in the gallery office to discuss terms of the Kunstschutz and the threats we experienced here yesterday."

"Monsieur Metternich," Philippe interrupts, approaching on his crutches. He has tied the red scarf around his neck. "I remember you. At the prison, the Cherche-Midi. You got me out of that hellhole. You arranged for the French doctors to see me."

Franz stands immobilized and listens intently before speaking with measured words. "Sometimes an occupation force, segments of it, go too far with their operations. The means justifying the ends. I don't agree with that kind of thinking."

Philippe shakes his head. "But why did you seek me out? Others were there too. Some of my friends were in worse condition than I was. Two of them died."

"I'm very sorry to hear that," says Franz, looking to the ground and back to Philippe.

"You saved my life," says Philippe, looking to his mother and back to the Nazi standing in front of him. "Why?"

"Because I asked him to help," says Mathilde, stepping close, lowering her voice. "I knew him. We met at the Louvre. He has his office next to Jacques Jaujard."

"Now he's the boss. Your Nazi boss," says Philippe, his eyes darkening.

"I tried Picasso. I tried your father. But they couldn't . . . I needed somebody like him." She gestures boldly with her chin at Franz, keeping him nameless for the moment, allowing the insult to soften Philippe's outrage. "Because I was desperate. I was desperate to save your life."

"Maman, you call up this Nazi every time you need help?" he says, hissing into her ear. "That's why he's here tonight?"

"Philippe," she says, flustered, stepping away from him. "You owe Monsieur Metternich your thanks, not your accusations." She looks to Franz and back to Philippe. She knows what she's doing. Not exactly lying, but also not exactly telling the truth. Mathilde feels time no longer stretches before her but festers and roils inside her. She is desperate to protect Philippe from the truth.

"Your mother and I knew each other in Alsace," says Franz, looking evenly at Philippe. He glances at Mathilde. "Go ahead, he is your son."

There is a long silence.

"It is difficult to tell it, our story . . . given everything," she says woodenly. She is staring at Franz, pleading with her eyes to not say anything further. She could lose her position, lose her son, lose everything in the name of honesty. "Our countries are at war. It makes it difficult, even impossible, to be friends."

"You knew each other from Alsace?" Philippe is shaking his head, trying to make sense of their words.

"It was a long time ago. I was seventeen."

"But we never stopped—" says Franz.

Mathilde widens her eyes, warning him off the topic.

"Never stopped what? Maman? Never stopped what?"

Here, Mathilde is amazed by the possibilities facing her. Either to invent a story that will satisfy Philippe or to tell the unvarnished truth. What it is people are born to do during their lives. To love or to deny the human instinct to love? To be good or to be evil? She feels ripped apart by the moment, as if she can no longer breathe in the waiting room of the train station, because to be a good person is the more difficult choice. A good person grows from being born and wanting to be whole, even if there are parts that have splintered and floated away. A good person will try to rebuild their parts. She feels her lungs burning. If she doesn't open the door of the waiting room, she will surely die an ignoble death. The only way out is by speaking honestly.

"We once—" Her brow pricks with sweat. It is difficult, physically difficult, to shape her tongue around the words.

"Maman? What are you saying?"

She does not see Philippe. She does not hear his disgust. She sees Franz standing on the hillock, his naked body shimmering in the light of the solar eclipse. She sees him crying at the train station, clasping the gold chain around her neck. She sees his eyelids fluttering softly in disbelief after recognizing her for the first time at the Louvre. She sees his hands reaching out to hold her. She sees him saving her son.

"We once loved each other, and perhaps we never stopped," she says at last.

CHAPTER FIFTY-SEVEN

Musée Ingres, 1941

Franz pulls a map from the inside of his uniform jacket and lays it out on Mathilde's desk in a far corner of the museum. They have left Philippe to brood. This knowledge of the past and his own obligation to a Nazi officer has shaken him deeply, and Mathilde can see that he needs time. The air is still tender between her and Franz, and so they both retreat into the urgent business of the moment.

"You can see, the evacuation routes for artworks from Paris have led to many destinations. To the west, to the south, and now in the southwest at Montauban. The red line indicates that art is also being transported to Germany by high-ranking officials."

"You're taking a considerable risk," she says, interrupting. "You're putting your life at risk, I mean, going beyond to help save some of the beauty."

He takes a deep breath and exhales slowly. "We have identified most of these works by train. There are also French individuals who are well aware of what is happening."

Mathilde thinks back to her meeting with Rose Valland, the curator at the Jeu de Paume in Paris, and her stories of works being stolen from the gallery by senior officials, such as Hermann Göring.

"I heard the Nazis are stealing the works. They're burning some of the paintings by the so-called degenerate artists. Can you do anything to stop them?"

"I am trying," says Franz. "We are applying pressure from international treaties and making everybody in the Nazi bureaucracy understand that art cannot be simply taken out of France. We have put bureaucratic controls in place in Paris, across France, requiring information about buyers and vendors, but of course, money is short, currencies are failing, people are easily bribed."

"What happened yesterday? Who was that Nazi who threatened to haul away our collections?"

"The longer the war goes on, the more extreme the Nazis will become. They want to silence the artists and intellectuals. They want to eliminate the gypsies, the Jews, the homosexuals, even the immigrants. We are living inside a dark, absurdist world. It will eventually be stopped, but for now . . . what you witnessed was one of Hitler's hard-liners likely frustrated with this remote posting, wanting more action for himself."

"And brutality."

"There will be more and more of his type scrambling to get to the top. I'm afraid my days are numbered."

Mathilde looks up from the map with alarm. "Meaning?"

"There have been rumblings about the bureaucratic roadblocks I've been putting up to keep the French national collection within its borders. The Gestapo came to my office with the French police. There have been some insinuations that I'm collaborating."

"By what means? What evidence?"

He hesitates, looks to the floor, over to the map. "My telegrams to you have been traced."

She bows her head in shame and regret at what she has allowed, what she has excused because of her weakness for Franz. She nods, showing she understands, but thinking of other incriminating evidence, she shakes her head. "Our train together? From Loc-Dieu to Paris. Did they find out about that?"

"Yes."

She places a hand on his shoulder, clasps the other over her mouth in horror that she has put him at risk.

"Mathilde, our work together is not the only evidence they will find if they decide to look. I have not shared everything with you about my actions with your colleagues, and I will not tell you. But please know, you are not to blame."

"They might send you to a work camp."

"They might shoot me. It's true. But, Mathilde, it was all worth it."

She touches her fingers to his neck, to his face, to his lips. "All these years," she says, shaking her head. "You've stayed the man I knew you to be."

"You have always been by my side, in spirit, at least. And now, at last, I have this moment with you."

"You have trusted me tonight with knowledge that could end your life if it was known. I feel I owe you the same truth." She crosses the floor slowly. "Come, sit with me. I have something to tell you that will put my life in your hands." Mathilde arranges herself in a wooden chair and directs Franz to sit across from her on a settee. She takes a deep breath. What she is about to tell Franz could be used against her, could deliver her to a French prison. But she does not hesitate. She carries a deep conviction that she can trust him.

What choice does she have? She must tell or stay forever in the waiting room. Mathilde begins by confessing about her habit of thieving. Glasses from the Café de la Rotonde, cutlery from the

Brasserie Lipp, sable round-head brushes from Picasso's studio, and the palette he used while creating some of his Cubist paintings, with its heavy patches of oil paint. She stole them as gifts to herself, to try to fill the gaping wound in her heart left by a life without a mother. And finally, she confesses to her role in the theft of the *Mona Lisa*, stuffed into the white pine box for two years in a Paris garret. "It was wrong of me," she says. "Cruel to hide her for so long, and then let others pay the price." She looks at Franz, whose face is unreadable. "And now she is here. It's true. Imagine what I am telling you now. *La Joconde* is in my care and I will do anything to keep her safe. You need to know that I am many things, but especially that I am a liar."

"I see," he says, looking to the floor. He stands quickly and walks away. She can hear him exhale in exasperation. Turning back to her, he continues, "I suppose I could have you court-martialled for aiding and abetting in the theft of a national treasure." She wants to choke back her emotion but, hearing this, her eyes fill with tears. He strides next to the window and looks out for a long time. "You were young. In search of your mother. Perhaps *Mona Lisa* filled a void that you desperately needed. I could think of you as a liar, a woman without any moral conscience. But I couldn't be sure. Only the thugs and autocrats are sure of what they do. I want to not know."

"I've made many mistakes in my life," she says, looking to the floor.

"Fate has delivered you a turn, Mathilde, but I will not deliver another blow. Your secrets are safe with me."

She crumples over in her chair, holds her face in her hands. All breath has gone out of her. She rises from her seat and slowly, carefully, reaches out for him. She did not know how much she has needed his forgiveness. In that moment, though the room is glazed in dark evening shadows, she feels bathed in something soft and luminous and she thinks of the rays of sacred light descending from peace doves in so many Renaissance paintings. If she could extend time, this would be the moment to work that magic. Because memories from the past can be heightened or diminished, such is the imperfect nature of recall over time. But here she is with Franz, whose kindness is as real as the touch of his hands holding hers tightly now.

"Make me one promise," says Franz, holding her close. "That if we both survive this war, we will meet again."

She smiles a little. "No uniforms?"

"At peace."

She thinks about how Picasso spoke of taking her apart during some of her modelling sessions with him years ago at the Bateau-Lavoir. How he would draw her in jagged pieces. It disturbed her a little back then but also gave her comfort, as though she was looking in a mirror and recognizing herself in the chaos. But not now. She is done bleeding. She is done being broken into ten thousand pieces. She wants to be whole.

Her thoughts travel from Montmartre during the Belle Époque to fly into the future. She thinks about giving a public lecture decades from now in a liberated, free Paris. Who can say for sure what will transpire over time? There is no telling how much devastation the Nazis will have inflicted during this war or who will be the victors. There might not be enough paper to map all the scars tattooed on the land, not enough grains of sand to absorb the tears of the heartbroken. But she can dream that someday there will be healing. That her first lover and friend may still be in her life. That is her right. To dream. The invaders cannot take that away from Mathilde.

She imagines walking slowly through the crypt of the museum and, with luck, steadying her on both sides are her grandchildren, two beautiful women, Philippe's daughters. They walk past the *Great*

Sphinx of Tanis and stop to reach back to an ancient universe, as she has taught them, to caress the giant paws of the lion before linking arms again with their grandmother. She dreams of giving a lecture in a small auditorium in the basement of the Louvre about a world-famous portrait of a silk merchant's wife, and how such a painting changed her life again and again. At last, Mathilde stands at the lectern and sips from the glass of water that somebody has kindly left for her. She looks out over the crowd and is surprised to see that all the seats are filled and people are still arriving, angling their bodies to press inside, many crouching to sit in the aisles.

Mathilde thinks her dream should stop there, but she cannot resist pulling more details from her lecture at the Louvre. In the front row, she sees an old man, bent with time and gentle grace. He is nudged by a small boy, one of his great-grandchildren, who sits beside his mother and his sister. Mathilde can hear the child's melodic voice: "Is that your friend?"

"She is, yes," he says. "My friend like no other."

"I like her."

"Yes," says the man, lifting his green-blue eyes to Mathilde.

"She is looking out to face everybody."

"Yes, but now she is speaking."

Years ago, long before the Second World War, I stood in front of a small Italian portrait at the Louvre museum. This painting, the *Mona Lisa*, was different from the other great pictures in the gallery. I didn't really understand exactly how back then. But I do now. It took me a long while. You see, life is complicated. It can be incredibly painful and messy. One day, we crumble, and we just can't find the energy to stand up. Another day we might feel so much power it goes to our heads and we end up doing cruel

> and unkind things. But the thing is, waiting for us, there is always a sunrise. And there are so many reasons to get out of bed. Love is the most compelling reason but so is believing in our own power. Look at how Leonardo da Vinci painted the *Mona Lisa*, as somebody with the strength of an oak tree, whom he painted while she talked with him in his studio in Florence. You can almost hear the sweet music she has listened to. You can feel what she has suffered and lost over time. In the landscape behind her, Leonardo shows us rivers that curl across time. And in one corner an old stone bridge spanning impossible waters. But look at the way Lisa Gherardini twists her body slightly in her chair, contrapposto, to have a good look at what's outside of her. You can see it in her eyes, how she has lived and endured, how she has honoured an empathy for others.

"What does empathy mean?" asks the boy, leaning over to his great-grandfather.

"Acceptance," says Franz.

Mathilde's voice carries over the auditorium. "It has taken hundreds of years to tell Lisa Gherardini's story. But look at her confidence. In the end, she trusts, as I finally do, that women belong to this world."

AUTHOR'S NOTE

While many of the characters in this novel are based on real people whose real names are used, their portrayal is fictitious, and the events surrounding them are both historic and imagined.

However, there are facts interwoven throughout this novel. Beyond its timeline, readers may be interested to know that in 1942, Franz Wolff Metternich, the head of the Kunstschutz Art Protection Unit, was dismissed by the Nazis and sent back to Germany. Although he was appointed by Hitler, Metternich was never a signatory to the Nazi movement and he returned to his life in northern Germany as a respected art historian and aristocrat. His collaboration with Jacques Jaujard, the director of the Louvre, prevented senior Nazi officials from looting the French National Museum collections. He was awarded the Légion d'honneur in 1963 from President of France Charles de Gaulle at the recommendation of Jaujard. After the war, more than 60,000 artworks were found in Germany and Austria, the result of intense plundering of Jewish estates. In 1949, an estimated 45,000 works were returned to their owners.

As is the case with many of the details and dialogue in this novel, Metternich's love affair with Mathilde was entirely invented in the name of fiction.

The character of Mathilde is inspired by Mathilde-Suzanne

Deutschmann, born in 1893 in Haguenau, Alsace. As a teenager, she worked in a restaurant in Paris. Allegedly, she was questioned by French police on December 17, 1913, as a person of interest and friend of Vincenzo's during the investigation of the stolen *Mona Lisa, La Joconde.* I obtained a scanned copy of the French police record and the "*procès verbal*" with Mathilde. After that, I invented.

The theft of the *Mona Lisa* from the Louvre on August 21, 1911, by the Italian carpenter and house painter Vincenzo Peruggia is well documented, as are the charges and court proceedings against both Picasso and Apollinaire following the discovery that Picasso kept two Iberian sculptures that belonged to the Louvre museum in his studio at the Bateau-Lavoir.

Picasso reflected on record that the artistic milieu of the Bateau-Lavoir during the early 1910s represented some of the best of his life, despite the grinding poverty. His invention of Cubism with Georges Braque is also well known, although his relationships with and treatment of women are more complex. I relied heavily on memoirs written by women, including two of Picasso's lovers, Fernande Olivier and Francoise Gilot. The indulgence in absinthe and opium was part of the bohemian flavour of the Bateau-Lavoir in Montmartre. However, when one of Picasso's close friends, German painter Karl-Heinz Wiegels, died of opium-related causes in the early 1900s, it is said that Picasso curbed his enthusiasm for the drug.

I visited the Bateau-Lavoir and spent time recording the ambience and urban design of Montmartre and, in particular, Place Émile Goudeau (previously Place Ravignan), while finding in original paintings and documents of the Musée de Montmartre the important historic context of the "Butte" during the early 1900s. The recreated atelier of Suzanne Valadon also proved useful for writing certain descriptive passages.

During recent research trips to Paris, I sourced many books from exhibitions and bookstores, including *Picasso à Paris* (Gilles Schlesser) and *Picasso Bleu et Rose* (Musée d'Orsay, Musée national Picasso-Paris, Hazan, 2019), and read memoirs by the wives and girlfriends of Picasso, including *Life with Picasso* (Françoise Gilot and Carlton Lake), *Loving Picasso: The Private Journal of Fernande Olivier* (Fernande Olivier), *Picasso: Women* (Hélène Parmelin), and *Picasso* (Gertrude Stein).

I have included several excerpts from poems translated into English from their original French and German. The lines quoted on page 59 are from "Poèmes saturniens" by Paul Verlaine, translated by Gertrude Hall Brownell, 1895, while the lines quoted on page 115 are from "The Secret" by Friedrich Schiller, from *The Poems of Schiller—Third Period*, translated by Edgar Alfred Bowring, 1874. The translation of Guillaume Apollinaire's "The Song of the Badly Loved" on pages 63 and 149 is taken from *Zone: Selected Poems by Guillaume Apollinaire*, translated by Ron Padgett, published by New York Review Books, 2015, and used with permission.

Vincenzo Peruggia's attempt to sell the *Mona Lisa* to Alfredo Geri and the aftermath of his trip to Florence is based on events widely reported in newspapers. Though he suffered from lead poisoning, Vincenzo served in the Italian army during World War I and later moved to France. He died at forty-four in a suburb of Paris, leaving behind a wife and a daughter.

ACKNOWLEDGEMENTS

I am indebted to Jennifer Lambert, editor-in-chief of HarperCollins Canada, for backing this novel in its nascent form as a draft outline. Having worked closely with Jennifer on both my debut novel, *Tuscan Daughter*, and *The Paris Thief*, I can attest to her brilliant eye and elegant editing, which lift me up to become a better writer every time. I am thankful for the tremendous work of my agent, Hilary McMahon, and international rights director Meg Wheeler, of Westwood Creative Artists, and to Frankie Edwards, editorial director of Headline UK (Hachette), the publisher taking *The Paris Thief* globally into the English-speaking world.

The Paris Thief allowed me to immerse myself in Paris, France, a city beloved and familiar, which I have long considered my other hometown. My love affair with the city began during the mid-1980s when I was a student and young journalist living in the Latin Quarter, close to the Luxembourg Gardens, La Coupole restaurant, and the Café de la Rotonde, where some of the novel's scenes are set.

Equipped with a Pentax camera and a notebook, I recorded the marches of the extreme right politician Jean-Marie Le Pen, the funeral of Simone de Beauvoir, and the reinvention of the Louvre by American architect I. M. Pei. While studying full-time at Sciences Po (L'Institut d'Études Politiques), I audited evening courses in modern art at L'École du Louvre, immersed in the art of the Cubists or the Futurists, before walking across the Seine back to my apartment, a haven of camaraderie with French friends, especially Cécile Fabre. My student card allowed me to enter the Louvre without any security checks. I remember the feeling of time being exquisitely slowed down while I wandered the shadowy halls of the museum, unguarded and alone, an experience that impressed upon me that the arts, like human rights, are an extraordinary privilege. Too often, we take them for granted. Since ancient times, tragically and predictably, masterworks have been destroyed and plundered by occupying regimes.

I wish to thank the staff at the Château de Chambord, particularly Alexandra Fleury, for the warm welcome and access to the entire château and its archives, and for providing me with enlightening journal articles, historic photography of the Nazi occupation of the Louvre, and Chambord itself, filled with thousands of wooden crates and monumental treasures, to become the largest depot of evacuated art during the Second World War. I am grateful for the invitation to sleep over as the only guest in the 480-room château one chilly night in November 2023. The book *Sauver un Peu de la Beauté du Monde: Chambord 1935–1945* (Alexandra Fleury) was an invaluable resource during the research of *The Paris Thief.*

Ma Vie de Châteaux, the diaries of the French archivist Lucie Mazauric, was critical to my understanding of a woman's life enduring hardships as a nomad travelling with and protecting artworks, notably from the Louvre's painting collection, including the *Mona Lisa*. Her little-known story of living rough and travelling in convoys from the Château de Chambord to safer abbeys and museums in the south inspired many of the textures and feelings of Mathilde in this book. The recent docudrama produced by Radio France *Rose Valland, la Résistante du Jeu de Paume* gives recognition, at last, to the remarkably brave and meticulous work of curator Rose Valland at the Jeu de Paume documenting the burning and thieving of artworks by senior Nazi officials, especially Hermann Göring, who, it was later discovered, had stolen at least a thousand works for his personal collection. The television series *The New Look* and classics like Truffaut's *Le Dernier Métro* provided atmospheric information, and I found emotional resonance in John Steinbeck's unvarnished telling of an occupied nation in *The Moon Is Down* and Anthony Doerr's *All the Light You Cannot See*. Both Jacques Jaujard and Franz Metternich are brought to life in the documentary/drama *Francofonia* (2015) by director Alexander Sokurov, which features edifying archival photography and re-enactments of the Nazi occupation of France and the regime's obsession with the national treasures of France.

None of the works moved from one château to another by French museum staff during the Nazi occupation ever suffered damage.

Around the world there are hundreds of thousands of works that need to be returned to their rightful owners. I admire the dedication of my friend Kamila Gourdie, for advocating tirelessly for the restitution of artworks stolen from Jewish families during the Second World War. There have been some significant wins and some very long battles. Our long promenades on the wooden boardwalk in the Beaches discussing the plundering that takes place during wartime and colonization spurred me on to write this novel.

Thanks also to many friends for wrapping me in their energizing, intelligent company through all the seasons, including the Soaring Sisters, Monica Gutschi, Rana Khan, Dale Frederick, Christine Raissis, Helen Hatzis, and Diana Aziz.

Novels take a long time to research and write, but even longer to get published. In the meantime, we lose loved ones and beautiful babies are born. My deep gratitude goes to my family for their endless support and cheering from the sidelines, to Dylan and Alexander for their sensitive insights, and to Geneviève, Hannah, and John for their critically important advance reads. I cherish many lush memories of Paris with my husband, John Terry, walking the city's streets all night, spending intimate evenings at the opera for ten euros a ticket, and, later, with our kids, on a tour with Olivier, stuffed into his little car, starting at Sacré-Coeur after arriving at sunrise from Canada and continuing to the Louvre for a photo in front of the *Venus de Milo*. By "Olivier" I refer to Olivier Bériot, a celebrated French costume designer, who was with me during much of the research for this book, although our walkabouts in Paris started decades ago when we were both students and penniless flâneurs.

RAISING READERS

Books Build Bright Futures

Dear Reader,

We'd love your attention for one more page to tell you about the crisis in children's reading, and what we can all do.

Studies have shown that reading for fun is the **single biggest predictor of a child's future life chances** – more than family circumstance, parents' educational background or income. It improves academic results, mental health, wealth, communication skills, ambition and happiness.[1]

The number of children reading for fun is in rapid decline. Young people have a lot of competition for their time. In 2024, 1 in 10 children and young people in the UK aged 5 to 18 did not own a single book at home.[2]

Hachette works extensively with schools, libraries and literacy charities, but here are some ways we can all raise more readers:

- Reading to children for just 10 minutes a day makes a difference
- Don't give up if children aren't regular readers – there will be books for them!
- Visit bookshops and libraries to get recommendations
- Encourage them to listen to audiobooks
- Support school libraries
- Give books as gifts

There's a lot more information about how to encourage children to read on our website: **www.RaisingReaders.co.uk**

Thank you for reading.

hachette UK

[1] OECD, '21st-Century Readers: Developing Literacy Skills in a Digital World', 2021, https://www.oecd.org/en/publications/21st-century-readers_a83d84cb-en.html

[2] National Literacy Trust, 'Book Ownership in 2024', November 2024, https://literacytrust.org.uk/research-services/research-reports/book-ownership-in-2024